c/3
117
921

		DATE DUE		

A MURDER
OF JUSTICE

ROBERT ANDREWS

A MURDER OF JUSTICE

A Marian Wood Book

•

Published by G. P. Putnam's Sons
a member of Penguin Group (USA) Inc.
New York

This is a work of fiction. Names, characters, places, and
incidents either are the product of the author's imagination or
are used fictitiously, and any resemblance to actual persons,
living or dead, businesses, companies, events, or locales is
entirely coincidental.

A MARIAN WOOD BOOK
Published by G. P. Putnam's Sons
Publishers Since 1838
a member of
Penguin Group (USA) Inc.
375 Hudson Street
New York, NY 10014

Library of Congress Cataloging-in-Publication Data

Andrews, Robert, date.
    A murder of justice / Robert Andrews.
        p.   cm.
    "A Marian Wood book."
    ISBN 0-399-15039-0
    1. Kearney, Frank (Fictitious character)—Fiction.
    2. Phelps, José (Fictitious character)—Fiction.
    3. African Americans—Crimes against—Fiction.
    4. Police—Washington (D.C.)—Fiction.
    5. Washington (D.C.)—Fiction. I. Title.
    PS3551.N4524M875   2004   2003064679
    813'.54—dc22

Printed in the United States of America
10 9 8 7 6 5 4 3 2 1

This book is printed on acid-free paper. ∞

Book design by Judith Stagnitto Abbate/Abbate Design

Thanks to Clifford McLain, master craftsman,

who kept our roof sound, our walls solid, and our morale intact.

FOR ANNA

The only affront that compares to the taking of a life is the failure of government to assure a commensurate response to murder.

—District of Columbia Judiciary Committee, February 2001

APRIL 6, 2001—a Friday. Edward Teasdale had just tilted back in his Barcalounger to watch the Orioles and Red Sox on CSN, when he heard the shots.

Bam . . . Bam . . . Bam . . . Bam . . .

Steady shooting.

Bam . . . Bam . . . Bam . . .

Silence.

Teasdale waited. No more shots.

Bayless Place in southeast Washington, D.C., used to be a quiet neighborhood. But in the last several years, Teasdale and his neighbors had gotten practice at what he sourly called "acoustical gunfire analysis."

This evening's shots had been evenly spaced.

One shooter. Somebody out there on the street wasn't in a hurry.

Seven shots, maybe eight.

Not a revolver. An automatic—probably a nine.

Teasdale glanced at the digital clock on the TV—seven thirty-two. He went to the window and pulled the curtain open just enough to get a glimpse of the street, then settled back into the Barcalounger.

Jason Johnson took the mound against Boston.

The day before, Hideo Nomo had thrown a no-hitter for the Sox against Teasdale's beloved Birds. Tonight, Teasdale wanted revenge.

The clock showed seven thirty-eight. Johnson had struck out the inning's second batter . . . no further gunfire outside. Teasdale grudgingly lifted himself out of the Barcalounger.

Might 's well take a look.

Standing off to the side, he unbolted and opened his front door. It was sunset. The sidewalks were deserted. Anyone who'd been outside had long before taken cover. The dark Ford Taurus was parked about halfway down the block in its usual place. Rhythmic bass thumps of a stereo driving at top volume rocked the air.

The sidewalks were still empty when Teasdale got to the car. In the street, glass nuggets glowed in the sun's last light. Bullet holes dimpled the door. Skirting the back of the car, Teasdale peered through the shattered window.

Blood darkened the windshield and dashboard. A Puff Daddy rap thundered from the Taurus's speakers.

Off to his right, Teasdale caught the brassy glint of empty cartridge cases on the asphalt. Here's where the shooting had been done, right here where he was standing, Teasdale figured. He aimed a finger pistol.

Bam . . . Bam . . . Bam . . . Just like that.

Teasdale circled around to get a more direct look into the front seat.

"Why, hello, Skeeter," Teasdale whispered.

The top of James "Skeeter" Hodges's head had been blown away. Teasdale smiled.

Another figure slumped in the passenger seat. Tobias "Pencil" Crawfurd, Skeeter's number two, was breathing.

Teasdale frowned. He waited a moment.

But Crawfurd kept breathing.

Teasdale sighed.

Inside his house again, he dialed 911. Finished with the call, he settled back to watch the game. Things were getting better. The Orioles were up by one.

"Oh, yes," Teasdale whispered into the empty room. He smiled.

Ten minutes passed before Officers Antwon Hawkins and Samuel Lawson responded, got Crawfurd on his way to the Hospital Center, and secured the crime scene.

Five minutes later, District of Columbia Metropolitan Police Department homicide detectives Frank Kearney and José Phelps arrived.

ONE

"Funny," José said.

"Funny funny?"

"Strange funny." José pointed through the windshield. "No spectators."

Ahead, on Bayless Place, an ambulance and three squad cars, light bars blazing blues and reds, yellow crime-scene tape, and flares like fireballs framed a Taurus with shot-out windows. A regular circus. A sure-fire crowd-draw anywhere.

Frank felt his gut go heavy. He'd seen violent death, some of it in wholesale lots. He'd never gotten used to it. But he'd learned to wall it off. He'd kept the wall in good repair. Through Vietnam, through the years on the force, the wall had shielded him from the soul-searing exhibits of the horrific things people did to one another. Lately, though, it seemed too much was getting through. Too much was following him home.

He pulled over to the curb. He and José got out and walked toward the lights and the Notorious B.I.G. rap blaring from the Taurus.

At six-two, Frank was an inch shorter than José, and at one-ninety, thirty pounds lighter. Frank had run track and cross-country at the University of Maryland. José had played football at Howard, switching in his junior year to boxing. They'd been together on the force for twenty-six years. Roommates at the academy, beat cops in every tough neighborhood in the District, and now plainclothes in Homicide.

But the years had done more than produce the force's two most senior detectives. Their off-duty lives had intersected and intertwined. The two men had supported each other through private triumphs and personal trials, through marriages and children, divorces and deaths. Years passed, and each became as comfortable with the other as he was with his own shadow.

One of the uniformed officers turned. Frank recognized Antwon Hawkins.

Hawkins walked toward them with the rolling swagger of a sailor on shore leave. One hand thumb-hooked over his pistol belt, he tossed José a casual salute with the other.

"Ho-zay can you see?" he singsonged.

José pointed at the car. "Who was that?"

"None other than the newly dead Skeeter Hodges."

As they walked to the car, Frank felt the heaviness ease. "Somebody finally got him?"

"Pretty good. Pencil Crawfurd was sitting in front with him."

"He get it too?" José asked.

Hawkins shook his head and frowned in disappointment. "Sam and I get here, he was unconscious. Looks like he took at least one in the shoulder. Hard to be in that car anywhere and not get one. We found eight shells . . . nine-millimeter."

"Where is he?"

"Hospital Center."

At the car, Hawkins pointed to the body slumped forward over the steering wheel. He turned his flashlight on the dead man. The top of the skull was missing. Contents of the brain pan were splattered on the dash and windshield.

Death smell, metallic like that of damp copper, radiated from inside the car. Frank exhaled through his nostrils. When he had to, he inhaled through his mouth, keeping it shallow. It didn't do any good. He'd known it wouldn't, but he did it anyway.

"Head shot at close range."

Frank felt in his chest the vibrations of Notorious B.I.G. going on about big booty bitches, and he reached in and jabbed at buttons until the CD player turned off and B.I.G. vanished in the middle of a "'ho."

"Who was the nine-one-one?" José asked.

Hawkins checked his notebook. "Teasdale." He spelled the name. "Lives over there." He pointed to a small brick bungalow halfway down the block.

Frank felt somewhat better walking away, putting the crime scene behind him.

"Skeeter finally got a dose of what he's been giving out," José said.

"Surprised somebody didn't do it sooner."

Closing the case might not be too hard, Frank half reasoned, half hoped.

Somebody out there somewhere. Still on an adrenaline rush, pupils dilated with excitement. King of the world. Immortal. Invincible. Absolutely bulletproof. And they'd talk. Absolutely had to talk. Because they wouldn't get credit for the score, for taking down Skeeter Hodges, unless people knew they'd done it.

A porch crossed the front of the Teasdale house. From the porch, four rocking chairs surveyed a tiny but well-kept yard guarded by a chain-link fence.

Frank rang the doorbell. From where he stood, he could see Skeeter Hodges's car. The ambulance and the patrol cars were still there, and the flares still guttering, and still no rubbernecking crowd. The door opened a crack.

"Police," Frank said, flashing his badge. The door closed. He heard the rattle of one chain lock being undone, then a second. The door opened.

Large man. Mahogany skin. Thick black mustache. Prominent, suspicious eyes. Orange and black Orioles cap, bill to the front. A sweater buttoned snugly across a heavy gut.

"In here."

Teasdale led Frank and José through the living room to a dining alcove. No woman around, Frank decided. No plants, pleats, or patterned fabrics. All straight lines, solid colors, and sturdy furniture. It was barracks neat, the way a meat-and-potatoes man would keep things. In the alcove, Teasdale took a chair on one side of the small table and motioned the detectives to chairs on the other side.

Frank and José sat down.

José started the questions, Frank took notes.

Teasdale was Edward Everett Teasdale. Sixty-one. District native. Four-year enlistment in the Air Force, service in Germany. Retired Metrobus driver. Spouse deceased. Lived on Bayless Place for the last thirty-six years.

"Tell us what happened this evening," José said.

Teasdale told his story in short, unadorned sentences. He told it methodically. A bus driver making all the stops. He finished and sat, hands folded on the table, looking at José and Frank.

Frank went first. "So you heard the shots at seven thirty-two."

"Jason was warming up."

"You heard shots, but you didn't go outside for five minutes."

"Six."

"What?"

"*Six minutes.* Didn't go out for six minutes. Waited till Jason put down the second batter."

"Okay, six minutes. Why'd you wait? . . . Besides wanting to see Jason, of course."

Teasdale gave Frank, then José, a long, disbelieving look. He frowned, a man who knew that there were such things as stupid questions.

"You live 'round here, and the shooting starts," he said patiently, as though explaining to a child, "you don't go sticking your damnfool head out your door."

"You knew it was James Hodges?" José asked. "When you looked in the car? How's that?"

Teasdale's eyes rolled at another stupid question. "It was his car," he said, again slowly, patiently. "It was where he always parked. Him and his buddy, that skinny bastard Pencil. Drive up every evening. Sit there for an hour, maybe two. That's how I know."

"They doing any business?"

"Not here. They just sit there." Teasdale's eyes narrowed. "Letting us know."

"Know? . . . Know *what*?"

Teasdale took a deep breath. "That Bayless Place was his."

"Why'd he have to prove that?" José asked.

"He just comes around. Sits there, just letting us know."

"When'd he move in?"

"February . . . no, March."

"You see anybody in the street before the shooting?" Frank asked.

"Like I told you," Teasdale said evenly, "before, I was watching the Birds. And after, I was watching the Birds. When Jason put down the second man up, that's when I went out. The street was empty. Nobody there. Nobody."

"You know anybody who'd want Skeeter dead?" Frank asked.

Teasdale half laughed. "Pick a page in the phone book."

It got quiet in the house as he looked steadily at Frank.

"Somebody's goin' to take his place, you know." Reproach was a knife in Teasdale's voice. "It's the way it's gotten to be around here." He swung his head back and forth. "Isn't one bunch of gang-bangers, it's gonna be another."

. . .

Back on the street, Frank saw a dark gray Jaguar parked beside the ambulance at the crime scene. As they got closer, he spotted Anthony Upton, the medical examiner. A tall, angular man, Upton was directing technicians to position a folding gurney by the Taurus's open driver's-side door.

"Nice night, Tony," Frank said.

Upton looked around and smiled.

Frank avoided looking into the car. Even so, the blood-copper smell reached out for him.

"Messy," he said. *As if it's ever neat.* He said it to have something to say, because if he didn't, he'd have to take another look inside.

"Shooter shot through the closed window," Upton said. "Slugs carried a lot of glass in with them."

"You see his buddy?"

Upton dismissed the question with a shrug. "He was alive."

"Restricted clientele?"

Upton nodded. "I got enough business with the dead ones, Frank."

Two techs had the white plastic body bag open on the gurney beside the car. The bigger tech reached in and easily lifted Hodges by the shoulders. He had the corpse halfway out of the car when his smooth motion jerked to a stop.

"Foot's caught," Upton said.

The tech heaved.

Frank heard a splintering snap. The tech stumbled back, the corpse in his arms trailing blood and brains.

"Muthafucka," the tech muttered. He recovered his footing. In a graceful ballroom maneuver, he swung and dipped, dropping his partner onto the gurney, faceup. Everything above the eyebrows was missing. Beneath the dark cavity, the eyes and mouth were wide open.

"Surprised, Skeeter?" José asked.

"Slugs exited the front," Upton said. "Probably somewhere inside the car."

. . .

José sat in the driver's seat, slapping the wheel in a slow funereal beat.

Upton had left in his Jag, following the meat wagon. He and Frank had inventoried, photographed, measured and sketched, and scoured the area for evidence, and an hour later, they were watching the forensic techs wrapping up the crime scene. The department wrecker was hooking up the Taurus. Tomorrow, all that'd be left would be glass on the street from the shot-up car. The glass would stay awhile, but eventually it would be gone too.

"Teasdale was right, you know," José said, still looking at the glass. He heard Frank say something in reply, but not exactly what. José surveyed the small houses with their neat yards that lined Bayless Place.

Once you had your street taken over by assholes like Skeeter, you were in for trouble. Even if you got rid of Skeeter, the damage was done. He had shown that Bayless Place could be had. Blood in the water. And there was always somebody else out there, circling, watching, searching out the cripples, the easy pickings. That's why Teasdale had seemed so angry. Teasdale knew what would come next. What for certain would come next.

José felt a weighted despair. Getting looked at that way went with the job. They pay you to be the thin blue line between society and the animals. But the Skeeters roamed free and the Edward Everett Teasdales stayed off the streets and made sure they locked their doors.

"You ready to go?" José asked Frank.

He'll live. He might not be able to do anything useful with that left arm, but I suspect he wasn't trying out for Olympics gymnastics before he was shot."

Dr. Sheresa Arrowsmith, a stocky woman with a glossy ebony

complexion, was an expert on gunshot wounds. "Didn't plan it that way," she'd explained to Frank and José when they had met her years before, "but you work trauma in the District, you get a lot of practice digging out slugs."

"Officer on the scene said it looked like he took it in the shoulder."

Arrowsmith nodded. "He did. But the bullet was tumbling when it hit him. It may have ricocheted off something in the car . . . may have been one that went through his friend's head."

The three began walking toward Intensive Care.

"He'd have been better off if it had hit him full force," Arrowsmith continued. "Would have drilled right on through the shoulder. Tumbling like it did"—she made a circling motion with an index finger—"it pretty much smashed up the rotator cuff."

She stopped in front of one of the ICUs.

Through the glass door, Frank saw Pencil Crawfurd, chest bandaged, a tangle of tubes running in and out of his body, his bed surrounded by electronic monitoring equipment.

"He's still out," Arrowsmith said.

"Any guess how long?" José asked.

"Maybe another two, three hours." Her eyes fixed on the motionless figure. She sighed, as if acknowledging how powerless all the tubing and electronics were to affect what would happen. "Maybe a couple a days."

"He starts coming around . . ." José offered Arrowsmith a contact card.

She laughed. "Save your card. All these years, José, I got your number."

TWO

Frank turned off Florida Avenue onto M Street, NE.

A dingy assortment of run-down row houses lined both sides of the street. The stark glare of mercury-vapor lamps washed over battered doors, raw-dirt front yards, plywood-patched windows sprayed with gang graffiti. A gutted mattress lay on the sidewalk. Farther on, a Safeway shopping cart, minus a wheel, leaned against a long-dead tree.

"Looks like all the shit in the world nobody wanted's been dumped here," José said.

"Little urban renewal needed."

José grunted. "A little nuclear bomb."

"Here we are." Frank pulled over to the curb.

The two-story brick row house stood out from its crumbling neighbors: bright yellow with white trim, azaleas and climbing wisteria. A black ornamental cast-iron fence set the property off from the rest of the neighborhood.

The gate opened and shut quietly. At the door, José rapped with the polished brass knocker. He was about to knock again when the door swung open. A compact black man in a black suit, white shirt, and black bow tie stood like a statue in the doorway.

Marcus was into his never-blink routine. Deciding against a stare-down standoff, Frank held up his credentials and badge.

"We're here to see Ms. Lipton, Marcus."

Marcus's eyes moved almost imperceptibly, first taking in the credentials, then scanning Frank's face as though he'd never seen him before.

"Wait." Marcus's shearing whisper was like a razor cutting through stiff paper. He swung the door shut. It made the heavy, cushioned sound of a vault closing. The snicking of a deadbolt followed.

Frank glanced out at the empty street, then at José. "I thought he was still in Lorton."

"No," José said. "Maybe a month, two months ago, I heard he was out. Nice uniform."

"Looks like he got religion."

"If you can call it that."

More time passed.

Impatient, Frank rolled his shoulders. "Think he's coming back?"

"I don't hear anything."

José had the knocker up when the deadbolt slid back. Another second and the door swung open. Marcus did a short rerun of the statue game, then motioned Frank and José in with a twist of his head.

Walking with feline grace, he led them down a narrow hallway and into a glassed garden room filled with potted palms, orchids, and climbing vines.

Sharon Lipton, a large, exotic woman, sat in an even larger wicker chair. Like a throne, the chair back swept out and up, forming an oval frame for her face. Beside her, a similar chair, empty.

"Thank you, Marcus."

Marcus gave the slightest nod. He waited for a moment, eyeing Frank and José in warning, then left.

Lipton watched him leave, then turned to Frank and José.

They offered their credentials.

With the back of her hand, she waved them off. "Sit."

The two men took seats on a small sofa. Lipton looked them over as if they were up for auction.

"You . . . you're Josephus Phelps . . . Titus Phelps's boy. And you"—she shifted to Frank—"you're Frank Kearney."

She continued looking at the two detectives, collecting more thoughts. She pursed her lips. "You the two who set up Johnny Sam."

José shrugged. "Johnny set himself up."

Lipton ignored him. "You said you wanted to talk to me." She settled back in the chair and rested her hands on the arms. "So . . . so talk," she commanded.

The thought came to Frank: She knows. She knows why we're here.

José did it. Without preamble, he did it. "Ma'am, somebody shot and killed your son, James."

Lipton's expression didn't change.

"It was over on Bayless," José continued, "and Pencil—"

Lipton cut in. "I know."

Her voice came from a dark cavern of grief and anger. It hung in the still air of the garden room. A heartbeat or two passed; then she brought her head forward a fraction of an inch. The motion carried an impression of searching.

"Where is he?"

"Medical examiner's."

"They gonna cut him up . . . my boy." The final, flat way she said it, it wasn't a question, it was an indictment.

"Medical examination could help us find who killed him," José said.

Lipton registered zero expression.

"And his car?" she asked, as though toting up a score to be settled later.

"Impounded, ma'am, for evidence."

Frank asked, "He lived here?"

"Yes."

"Could we see his room?"

"Why?"

"There might be something there that could tell us something."

Lipton shook her head. "Not gonna have my boy's room tore up."

"We won't disturb a thing, ma'am," Frank said. "We would like to look, though."

"I don't let you," Lipton said sullenly. "You gonna get a warrant."

"We could," Frank said.

Lipton fixed Frank with a poisonous stare. Then the venom drained away, and only sadness remained.

"Marcus?"

She hadn't raised her voice, but Marcus instantly appeared in the doorway. She motioned toward Frank and José. "Take these . . . these *gentlemen* to James's. They gonna look around."

Marcus led the two toward the back of the house, through the kitchen and down a short hallway. In what was apparently an addition to the original house, he opened the door. A cathedral ceiling vaulted over a king-size bed that faced a wall-to-wall cabinet filled with stereo gear and a massive flat-panel TV. On the other side of the room, a recliner chair, a leather sectional sofa, a small wet bar, and another flat-panel TV.

"Turn all that stuff on at one time," José said, "you black out the neighborhood."

Marcus stationed himself by the door and folded his arms across his chest. The only thing that moved were his eyes as he followed the two detectives working their way around the room, Frank to the right, José to the left.

Without a warrant, you didn't get down to squeezing toothpaste out of the tubes, dismantling furniture, or even emptying the contents of drawers on the floor. But there were trade-offs. In the time you took to get a warrant, somebody could go through the place before you.

A walk-in closet: fourteen suits, a dozen or so shirts on hangers under plastic covers, and, Frank counted, twenty-three pairs of Nikes and sixteen athletic jackets of NBA teams.

Frank couldn't find a Wizards jacket.

With Michael Jordan, you'd think . . .

The door beside the closet led into a marble-and-tile full bath complete with steam shower and whirlpool tub.

Another door led to a garage that opened onto the alleyway running along the backs of the row houses. Skeeter could come and go without mama's knowing.

On the nightstand by the bed, a Uniden radio scanner and a large white telephone with a bank of speed-dial buttons and a row of LEDs.

"Secure phone," José said.

Frank jotted down the number. The nightstand also held several magazines, *Ironman, Basketball Digest, Sports Illustrated.*

José had finished his side of the room and was standing on the other side of the bed. He pointed to the *Ironman* cover, where an improbably muscled man and woman were showing nearly everything while rollerblading on a Venice, California, beach sidewalk. "Those two probably got muscles in their shit," he said.

Marcus spoke for the first time. "You two finished?"

Frank and José exchanged glances.

"Take us back to Ms. Lipton, please," Frank said.

Lipton hadn't moved from her wicker chair.

"You find what you wanted to find?"

"Thank you for your help, Ms. Lipton," José said.

"Didn't leave anything behind, did you?" she asked, eyelids heavy.

Frank ignored her.

"Do you have any notion who killed my boy?"

"No," José answered softly. "No, ma'am, we don't." He let the silence ripen, then asked, "Do you?"

Lipton sat back in her chair. Her face suddenly seemed to wilt. She shook her head. "Would it do me any good to tell you?"

"I don't know, ma'am," José said very deliberately, in a low voice. "I don't know if it would do you any good or not."

"How do you mean that . . . you don't know if it would do me any good or not?"

José lowered his voice even more. "Nobody can tell you that except yourself."

Lipton stared at José a long time, things going on behind her dark eyes. "How many times my boy hit?"

"We don't know, Ms. Lipton," Frank said, "not yet."

"My boy dead, and that Pencil gonna live . . ." Lipton mused, trailing off as if she had banked something she had to think about later. She assumed a businesslike tone. "When we get his car?"

"Like I said, Ms. Lipton, it's at impound. We'll be going over it for evidence."

"Evidence?" Lipton's mouth tightened. "Evidence against who?"

"Just evidence," José said evenly.

"How long?"

"Beg pardon?"

"How long before we get his car?" Lipton's exasperation was growing.

Frank watched as Marcus, standing behind her, stirred restlessly, gunner's eyes locked on the two detectives. Frank became aware of the weight of his own shoulder holster and the drape of his coat over his left armpit.

Him first. Then . . . then her?

"Can't say, exactly," José said.

"Can't? . . . Or won't?"

"Can't, ma'am. I can't say right now, and you know that. As soon's we can, that's all I can say."

For several heartbeats the four remained motionless, trapped in amber.

Frank broke the silence. "Ms. Lipton. Your son's killer . . . you have any idea . . . any guess?"

Lipton took a deep breath. She held it, then let it out, rocking ever so slightly in rhythm with music only she could hear.

"Idea?" she said in a hard-edged whisper. "I got an *eye*-dea. I got an idea that you folks did him in." She paused as though listening to her own thinking coming back to her. "Yes," she said with finality, "I think I'm looking at the people who did my boy in."

Frank was unlocking the car when José's cell phone chirped. José stood head thrust forward, phone pressed against his ear, massive body locked in place, as if the slightest movement might break a fragile connection. Then, almost imperceptibly, he nodded. His shoulders relaxed. He turned.

"Daddy," José explained. "Wants me to drop by."

"Want to skip coffee?"

José gave Frank an incredulous look. "Not with your turn to buy."

Adair set the orders of hash browns in front of the two men. Steam rose, fragrant and seductive, heavy with oil and paprika. Frank reached down the counter and snagged a bottle of Tabasco. After dousing his potatoes, he passed the hot sauce to José.

Adair watched, then gave out his usual warning. "Stuff'll rot your gut."

José came back with his usual reply. "Hasn't yet."

Adair ran a rag over the already clean counter in front of them. "Word is, Skeeter Hodges got whacked tonight."

José held up the Tabasco bottle. "Empty."

Adair sighed, reached under the counter, and came up with another bottle. He held it just out of José's reach. "And Pencil Crawfurd caught a few," he added. He looked at José, then Frank.

Frank raised his empty mug for a refill, pointedly saying nothing.

Adair took the hint and gave up on the fishing. Sighing again, he handed José the Tabasco and collected both mugs. "Whoever zapped those shits," he said, returning with the refills, "did us all a favor."

"Isn't hunting season for humans yet in the District," José said.

"Too bad," Adair replied over his shoulder as he walked away, down the length of the counter.

José and Frank picked at their hash browns. More out of needing something to do than being hungry. Leaving their plates half full, they drank their coffee without talking. Adair had gone to a booth at the back, where he sat working on the books.

Just the three of them in the place.

Night traffic sounds from outside joined with the gurgling of hot water in the coffee urns.

José looked around. "Lonesome is an empty diner at night." He took another sip of his coffee.

"Skeeter was what . . . thirty-four, -five?"

"Six. Thirty-six."

"Old to be living at home."

José considered this, then shook his head. "Advantages . . . Pretty much come and go as he wanted. Besides, with mama and Marcus there, he could tomcat around town all he wanted and come home to twenty-four/seven room service and security."

"That, and a twenty-four/seven alibi," Frank conceded.

"Sure was into high-tech."

The flat-panel TVs, the circuit boards, the scanner, and the secure phone.

"Pac-Man generation," Frank said, still putting a follow-on thought together. "You think about it, Hoser . . . how much Skeeter's business depends on communication. He can get stuff at Radio Shack or off the Net . . . scanners, bugging equipment, scrambler phones . . . stuff that's years ahead of anything we've got."

"What's more," José said, "he doesn't need a court order to use it. Something else . . . ?"

"Yeah?"

"Notice how eager Mama Lipton was to get his car back? We oughta have R.C. take it apart." José said, adding it to a mental checklist. " 'Nother thing—Skeeter's organization."

"Who's gonna inherit?"

"Yeah. Takeovers in that line of work get messy."

"Might tell us who had the motive and the balls to go after him," Frank said.

José scribbled a reminder in his notebook, then sat pensively as though something else was calling for his attention.

"Yeah," he said finally. "The chair."

"Chair?"

"Babba Lipton. The chair she was sitting in . . . with the big round back."

"Yeah?"

"Remind you of something?"

It wasn't until José asked that a memory flashed to Frank like a falling star. He struggled with it, trying to give it definition, time, place.

"Huey Newton," José hinted.

Instant clarity: The Black Panther poster. Huey Newton. Black leather jacket. Black beret. Shotgun in one hand, spear in the other. Sitting in a thronelike wicker chair. Brooding hate and malevolence.

"When we came in," José continued, "I knew she knew. The way she was waiting for us, sitting in that chair."

Frank put down his mug. "Yeah. She had a hard time. She's a tough lady."

"Yes. No."

"Yes? No?"

"Yes . . . she had a hard time. No . . . tough is raising a good kid. It's easy to do what she did."

"What'd she mean by that crap about her looking at Skeeter's killers?"

José shook his head. "Partner, I done finished with my psychoanalysis for the night. We got to get back to detecting."

Frank drank the last of his coffee. "Might not be too hard."

"How?"

"Guy who did Skeeter's out there somewhere"—Frank thumbed over his shoulder—"still on a high . . . pupils still dilated with excitement . . . king of the world. Absolutely . . ."

"Out there feelin' bulletproof," José said.

"Absolutely bulletproof."

José tried to picture the killer, but Teasdale's living room came on instead.

Teasdale in his button-up sweater sits in his Barcalounger. TV reflections flicker across the big man's broad face.

Somewhere off in the distance, he heard Frank. "And he'll talk," Frank was saying.

Bedtime. Teasdale fires the remote at the TV. The tube dies.

"He'll talk . . ."

Teasdale gets up. He checks the locks. The curtains are closed. But Teasdale pulls them tighter anyway.

". . . absolutely have to talk . . ." Frank batted his empty mug between his hands. Back and forth over the countertop. ". . . get credit for the score . . . big man . . . capping Skeeter Hodges . . ."

José caught his own image in the mirror opposite the counter. "What kind of life is that?" he asked himself quietly.

Frank closed his hands, capturing the sliding mug. "What?"

"Oh," José said, "thinking about . . . how we have to live." He stood and reached for his wallet. "How much we owe?" he asked Adair.

Frank shot him a puzzled look. "You forget," he said, "it's my turn."

THREE

Trumpets . . . church bells . . . ghostly voices . . . a Morricone score out of an old Clint Eastwood spaghetti western.

In semidarkness, a crouching figure holds the pistol in a two-handed combat grip, aiming it into even darker shadows. A lightning flash. Skeeter Hodges sits in the Huey Newton wicker chair.

Motionless as a manikin, he sits . . . waiting.

Blood erupts. Skeeter's head explodes.

In slow motion, the shooter turns.

The bells and the voices surge.

And the figure faces him. And a lone trumpet searches his soul. The pistol finds his eyes. And the bore of the muzzle reaches out and engulfs him, and he stares into the darkness at the end of the world.

The trumpets . . . the bells . . . the voices . . . pound in a hellish apocalyptic crescendo. . . .

Frank opened his eyes as the first jet of the morning from Reagan National screamed overhead, clawing its way north above the Potomac.

He lay twisted in the sheets. Motionless, he stared at the ceiling. His pulse beat furiously in his throat. The jet engines faded and his pulse slowed and the dream fragments drifted away.

He rolled over and shut his eyes, but his legs had cramped during the night, and his lungs felt musty, like a room that'd been shut too long. He sat up and swung his feet to the floor. He yawned, stretched, and looked around the bedroom, eyes coming to rest on the two windows overlooking the courtyard garden at the back of the house. Blue sky framed a sun-dappled oak. Plaster walls and heart-pine floors glowed from sunlight coming down the hallway from the front of the house.

Sixteen years before, when he'd bought the dilapidated row house on Olive Street, all the windows had been painted shut. A contractor had wanted to install thermopaned windows. The more Frank thought about it, the less he'd liked it. Old houses had old windows. So he'd learned how to disassemble the original windows, strip layers of paint, replace pulleys and sash cords, and he'd put everything back together so it worked as it had when the house had been new and Grover Cleveland had been president.

It was warm enough to run in shorts and T-shirt, and ten minutes later, he was striding at an easy pace down M Street. He crossed Key Bridge, ran along Teddy Roosevelt Island, then down the riverside path to Memorial Bridge. Once across the bridge, he circled the Lincoln Memorial, then picked up speed for a hard run up the Potomac and back into Georgetown.

Despite the exertion, the dream kept replaying. *Skeeter's head . . . the pistol . . . Skeeter just sitting there . . . a captive actor in a deadly play . . . the shot.*

He finished the run winded, sweaty, and nagged by a rasping sensation that something somewhere somehow had gone very badly wrong.

A half-hour later, showered, shaved, and standing at the kitchen counter, he sipped coffee and scanned the *Post.* Skeeter's killing ranked front page above the fold, complete with photos. Bad-boy rating about eight or nine on a scale of ten, Frank figured, reading between the lines. A follower of the flamboyant Juan Brooks. Inherited the business when Juan got life in max security at Marion, Illinois. Then the obligatory boilerplate editorial equation: Young boys plus inner-city poverty plus guns equals crime.

He felt a brushing against his trouser leg and looked down.

"Hello," he said to Monty.

The big gray cat sat with the steely expression of a drill sergeant. Cats had always intrigued him—how they watched people in the curious but detached way people watched parades. But until Monty, Frank hadn't thought of himself as a cat person.

Frank tapped the newspaper. *"Les Misérables,"* he explained.

Monty wasn't interested.

Monty had literally dropped into Frank's life. Frank had been laying a patio in his courtyard one Saturday. He'd been on his knees, tapping a brick into place, when a very thin kitten landed in the impatiens by the wall. Frank was startled, and assumed the animal had jumped or fallen from an overhanging branch of his neighbor's tree. Showing no fear, the kitten approached Frank and sat just out of reach. For an hour, it watched him work. When he went into the kitchen for a beer, the kitten followed.

The cat didn't beg. It just sat, staring, beaming a telepathic command. Frank obediently opened a can of tuna.

The cat made himself at home. He had no collar. Frank put an ad in the lost and found. He watched for lost-cat flyers taped to Georgetown lampposts. The first week, he hoped an owner would show. The next week, he was afraid one might. One never did, and Monty took over as master of the small row house on Olive Street.

Food!

Frank saluted. "Right away, sir." In the years with Monty, he'd come to the conclusion that if cats could talk to humans . . . they wouldn't.

Monty had accumulated a variety of bowls from Kate, José, and a loose coalition of neighbors Frank had come to think of as "the Olive Street Gang." From a cabinet, he picked out a bowl featuring a Delft-blue cat with a crown.

"This okay?"

Move it, move it.

Frank filled the bowl with dry food and put it down near Monty's swinging door that led into the garden. Monty sniffed at the offering, then grudgingly tried a bite. Soon the food was disappearing, swept up by a furry vacuum cleaner. As he finished his coffee, Frank watched the big cat eat. Then, after stuffing the newspaper into a canvas briefcase, he went through the ritual of setting the alarm system and locking up the house.

On his front steps, Frank glanced up and down the street, taking a second or two to recall where he'd had to park the night before. He found his car on Thirtieth Street and said a silent thank-you prayer for no new dings and the still-intact side-view mirrors.

WGMS was playing the *1812 Overture.* It was too early in the day for booming cannons, so Frank switched to WOL and Joe Madison. Concentrating on the Pennsylvania Avenue traffic, he paid little attention until he realized that Madison was talking about Skeeter Hodges. He turned up the volume.

Madison was refereeing a bare-knuckle brawl between Oliver North and Sarah Brady. North, the former Marine, was arguing against gun control, while Brady, the gun control activist, was arguing for. The two counterpunched with the now familiar prefabricated sound bites—Second Amendment rights, Founding Fathers' intent, the definition of an organized militia.

All the old answers. Any new questions?

Madison cut in.

"We got a call from a listener, Mrs. Frances Morrow. Mrs. Morrow, you're on."

"*Mis*-tuh Madison—" An assertive chocolate-brown voice. Frank tugged at a memory, then gave up.

"Where you from, Mrs. Morrow?"

A pause. Then, crossly, "Eads Street." As though laying down a challenge, she added, "Forty-five-oh-*four* Eads Street."

Again the voice sounded oddly familiar, and Frank recognized the address. *Two blocks from Bayless Place.*

"Go ahead, Mrs. Morrow. You got words for Mr. North and Mrs. Brady?"

"I do, Black Eagle," she said, using Madison's nickname. "Where *you* folks live?"

Dead air.

Frank imagined North and Brady, sensing a trap, exchanging wary glances.

"*Well?*" Morrow demanded.

"Ah"—North cleared his throat—"Great Falls. Great Falls, Virginia."

"Potomac," Brady answered, her voice tentative.

"Unh-hunh! *Yeah,*" Morrow replied, a sneer in her voice. "An' how many a your whitebread friends in *Puh-toe-muck* or Great Falls ever had to chase drug dealers off *their* front porches?"

More dead air. It hung there, embarrassing, like a bad smell.

"I tell you how many!" Morrow's voice rose with indignation. "*None!*"

Frank rapped the steering wheel and smiled.

Frances Morrow bored in. "You give us all these downtown arguments about the Constitution. . . . You're talking about *Puh-toe-muck* living. About how you folks in Great Falls live. I tell you what"—righteous anger rolled in her voice—"I tell you *what*— you come down to where *I* live. Or you go over to Bayless Place. You'll find one thing, Mistuh North, Missus Brady—you'll find the only thing wrong with guns is that the wrong people got them."

Madison, recognizing a dramatic closing line when he heard one, took a break for a commercial. Frank imagined North and Brady wondering what the hell had just hit them.

. . .

Two large wooden desks dominated the center of Frank and José's small office. Years earlier, they had pushed the desks together so they could work facing each other. A random collection of file cabinets and bookcases lined the walls. Above the bookcases on one wall was an Ipswich Fives dartboard that Frank had picked up in a London secondhand shop, surrounded by holes in the drywall attesting to sloppy marksmanship. The single window faced south, its sill home to an eclectic parade of potted plants over the years. Today, a variegated pothos shared its perch with a struggling African violet that Frank had bought at Eastern Market and a spider plant that Tina Barber had given José.

José stood looking out the window. He turned slowly when Frank walked in. He glanced up at the wall clock.

"You run this morning?"

"Yeah." Frank saw that José had already made coffee. He picked his mug up off his desk; regarded the dark brown remainder of yesterday's coffee, poured it out, then poured a refill. The coffee was scalding.

"Frances Morrow," he said, and blew across the steaming mug, "on—"

"Joe Madison this morning."

"Yeah." Frank tried another sip. "Where'd we—"

"O'Brien case."

Gears meshed. The picture materialized. Big woman. Filling the doorway of the small brick house. "Gray sweats," he recalled.

"Redskins jersey," José added. "Mean like no tomorrow."

The phone rang. José answered. Listened. Hung up.

"Emerson wants to see us."

Walking down the hallway toward the stairs, Frank noticed a weariness around José's eyes.

"You sleep last night?"

José shook his head. "Going home, I stopped by Daddy's."

"Oh?"

"He wasn't home. Mama said he was still at the church."

A single light far up in the rafters illuminated the altar and pulpit. His father sat in a front pew, head bowed.

José put his hand on his father's shoulder. Titus Phelps reached up and covered his son's hand with his own.

"Getting late, Daddy."

His father looked at him, then to the altar. He moved over. José sat down beside him.

Titus Phelps paused as if listening to a voice inside himself. "Just sitting here, talking with Jesus."

"You heard about over on Bayless Place?"

His father turned to him. "You ever wonder, Josephus, what keeps us safe? Truly safe?"

"Go on, Daddy."

"You're my oldest son . . . a policeman. You're strong . . . you're smart. But you can't keep us safe."

Titus Phelps listened to his private, inner voice, then nodded in agreement.

"It's inside us, Josephus, the power to keep ourselves safe. So we don't have to fear the night. So we can trust our neighbors." He paused, then, voice picking up momentum, continued: "That power is in us. Each of us. And if we don't use it, it goes away. And if that happens, we won't be safe, no matter how many police we have . . . even if they're all as strong and as smart as my son."

The words had rolled through the church toward the farthest pews in the back. José knew he'd heard the beginnings of a sermon yet to be preached.

. . .

They were now at the stairway. Frank reached out and squeezed José's shoulder. "Let's see what's on Emerson's mind."

They pushed into Emerson's outer office at eight-fifteen.

Shana looked up from her computer and frowned petulantly. "He's been waiting." She snapped an index finger toward Emerson's door. The inch-long scarlet fingernail resembled a bloody talon.

Frank felt an acid clot of irritation in his throat.

Emerson stood behind his desk, a green glass slab supported by two matte black metal sawhorses. Resplendent in a creamy silk shirt and an Italian designer tie, he held a folder several inches thick. He studied the contents for a moment or two after Frank and José entered. Then he closed the folder and held it up.

"Looks like somebody did some street cleaning."

"Somebody did murder one," José said.

As if he hadn't heard or didn't care, Emerson regarded the closed folder in his hands. "Hodges was a busy boy," he whispered to himself. He got a sly look that put Frank in mind of something slithering through the grass.

"He's in cold storage now," Frank said.

Emerson continued staring thoughtfully at the folder. Then, as if the comment finally registered, he put the folder on his desk and looked at Frank.

"Oh, no. Skeeter's got one more job to do. A job for us."

Without having to look, Frank knew that José was doing his slow eye-roll. He looked anyway. José was.

He looked back at Emerson. Emerson's eyebrows were raised in a question mark.

"Beg pardon?" Frank asked.

"I said, 'How many people you think Skeeter clipped?'"

"Rounded off to the nearest hundred?"

"Get serious."

José yawned. "Belt-and-suspenders estimate? Fifteen. Twenty. Most of them competitors."

"Okay. And how many times did he go to trial?" Emerson asked.

"None." Frank shook his head.

Emerson sat down in his high-backed black leather chair. It looked like it came off the bridge of the starship *Enterprise*. He tilted back. "And why was that?"

"Why was what?" José asked.

"Why didn't he go to trial?" Emerson eyed the space just in front of him, the question hanging there, rotating slowly in midair. "I'll tell you why," he said, eyes still on the question. "Witnesses died, disappeared, or suddenly got Alzheimer's."

"Or they'd swear Skeeter was singing in the choir or babysittin' their kids," José added.

Emerson shifted his gaze to José, then to Frank, and back to José.

"We have cases where we know Skeeter was involved, but no evidence. But now, like you say, he's no longer on the street. We don't have to bring him to trial. We only have to dig a little. Push a little. Bend a little."

He tilted forward and pushed Skeeter Hodges's folder across the glass. "So why don't you two see if some witnesses have reappeared or had a miraculous memory cure?"

"What you want us to do," José said, "is pin a bunch a cold cases on Skeeter so we can make our numbers."

Emerson's lips thinned. "I want you two to do some retrospective investigation," he said tightly. "Bring justice. Is that too much to ask?"

"What you're asking us to do," Frank countered, "isn't investigating, it's picking through a garbage dump."

Emerson's face flushed. He jabbed an index finger at the two detectives.

"You two prima donnas," he shouted in a strangled voice, "are not . . . by God . . . going to fucking define . . . what your job is in this goddamn department!"

His eyes bulged and his finger trembled as he went on. "There are procedures . . . recognized procedures . . . legal procedures . . . for closing cold cases. And you will damn well get busy, or you will turn in your badges."

Winded, Emerson paused. "Is that clear?" he asked in a flat, metallic voice.

"Clear . . ." José hesitated, then tacked on a silent "But . . . ?"

"Yes?" Emerson asked.

"You mind if we track down Skeeter's killer while we're at it?"

José shook his head. "You had to know *that* was coming," he said as they walked down the hall from Emerson's office.

Frank felt the knot of anger tight in his stomach. "Emerson the weatherman."

"Hunh. Weather*vane*."

They stopped at a door with a sign that said "Records—Modus Operandi." Frank tapped his five-digit access code into a keypad set into the wall beside the door.

Nothing.

Frowning, he entered the numbers again. Again, nothing.

"Damn thing's fighting you," José said unhelpfully.

Frank mentally went over the access code again. *Bank PIN, Social Security number, health insurance group number, frequent flyer account number.* "I thought it was only the army that made people into numbers."

He tried a third time. The door unlocked with a metallic click, and Frank pushed through. Battered ranks of old-fashioned file cabinets filled the left side of the cavernous room. On the right, records analysts sat at four rows of desks. The analysts, mostly women, faced their computer screens with a vacant stare—the empty look of combat veterans who'd seen too much and who knew they were going to see more.

No one looked up as Frank and José made their way to a desk in the last row. There, a small-boned woman with short-cut iron-gray hair leaned forward, her fingers racing across her computer keyboard like those of a concert pianist at a Steinway. They stood watching until she looked up.

Eleanor Trowbridge intrigued Frank. R&MO's senior analyst was a constant in a constantly changing world. She'd had the wrinkles and the gray hair when he and José had first met her twenty-six years before. She knew damn near all there was to know about crime in the District. She'd turned in her battered Olivetti typewriter for a Gateway computer, but she was still the person you went to if you wanted to make sense of things that didn't make sense to anybody else.

José started to say something.

Before he could, Eleanor swiveled her chair around to a file cabinet and pulled a thick file jacket from a drawer. "James Culver Hodges. Aka 'Skeeter.'" She handed it to José.

José flashed a look of surprise, then smiled. "While you're at it, got any picks for NBA playoffs?"

"Maybe the Powerball numbers?" Frank asked.

"Elementary, gentlemen," Eleanor said, sighing. "Point one, Mr. Hodges is newly dead."

José's smile turned wry. "Bingo."

"And you two want me to find you some cold cases you can bury with Skeeter?"

"Double bingo," Frank said.

Eleanor looked at the two detectives over the top of her glasses. "This afternoon? After five?"

Back in the office, the answering machine flashed insistently. Frank jabbed the answer button.

"Frank?" The words came out burgundy. "Call when you can."

José watched the smile gathering at the corners of Frank's mouth. "Woman's got a voice."

Frank nodded and slouched comfortably into his chair. "She does indeed."

He never thought about Kate without a flush of warmth somewhere between heart and stomach. He didn't remember a world before her and couldn't imagine a world after. He caught occasional reflections of himself in her, and it always surprised him, the goodness he saw there. Part of him marveled that the two of them had found each other, while another part worried how he'd be if she weren't there.

José watched Frank's smile grow. "I know what you're thinking."

"Yeah?"

"Yeah. Meantime, you want to do . . . what?"

Frank thought about Kate some more, then sat up, took a deep breath, and surveyed his desktop. The overflowing in-box drew his eyes.

"We could"—he waved at the mound of paper—"get some of *that* done."

José looked at his own in-box in distaste. "Let's *not*. Let's go check the street."

Frank reached for his phone. "Let me call Kate first."

"I'll get the car."

Frank picked up the phone and hit a speed dial. He looked out toward the Mall. The wind had picked up; the flags atop the Smithsonian castle stood straight out. How long, he wondered, had it been since he'd taken the time to—

"Hello."

The Smithsonian and its flags vanished, and he felt warm in his chest.

"José says you've got a voice."

"Doesn't everybody?"

He waited several heartbeats. "You're back tonight?"

Kate gave him a flight number.

"Missed you," he said.

"It was only a week."

Several more heartbeats. "Oh?"

Kate laughed. "You've got a voice."

"Doesn't everybody?"

Another laugh. "No."

FOUR

The maroon Crown Vic idled at the curb, José at the wheel.

Still thinking about Kate and dinner, Frank got in.

José dropped the car into gear and pulled away. "Thought we might check the Rolex market."

Ten minutes later, Frank and José sat in the car, watching as Waverly Ngame assembled his stand across the street.

First out of the white Dodge van, a longish rectangular folding table, the kind you see in church basements and at catered receptions. Ngame locked open the legs. With a toe, he nudged wood shims under them, working around the table until it was steady on the uneven brick sidewalk.

Ngame disappeared into the van. He came back out with racks of white plastic-coated wire-grid shelving under both arms, and a grease-stained canvas bag in his left hand. In swift, practiced motions, he picked the largest of the shelves and braced it upright on the side of the table facing the street.

Holding the shelf with one hand, he reached into the canvas bag with the other and brought out a large C clamp. He twirled the clamp with sharp snaps of his wrist, then opened the jaws just enough to slip over the shelf and the table edge. He tightened the clamp, and moved to repeat the process on the other side of the table.

Almost magically, more shelving and more C clamps produced a display stand.

Back into the van.

This time, Ngame reappeared with large nylon bags of merchandise. Several more trips, and Gucci handbags hung alluringly from the vertical shelving while Rolex watches and Serengeti sunglasses marched in neat ranks across the top of the folding table.

In the street, by Ngame's van, a crow worried at the flattened remains of a road-killed rat.

With a little finger, Ngame made a microscopic adjustment, poking a pair of sunglasses to line up just so with its neighbors. He didn't look up from putting the fine touches to his display.

"Detectives Phelps and Kearney. Good morning, sirs."

As a boy in Lagos, Ngame had learned his English listening to the BBC. He sounded like a Brit announcer, except that he had a Nigerian's way of softly rounding his vowels and stressing the final syllables of his sentences.

"How's business, Waverly?" José asked.

Ngame gave the sunglasses a last critical look, then turned to face José and Frank. He was a big man, almost as big as José, with shiny blue-black skin.

He smiled, unveiling a mouthful of perfectly straight glistening teeth. "This is America!" The words exploded with exuberance. A-mare-uh-*cuh*! "Business is *always* splendid!" He waved a large hand down the crowded sidewalk—*his* sidewalk—taking in potential customers—*his* customers. "One is free to sell and free to buy . . . buy and sell."

He caressed a handbag. "This purse, for example—"

José pulled Ngame's string. "Mr. Gucci gets his cut?"

Ngame got the tried look of a long-suffering teacher with a slow student. "Detective Phelps! Do you suppose this is a real Gucci purse?" He swept a hand over the watches. "Or that these are real Rolexes?"

José's eyes widened. "They aren't?"

"And do you suppose that any of these good people who come to my stand *believe* they are buying real Guccis or real Rolexes?"

José opened his eyes wider, spinning Ngame up more.

"And do you suppose that my customers could buy a *real* Rolex?"

"Oh?" José said encouragingly.

"So who is hurt?" Ngame was into it now, eyes wide in enthusiasm, hands held out shoulder high, palms up. "Not Mister Gucci! Nor Mister Rolex! As a matter of fact, Mister Gucci and Mister Rolex ought to be *pleased* with me—*pleased!* Yes, pleased. My customers have learnt good taste here at my stand." Ngame's chin tilted up. "When they get wealthy, they'll buy the *real* Gucci and the real Rolex."

"Like Skeeter Hodges," Frank said.

Ngame gave Frank a heavy-lidded, somber look. "He didn't buy here. He kept the real Mister Rolex in business."

"What's the talk?" José asked.

Ngame looked up and down the sidewalk. He did it casually, but he did it.

"Conjecture?" Con-jec-*ture?*

Another glance, this time across the street. "From the Puerto Ricans I hear it was the Jamaicans. The Jamaicans tell me it was the Puerto Ricans. And the blacks"—Ngame shrugged—"the blacks all point their fingers at one another."

"No names?" Frank asked.

Ngame shook his head. "No pretender to the throne. But then again, Detective Kearney, it was only last night."

Ngame reached down, then came up with a watch in his hand, gleaming gold in the morning sunlight.

"A Rolex President? I will give a discount."

A block north of Waverly Ngame's stand, Frank and José made their way down an increasingly crowded sidewalk.

"Like I care."

Frank angled his head slightly to catch the disembodied male voice behind him. It had a demented quality, like that of a man talking to himself.

"The garbage?"

The pitch rose.

"Ten dollars?"

The voice came nearer, and passed to Frank's right.

"Mary? Mary?"

A lanky white kid in baggy jeans and a Bulls sweatshirt walked by. He held a cell phone out at arm's length, as if that would somehow put him in visual contact with Mary? Mary?

"Shit," the kid muttered.

José and Frank watched him walk on. Another couple of steps, and he was punching another number into his phone.

"Voices everywhere," José said.

"Schizophrenia or Sprint?"

The 7-Eleven had a frayed, secondhand look, as though time had been working it over with an eraser. A ragged man sprawled on a bench near the entrance. Close by, a clear plastic bag stuffed with blankets, aluminum cans, and scraps of unidentifiable clothing. Over his head a sign warned "No Loitering—Violators Will Be Prosecuted." At the curb, a battered and rusting ten-speed bike, stripped of its front wheel, was Kryptonite-locked to a parking meter.

Frank stopped to take in a faded poster in the 7-Eleven window. It carried an image of a gold-foil District Metropolitan Police Department shield; above the shield, "Official Location," and below it, "Police Community Work Station." Malcolm Burridge, the previous mayor, had had these posters put up after a wave of convenience-shop holdups and killings. They hadn't stopped the killings, but they'd made one of Burridge's political fat cats a little fatter with the proceeds from the printing contract.

"Hex sign," Frank thought he heard José say. He looked at his partner. "What?"

José was looking at the poster too. "Hex sign," he repeated, "like on those barns . . . up in Pennsylvania . . . Keep away the devil."

Kim Tae Ho looked up from the *Post* sports section. Two blurred foreigners. The first through the door black and big. Kim's right hand dropped under the counter, under the cash register. At the same time, he ducked his head to peer over the top of his reading glasses. His hand came up from below the counter.

"Ah! Mr. Phelps. Mr. Kearney." He smiled.

"Mr. Kim." José took his hand.

"Mr. Kim," Frank said, shaking the man's hand after José.

"You still keeping the forty-five under the counter, Mr. Kim?" José asked casually.

Kim widened his eyes. "Mr. Phelps! A private citizen cannot possess a handgun in the District. It is illegal."

Frank glanced around. A male customer at the back rummaged through the beer cooler; otherwise the place was empty.

"Somebody shot Skeeter Hodges last night, Mr. Kim," Frank said.

"Yes."

The pinched way Kim said it, Frank knew there wasn't going to be any more.

"You hear any talk?" José asked.

"No." Kim looked past the two men.

Frank heard footsteps behind him. The man from the cooler stood there with a tall can of Wild Bull. Frank stepped aside. Wordlessly, the man set the can on the counter and pulled a couple of rumpled singles out of his pocket. Frank noticed the man's hand trembled ever so slightly.

Kim made change and slipped the can into a paper bag. He stood still and watched the man leave. The door closed. Kim's eyes came back to Frank and José.

"No," Kim repeated. The tension in his voice had disappeared. "There is no talk. After a killing, there is usually much discussion of it. Such as after a baseball game."

Frank thought of Edward Teasdale, sitting in his Barcalounger, watching the Birds shut down the Red Sox.

"You knew Skeeter?"

"Oh, yes." Kim's face tightened.

"And . . . ?"

"He held me up." Kim pointed. "He walked right through that door and he held me up."

The forty-five . . . when was that?" Frank asked.

He and José stood on the sidewalk outside the 7-Eleven. The man on the bench hadn't moved. Frank glanced at him to see if he was breathing.

José massaged the back of his neck. He looked at the man on the bench too. "Two, three years ago. June . . . no . . . July. Yeah, July. Right after the Fourth."

Frank placed it. He and Kate, just back from Spain. An epidemic of violent holdups and dead convenience-store owners in Southeast, near Eastern Market.

"Cecil and Forrest . . . ?" The last name floated just outside Frank's reach.

"Gibbons," José furnished.

It had been a hot summer night, and the 911 dispatcher had reported shooting inside Kim's 7-Eleven. First officers on the scene found the Gibbons brothers sprawled among toppled shelves of canned goods. Each had been killed with a single headshot: Cecil between the eyes, Forrest through the right temple. Cecil's fingerprints were all over a SIG-Sauer, and Forrest still clutched a Glock 17. Forensics connected both weapons to the earlier Southeast killings.

Kim had claimed that the Gibbons brothers and a third gunman had gotten into an argument. He—Kim—had ducked behind the bullet shield by the cash register. The third gunman had fled after shooting the Gibbonses. The convenience-store killings stopped. The alleged third gunman had never been found, nor had the forty-five he'd allegedly used.

The man on the bench yawned.

"Might try that, one a these days," José mused.

"Sleeping on a bench?"

"Fella makes it look comfortable." José checked his watch. He pointed down Seventh Street toward the nineteenth-century rambling brick building that was Eastern Market. "What say we buy Gideon a roll?"

Mid-morning shoppers filled the market's aisles. Gideon Weaver's stall was empty. A broad counter ran around the three walls. Above and below the counter, bookshelves. Bibles crowded the counter and the shelves: Leviathan family Bibles, small vest-pocket testaments. Bibles in Braille. Spanish, French, German Bibles. Bibles in Kiswahili, Bihari, Shona. A cigar box minus its lid sat on the counter next to a portable CD player. Several tens, fives, and singles lay in the box, and "Lead On, O King Eternal" came from the CD player. Taped above the box and the CD player a paper banner—"Message of the Day."

" 'With the ancient is wisdom, and in length of days, understanding,' " Frank read aloud.

"Job Twelve, twelve."

Frank turned to José. "For sure?"

"Coffee and a roll?"

"Sure."

Frank knew he'd lose. Never do Bible bets with a preacher's kid.

Bean There used to be a soda fountain named Cherry's. Cherry had had the business for forty years before he retired and moved to Arizona. Two employees had bought him out, and latte, cappuccino, and a dozen variants of espresso had replaced banana splits, hot fudge sundaes, and of course, the signature cherry sodas. Bean There had, however, kept the round marble-top tables and the drugstore chairs with their curling wrought-iron backs and legs.

Frank watched José fix his coffee. Two spoons sugar, half-and-half to muddy brown. "How much coffee you think we've drunk?" he asked.

José didn't hesitate. "Least two thousand gallons."

Frank stared.

"Minimum." José made a show of his first sip, taking it slow.

Frank dismissed it with a laugh. "That's bullshit, Hoser—two thousand *gallons*?"

"Minimum," José repeated. He sat quietly a moment for effect, then: "Okay. Cup of coffee is about eight ounces?"

"Minimum."

"Okay, if we drink four cups a day that's thirty-two ounces. Every four days . . . a gallon?"

Frank ran over the math in his head. "Yeah?"

"Well, that's ninety gallons a year. Times twenty-six years . . ."

Frank tried to picture two thousand gallons of coffee.

"That's if we just drink an average of four cups a day," José added, "an' you know, there been days—"

"Josephus and Franklin, our wall by day and night." The voice came grating and rumbling, like a granite landslide.

A massively muscled man drove his motorized wheelchair up to the table.

"You were by my stall. I knew you'd stop here."

Southeast Washington's eyes and ears belonged to Gideon Weaver. A stray bullet during the '68 riots had ended his career as a car thief, but a hospital conversion by Titus Phelps had put Weaver in a new set of wheels and on the path toward becoming an inner-city missionary.

"Coffee and a roll?" Frank asked.

"Man does not live by bread alone, Franklin, but Deuteronomy doesn't say anything about cappuccino and a bear claw."

Frank put the coffee and roll on the table in front of Weaver.

"Thank you," he said. He bowed his head in brief prayer, then looked up at Frank and José.

"James Hodges," he said.

"You hear who?" José asked.

Weaver shook his head. "People don't know. They did, they'd talk, and I'd hear."

He got a reckoning look, a man making an inventory, or weighing the value of a soul. "A tragic figure," he offered slowly.

"You knew him?" José asked.

"He lived here in Southeast." Weaver's voice lifted at the end. As if to say, "I know everybody in Southeast."

Frank asked, "Personally?"

"Franklin." Weaver arched his eyebrows. "I *said*: 'He lived here in Southeast.'"

Frank raised both hands, palms toward Weaver.

With a smile, Weaver accepted Frank's surrender. "There was a lot written about James. His association with Juan Brooks."

"We know," Frank said, "but how'd *you* see him?"

Weaver worked at the bear claw with the side of a fork. He separated a piece, dipped it in his coffee, took a bite, and smiled in satisfaction. The smile went away and he put the fork down.

"James was a man who wanted to be king."

Frank and José looked at each other. They both eyed Weaver.

"King," José repeated.

Weaver took a moment to answer. "Yes." He paused and nodded as if in agreement with himself. "I never thought of him *that* way. Until now—until you asked. 'King' just . . . just came out."

"And what made it come out?" José asked.

Weaver considered this. "Do you know Belial?"

"No," Frank replied.

"A fallen angel," José answered.

Weaver rewarded him with a glance of approval. "James could have done much good. But he took the talents God gave him and turned them to evil uses. Still, it always seemed to me that he was searching for redemption. Trying to buy his way back into grace."

"He had a head for business," Frank put in.

"Numbers *and* people," Weaver said.

"People?" José asked. "How 'people'?"

"People underestimated him. Dropout. Child of the projects. A boy who didn't know his father. The hustlers thought that they had a good recruit. Their mistake. They'd give James a little slack, a little headway—he'd hustle *them*."

"You said 'king,'" Frank reminded Weaver.

"Folks bowing to him—James hungered for respectability." Weaver wagged a warning finger. "Not just *respect*. Difference between respect and respectability. . . . You can get re-*spect* because you got a gun in your hand. Or a hundred-dollar bill. What James wanted was respec-ta-*bil*-ity—something people give you without you asking. Without the gun or the Benjamin."

FIVE

Capital Mortgage." José pointed to the next door down the hallway.

The Majestic theater had opened in the 1920s, and generations of kids had grown up in Southeast spending Saturdays at double-feature westerns and horror movies. The theater folded in the 1970s. For years, it stood empty, a shelter for the homeless and an incubator for rats. Then developers reinforced the art deco façade, ripped out the rows of gum-bottomed seats, gutted the interior, and rebuilt the Majestic as an odorless, fully carpeted, color-coordinated office building. A Rite Aid drugstore, the inevitable Starbucks, and a branch of the Riggs Bank took up the ground floor. Capital Mortgage shared the second floor with an assortment of lawyers, dentists, and trade association lobbyists.

Capital's reception area conveyed an impression of rectitude: sturdy, unpretentious furniture, navy wool carpet, pale-blue walls hung with large black-and-white photos of old Washington, and a conservatively dressed receptionist with a Jamaican accent who offered a choice of V8, orange juice, or bottled water.

Frank and José waved away the receptionist's offer. They settled into armchairs, José picking up a *New York Times*, Frank a *Newsweek*.

José rattled the *Times* and groaned. "Shouldn't do it."

"Do what?" Frank asked.

"Kiss those Chinese asses." José held up the paper. Front-page headline, the Chinese demanding an apology for the EP-3 spy-plane incident.

"Can't just let them rot there."

José shook his head. *"Apologize,"* he muttered with contempt. "Bush got himself off on the wrong foot. You the new guy on the block, somebody's gonna test you." He was searching for the sports section when the receptionist got up and walked to a closed door.

"He's off the phone, now." She opened the door.

Simultaneously Frank saw Lamar Sheffield and the Capitol building. Sheffield sat at a large desk, and behind him, the Capitol filled a picture window.

Tom Kearney, Frank's father, had once remarked that Sheffield was a double for Nelson Mandela. Ever since, Frank thought Mandela when he saw Sheffield: a man with a starched backbone and silver hair, a man whose eyes said quietly that he had known fear and had mastered it. Both men had learned much about themselves while serving time in prison . . . Nelson Mandela for resisting apartheid, Lamar Sheffield for executing three of his criminal associates who had disobeyed his order to stay out of the drug business.

At first glance, the view of the Capitol seemed to demand a larger, grander office. But after you took in the Azerbaijan carpet, the well-aged club chairs upholstered in butter-soft leather, the walnut credenza with the silver-framed family photos and the Waterford crystal decanters, the room was not so much an office as the private hideaway of an old friend. A place where you could believe what you heard.

"I don't suspect you're here for refinancing," Sheffield said, getting up to shake hands. He had a surprisingly round voice, something, Frank thought, like Nat Cole's.

"Should we?" Frank asked.

"If you wait, rates may go up," Sheffield said, "but on the other hand, they may go down."

"And Capital Mortgage wins either way," José said.

"Only if we're smart," Sheffield said dismissively, as he led them to the club chairs. He sat, carefully hitching up his trouser legs to protect the crease. "And that's what you're here for, isn't it . . . to get smart? Skeeter Hodges?"

"Yeah, Skeeter. We'll settle for a little less dumb," Frank said.

Frank studied the man he and José had sent to Lorton twenty years before. Times had been changing around Sheffield. Prostitution, gambling, and loansharking had been sufficient to satisfy humanity's basic sins—sins that history and longevity somehow legitimized. Drugs, however, were different in Lamar Sheffield's view. They corrupted humanity in a way the old sins couldn't. A man had to be a man. Stand for something, even in the face of the inevitable. And so Sheffield had killed Mookie, Travis, and Snake, knowing what it would mean. And Frank and José had taken him in, and Sheffield had done hard time in Lorton at an advanced age— something that would have killed most men. But he had come out leaving one life behind and started a new one. Yet the old ties remained: people talked to Lamar Sheffield—residual perks of a reputation earned by a lifetime on the street.

"No word out as to who might have done it," Frank said.

Sheffield frowned. "There's always talk. Sometimes before. Most always after."

"You haven't heard anything about Skeeter?"

Sheffield smiled mockingly. "You talking to the other mortgage brokers in town?"

"Other brokers don't have such nice offices," José said.

"Or such rap sheets," Sheffield came back. "You thinking about a hit? Man gets shot in his car in that business, you know it was a hit."

"A competitor?" Frank asked. "I thought he didn't have any."

"Never can tell. It could have been one of his own people," Sheffield said sadly. "No loyalty these days. Too much on the table. Your best friends get greedy and you end up with a bullet in the back of your head."

"I heard it happens that way, Lamar," Frank said.

"Curious thing about Skeeter," Sheffield mused. "How he managed to slip by you folks with the badges. Took over when Brooks got sent away, and just dropped out of sight."

He paused to think about it. "A matter of style," he finally said. "Skeeter didn't wear the diamonds and fur coats, didn't charter planes to the Vegas fights. He paid attention to business."

"You think he may have had top cover?" José asked.

"Like I said, there was a lot on the table. Skeeter was in big business. Bound to have some investors."

"But you don't *know* if he did or didn't have cover," Frank said.

Sheffield leaned back in his chair and laced his fingers together. "Look, Frank," he said patiently, "when I got out, Skeeter was just another kid on the street with a couple of friends who'd do what he told them. Then he tied in with Juan Brooks. When the feds got Brooks, Skeeter came out top dog.

"Man was like one of them trapeze acts in the circus," he said reflectively. "He'd do the damnedest things. I'd hear about him tying up with the boys from Medellín. I thought he was in over his head. Those were hard boys playin' hard games. I'd say he was gonna fall. I'd *know* it. But he never did. Man does things like that . . . knows he's got a net."

Sheffield thought some more about it, then nodded. "Knows he's got a net," he repeated.

Frank and José stood.

"John doing okay?" Frank asked.

Sheffield's eyes flicked to one of the larger photos on the credenza: Lamar Sheffield standing beside a tall young man on a basketball court. The young man wore his father's smile and a Dartmouth jersey.

"Could be better. Killings aren't good for the real estate business."

"Helps if you're buying," José said.

Sheffield shook his head. "But the profit's in the selling."

. . .

For going straight, he stays in touch," Frank said when they were in the hallway.

"I played football at Howard," José said.

"Yeah. So?" Frank replied.

"I'm not on the team anymore . . . but I still know the lineup."

SIX

"Fresh?" Frank asked. He was already measuring grounds into the coffeemaker.

José nodded. He opened Skeeter Hodges's file jacket and spread an assortment of documents across his desk. "Lot of reading."

Frank switched the coffeemaker on. "Skeeter had a long run."

For the next hour, the two men worked through the files, taking notes, reconstructing Hodges's life as seen through the prism of his brushes with the law. Frank came across a photograph of him in cap and gown, smiling into the camera, and behind him, with the same smile, Sharon Lipton, then a handsome woman in silk dress and dramatically sweeping brimmed hat.

"Boy and happy mother?" he guessed, holding the picture up for José to see.

Over the top of his half-round reading glasses, José gave the photograph an appraising look. "A real mama, all right." He sifted through the papers on his desk until he found a rap sheet. Tilting back in his chair, he eyed the document.

"Sharon Stilton Lipton," he read, "aka 'Babba,' 1979, possession of narcotics, intent to sell . . ."

Fourteen, Frank thought, *kid would have been fourteen.*

". . . 1980, solicitation for prostitution." José shook his head. "'Eighty-two was a busy year . . . two charges receiving stolen goods, one sale of narcotics."

Frank looked at the graduation picture again: Hodges, grinning with a kick-ass confidence. Proud mama, a hand on her son's shoulder.

Hand . . . A special kind of hand on a kid's shoulder. The encouraging squeeze you gave before you sent them out . . . to the first day of school . . . away for the first camping trip . . . back into a game already lost . . . off to basic training at Fort Jackson . . . when you tried your best to pass on a small measure of your own strength, of your own knowledge about the world. Where was Babba Lipton sending her son?

"Helluva education *he* got," he said.

José slipped the rap sheet into the file. "Another testimonial for home schooling."

Frank pushed his chair back, stood up, stretched, and walked to the window. Several blocks away, the trees along the Mall were greening up after winter. Off to the right, the castle towers of the Smithsonian, brick-red under the late-morning sun.

To the left, the Capitol crowned Jenkins Hill. All his life—as far back as he could remember, anyway—the massive building, white and shining, had reminded him of pictures of monasteries in Tibet. Every so often, he'd idly wonder how he'd come to think of it that way. The Hill certainly wasn't a hangout for holy men. He'd probably made the connection as a kid, he thought. Back when he'd known for certain—without any doubt—that you could always tell the good guys because they wore the white hats.

The James Hodges that emerged from the files didn't resemble the morning papers' romantic spin about a charming and only slightly roguish urban outlaw.

A hot-out-of-the-box start in 1981—sweet sixteen and charged with assault with a deadly weapon. Charge dropped. A year later, a suspended sentence for heroin possession. *Thanks, mama Babba.*

Grand theft auto gave Skeeter a year at Lorton and new contacts for his life's work. There, he met one of Juan Brooks's lieutenants.

For years, Juan Brooks had been the District's kingpin of kingpins. A logistics genius, he built an organization of over five hundred street retailers and Uzi-toting enforcers, a ruthless enterprise that smuggled, packaged, and retailed hundreds of kilos of cocaine in the District each month.

Just days out of Lorton, Skeeter signed on with Brooks. By 1991, he had climbed the rungs to become a senior executive in Brooks's multimillion-dollar monopoly.

Then, in December 1992, Brian Atkins bagged Brooks. Got him big-time, life without parole. Brooks went off to an isolation cell in the maximum-security lockdown of the federal penitentiary in Marion, Illinois.

Atkins, head of the FBI's Washington Field Office, got hero treatment: the cover of *Newsweek*, a *60 Minutes* segment with Mike Wallace, a well-publicized lunch with President Clinton, a profusion of lawman-of-the-year awards, and a promotion to headquarters.

Skeeter went to work, picking up pieces of Brooks's empire and adding chunks of his own. But where Brooks had left the street work to his enforcers, Skeeter had kept his hand in. One informant reported Skeeter's holding forth about how great leaders led from the front, not from the rear. And so Skeeter Hodges had been at the front on Bayless Place, planning his next campaign, when somebody walked up and blew out his brains.

Frank saw a flag being raised over the chambers of the House of Representatives. There were other flagpoles on the Capitol roof. All day, a handful of congressional employees would be up there, raising scores of American flags—raising them, then immediately lowering them. They'd fold the flags and box them, and later, members of Congress would send them to their more important constituents with a certificate saying that the flags had flown over the Capitol.

Frank realized José was standing beside him, watching the flags. "Congress at work," he said.

"Wonder what it would be like, being a flag raiser?" José asked.

"Lot of ups and downs."

"Like us."

"Ups and downs?"

"Job never finished."

José watched a flag go up, come down.

"My stomach thinks my throat's been cut." Frank complained.

José turned away from the window. "Get carry-out and find a bench on the Mall?"

Ruth threw in a pint of potato salad with the salami for Frank and the pastrami on rye for José. They walked across Constitution Avenue and found a bench under a hundred-year-old water oak on the Mall, facing the National Air and Space Museum.

José motioned to Air and Space. "Haven't been there in a long time."

Frank looked at the huge building. He liked going there. But he couldn't remember the last time he'd been. You live in a city like D.C. and the only thing you see is killers and dead people. He unwrapped his sandwich and took a small, experimental bite. The salami was slick and spicy on his tongue, and there was just enough mustard to make his eyes wrinkle slightly. He sat back and watched a runner make her way down the Mall. Skeeter Hodges and the dream came back in faded tones.

"I was thinking, Hoser . . . maybe Emerson was right."

"That Skeeter's a key to the cold-case locker?"

"He liked working the street personally."

"So he had to whack a lot of guys."

"One way to thin out the competition."

"Business killings."

"So to speak."

"Yeah. So to speak."

"So what you're sayin' is he was good at his business."

"Or very lucky."

They took their time with their sandwiches and the potato salad, then sat drowsily for a quarter-hour under the springtime sun.

When they got back to the office, the answering machine held two messages: Kate, with her flight number and ETA, and Eleanor, saying the printout was ready. Frank punched the machine and listened to Kate's message one more time.

You asked for it." Eleanor indicated a stack on the desk beside her computer.

"Damn," Frank sighed. The printout was at least six inches thick.

"You were right," José said. "Lot of trees died for that."

Eleanor shrugged. "Just the cold cases since 1990."

"How many?" José asked.

"Fifteen hundred and change."

Fifteen hundred. One thousand five hundred unsolved homicides. In ten years.

"But the rate's going down," José protested.

Eleanor rapped out a riff on her computer keyboard, scanned the results on the monitor, and nodded.

"The *homicide* rate is," she said. "In 1990, we clipped off four hundred eighty-three citizens. In 1999, we dropped down to two hundred forty-one. But"—she threw her hands up—"look at the closure rates. In 1990, you guys were closing fifty-seven percent of the cases one way or another. In 1999, with half the killings, you were closing only thirty-seven percent of the cases. Over the ten-year period, we had almost four thousand homicides. Of those four thousand, over fifteen hundred are still open."

Frank looked at the stack of cold cases, still trying to get his head around fifteen hundred unsolved murders in ten years.

"Sweet Jesus," José murmured.

In the hallway, headed back to their office, José muttered, "Fifteen hundred . . . One *thousand . . . five hundred . . .*"

"Numbers," Frank said absently. "Somebody said one death is a tragedy, a million's just a statistic. I wonder where fifteen hundred comes down?"

They were passing Emerson's office. José jerked a thumb toward the door. "We'd been good at cooking the numbers, *we'd* be sitting behind glass desks and have nasty-ass secretaries with long nails and big tits to guard the front door."

"Remember what your uncle says about ifs?"

José laughed. *If my daddy hadn't died in the poor house, I'd be a rich man.*

"What say we work on that"—he tapped the printout Frank was carrying under his arm—"till six or so, then go out for ribs?"

"Give me a rain check. Kate's coming in at seven."

● SEVEN

At six twenty-five, Frank pulled into the C terminal parking garage at Reagan National, and found a slot on the third level. An arrival screen showed Kate's flight due to arrive at seven-ten.

Getting to appointments early. A security compulsion, a shrink once told him.

He locked the car and found the elevators to the pedestrian walkway.

Sometimes a cigar is just a cigar. Hadn't Freud said that? And it might be that you get to airports early because you don't want to risk getting tied up in traffic and miss your plane.

But tonight Kate was the reason. It was like one of those "If you do this, that'll happen" things you made up as kid—if he got there early, she'd walk through the passageway door sooner. Or at least on time, which was getting to be a minor damn miracle.

Getting through security with his pistol ate up several minutes. A manager had to be sent for. The man had checked Frank's badge and credentials with anxious uncertainty, then sent for *his* manager.

Taking a back-row seat opposite Kate's arrival gate, Frank eyed the crowd. He always found people-watching more interesting at National than at Dulles. He thought it might be that people making the relatively short hops out of National to Orlando, Pittsburgh, and Cleveland carried themselves with more energy than those anticipating the long-leg runs out of Dulles to Berlin, Tokyo, and Buenos Aires.

Fifteen hundred cold cases. Fifteen hundred dead people. How many living relatives of those cold-case victims? Say five? Okay, five per. That's . . .

Now, only partially aware of the airport crowd, Frank worked on the mental arithmetic.

An airline ground agent opened the gate door, and travelers began rounding a corner in the passageway.

Kate's smile caught him while she was still down the passageway. Frank got up to meet her. The arithmetic faded into the shadows.

A tweed jacket and pale-blue silk blouse highlighted short blond hair and blue eyes. Before they touched, he felt the warmth between them. They came together and kissed briefly. His hand at the small of her back, he felt the firm, assertive curve of her hip.

"Long time," he said, feeling his chest tighten.

"Six days?"

"It's all relative. You hungry?"

"Understatement."

"It's warm enough to sit outside."

"La Brasserie?"

La Brasserie's terrace faces Massachusetts Avenue, a few blocks east of Union Station. Schneider's Liquors sits across the avenue, along with a bagel bakery and the offices of a conservative think tank funded by a Colorado beer baron. But despite the view, there was something about the place that was truly French.

"Okay," Kate said as the waiter left. "You've heard all you want to about a city lawyers' conference at Harvard. Your turn."

"Hoser and I got the call just before eight, Friday night. . . ." Over his roast veal and her sole meunière, he filled in the details: Teasdale's discovery, the murder scene, Skeeter Hodges's history.

A tarte Tatin arrived for dessert, its apples bubbling in caramel under a puffed dome of pastry crust. The waiter punctured the crust. Like a balloon with the air let out, the tarte collapsed. A tendril of warm cinnamon teased Frank's nose. As the waiter did the dissection, scooping thin-sliced apples, crust, and sauce onto two plates, Frank pulled a single folded sheet of paper from his coat jacket and handed it to Kate.

"Your boss's press release," Frank said.

She unfolded it and glanced at the banner across the top. "Two months ago." She read the brief statement, then looked at him questioningly.

Frank pointed to the sheet of paper at Kate's elbow. "The mayor of the District of Columbia says the homicide closure rate is sixty percent."

She nodded.

Frank speared a bit of apple and pastry and brought it cautiously to his lips. It was still hot. He put the fork down to let it cool.

"It's not. I've done some back-of-the-envelope figuring. My grocery-store arithmetic puts *solved* cases down around thirty–forty percent. You only get to the mayor's numbers if you add in the cases closed administratively. And what that release ignores is the impact of the cold cases."

He tried the *tarte*. It had cooled just enough. The first taste made you listen for angels singing.

"What about them?"

Kate was giving him an impatient look. He thought better about going for another forkful.

"Over fifteen hundred in ten years." Frank went back to the mental math he'd cranked out while waiting at National. "So you're a citizen of the District. You live east of the river"—Kate understood he meant the Anacostia, not the Potomac—"maybe in the projects, maybe in a little house on what used to be a nice street but now's a shooting gallery."

He paused to retrieve more of the airport math. "East of the river, most of those fifteen hundred cold cases probably come within a five- or six-mile radius of your house. Now think about it. . . . Each of those people might have five relatives. Maybe three or four friends. Multiply the eight or nine people who knew the victim by the number of cold cases. Now we have almost fifteen thousand people who see that people they know get killed and other people they know get away with it. Fifteen thousand people learn that lesson in their personal lives."

"Something else."

"Oh?"

"Enemies of the victim," Kate said. "Even if they didn't do the deed, they also learned that they can get away with murder."

"Nobody pays."

"What you mean is, nobody gets *revenge*." Kate's eyes narrowed. "That what you're saying? How about justice?"

Frank thought about that. "Revenge? . . . Justice? You're a lawyer, I'm a cop, we see them differently."

"Tell me."

"I think you see revenge and justice as distinct things."

"And you don't."

"*Different*, but not distinct."

"I thought lawyers had cornered the market on wordsmithing," Kate said. "How's different different?"

"Revenge is different from justice, but it's *related*, not distinct."

"How?"

"Revenge and justice are yin and yang. Always together, always in a dynamic . . . push-pull." Frank hooked his index fingers together and pulled them against each other. "Government doesn't work when people gun each other down in the streets to settle scores. Government says, 'We will settle your scores. You people stop shooting each other. . . . Pay taxes . . . obey laws . . . serve on juries.'"

Kate nodded. "Be nice and we'll take care of the bad guys."

"That's the deal . . . the contract. Government serves up justice as a substitute for revenge."

"And when government doesn't serve up the justice?"

Frank cocked his hand up, then down in a seesaw motion. "Balance swings toward revenge. I'm not so sure people in Skeeter Hodges country think much about justice in the abstract. Not when they're worried about getting shot in the street. Most of them just want the shooting to stop. But if they've lost a friend or relative, they want somebody to pay."

"And if government doesn't make somebody pay through justice—"

"Friends or relatives will take out the payment themselves."

Kate put one hand on the press release. "You think the department's drawing attention away from the cold cases by talking about closure rates?"

"About inflated closure rates," Frank corrected. "You're reading my mind again."

She tilted her head slightly to one side. "And how long have you been on the force, Lieutenant Kearney?"

Frank didn't say anything. A challenging, professional edge had crept into Kate's voice.

"Well?"

He sat without speaking. His eyes fastened on the press release. Days, months, years on the force—the credit scrabbling, the blame-gaming, the sucking up and the kicking down. A twinge of loss, dark and draining, made him wince. He put his napkin on the table beside his plate, took a moment or two to smooth out the wrinkled linen.

"Terry Quinn"—he said the name and saw Quinn's face, how Quinn would squint, looking through cigarette smoke—"Quinn took José and me out for drinks the night we transferred to Homicide. 'A good detective may be disappointed,' he said, 'but he's never surprised.'"

Kate handed the press release back to him. "And this surprises you?"

He held the paper out and looked at it before folding it and putting it back in his pocket. "Yeah," he said, feeling angry with himself, "it does. When Eleanor came up with those numbers, I felt everything . . . just . . . just stop."

Flashing images:

Eleanor's printout of fifteen hundred unaccounted-for deadly sins.

The M.E. tech wrenching Skeeter Hodges's broken-headed body out of the car.

"Every so often something happens that holds up a mirror that you see yourself in."

"What do you see?"

"A guy who thinks he's a professional, who wasn't paying attention to what was going on in the rest of the department."

"You're being hard on yourself." Kate leaned forward, her voice now softer.

"No. Just realistic."

She shook her head. "You aren't a realist, Frank. You and José—two peas in a pod. Two idealists. Two crusaders out for cosmic justice."

"Cosmic justice?"

"Something that will make everything right for everybody all the time."

Frank laughed. "You are absolutely full of shit."

"Am I?" She leaned further forward. She put a hand on Frank's forearm. "Why'd you become a cop?"

She has a way of bringing you face to face with truth, he'd told his father once.

And that's why she's a good lawyer, his father had said.

"Why'd you become a cop?" she repeated.

"I told you before."

"Once more, come on."

"Kate—"

"Once more, Frank. Say it."

"To keep bad things from happening to good people," he recited.

It was something he had said to himself coming back from Vietnam. That'd been a long time ago. Some things change as you get older. This hadn't been one of them. Once he'd said it, he couldn't get away from it. It had stayed with him all that time. And with any luck, it would probably last out his run.

Kate studied him thoughtfully for several moments, then: "Why?" She asked tentatively. As though it had come from a partially formed thought.

"Why?" Frank felt that she had opened a door into darkness.

She nodded. "Yes," she said, now sounding more certain of herself. "*Why* do you care?"

Frank's eyes drifted out to Massachusetts Avenue and Third Street. A bicycle messenger weaved his way through cars stopped at the traffic light. Over at Schneider's, a truck driver loaded cases of beer onto a handcart. The bicycle messenger ran the red light, crossed Mass Avenue, and disappeared up Third, ignoring the "Do Not Enter" sign.

Frank realized Kate was watching him, waiting. Part of him stayed with her, while another part went off searching something coherent. Anything that'd make sense to Kate and to him.

Images—

Slapping sounds of bullets hitting flesh . . . bodies ripped apart . . . muddy boots protruding from ponchos . . . the putrid odor of death . . .

He zoomed in across Mass Avenue. The beer guy unloaded the last case, cocked the handcart back, and wheeled it into Schneider's.

"You see how little it takes to kill somebody. How one instant, life is there. The next, it's gone. Just . . . *gone* . . . " Frank snapped his fingers. "Life shouldn't go away like that. It oughtn't be there for the taking."

Kate sat silently. "You're in homicide," she finally said. "When you go to work, the bad thing has already happened. Somebody's been killed."

"You can't stop the *last* bad thing. But maybe you can the *next* bad thing."

He put his hand to work straightening the napkin beside his plate.

"And there's this indictment sitting in our office. Fifteen hundred cases where we haven't caught somebody. We've been hiding the truth. Hiding it from the public, hiding it from the mayor, hiding it from ourselves."

Frank paused. An ambulance, sirens screeching, made its way east on Massachusetts Avenue.

She smiled. "You know, you're very handsome when you're passionate."

"I thought I was very handsome all the time."

He felt her nudge his leg with her foot.

"Let's go," she said. "It *has* been a long time."

"Your place or mine?"

Kate got up quickly. "Mine. It's closer."

EIGHT

Still savoring Kate's warmth and traces of her perfume, Frank fit his key into the lock and turned. He pushed the door open and stepped into the entryway.

It took a second for him to realize that the alarm had been switched off. At the same time, he heard the sound of metal sliding on metal. Reflexively, his hand moved inside his jacket.

His father stood in the kitchen doorway down the hall. He held a frying pan in one hand.

For a frozen moment, the two men faced each other.

Tom Kearney broke the spell. "Breakfast?" He smiled and waggled the frying pan. "Beat you to the draw."

Frank felt the tension between his shoulders disappear, and he eased the Glock back into its holster.

"What're you doing here?"

His father gave him a longish look. "Shaker lathe. Remember?"

Shaker lathe? Shaker lathe? His father might as well have been speaking Swahili.

Tom Kearney still held the frying pan up. "You're not the one who's supposed to be getting short-term memory loss. You and Kate," he prompted, "weekend before last . . ."

It came back: The old stone millhouse his father had converted into a woodworking shop. Outside, the waterwheel slowly turning. Inside, he and Kate stood watching his father at a router, cutting a precise channel through a thick cherry post. Overhead, the massive oak shaft groaning and creaking as it turned the web of pulleys and leather drive belts. On a low bench, a chest of drawers in progress.

Kate had mentioned the absence of electric tools. That led his father off on a tutorial about nineteenth-century cabinetry. And Kate had said something about Hancock, Massachusetts, and the Shaker village. And then his father . . .

"Oh," Frank said, putting the memory together, "oh, yeah."

His father still had the quizzical look, as though still unconvinced that Frank had made the connection.

"Where's your truck?"

Tom Kearney lowered the frying pan and returned to the range. "Up at Judith's."

"Oh."

His father's eyes narrowed. "How'd you mean that?"

"What?"

"That 'Oh' of yours."

Frank grinned. "Just happy to see you in town. I ran into Judith the other day, coming out of Dean and DeLuca. She seemed happy too."

"Really?"

It was clear, the way his father asked, that Judith Barnes's being happy was important.

"Getting serious, Dad?"

Tom Kearney cocked his head, and his eyes drifted off into mid-distance somewhere above Frank's head. "Yes," he said slowly, "yes, it is." He set the frying pan down and leaned back against the counter. A man coming to a conclusion he'd been working on, thinking about, but not putting it into words. "For a while after Maggie's death . . ." he trailed off. "No . . . for a *long time* after . . . I prided myself for getting on with my life. I fixed up the millhouse, got into serious cabinetry. Got to believing I didn't need anybody . . ."

"Then Judith?"

"Then Judith." Tom Kearney nodded. "You live long enough, you get to know something about yourself. I'm one of those people who has to share. If we don't . . . if we can't . . . there's something good in us that atrophies. It just withers away."

He stood there, thinking about that, then turned and picked up the frying pan.

"Scrambled? Or fried?"

Frank sat at the harvest table, sipping coffee, and watched his father at the stove. He traced the ancient scars in the tabletop with an index finger.

Been what? Five? No . . . six months.

Six months since the early-morning phone call and the strangled words. Then the long weeks later, watching his father grit his way through physical therapy. During those grueling sessions, Frank understood how a younger Tom Kearney had gutted it through World War II—jump school at Fort Benning, parachuting into Normandy, and, finally, in muddy combat boots and no longer young, drinking captured champagne in Hitler's Eagle's Nest.

Fast forward—the murder of Mary Keegan, the frantic search for her killer, and the lives that search changed. Among them Judith Barnes's and his own father's.

"Hello, furry one."

Tom Kearney looked down at Monty. The big cat had come out of nowhere and was winding around his legs.

"A little egg?"

Monty sat staring raptly at Frank's father.

With one hand, Tom Kearney found a saucer in a nearby cabinet and, with the other, deftly scooped up a heaping tablespoon of scrambled eggs.

"He won't eat eggs," Frank said.

Monty was into them before Tom Kearney could get the saucer on the floor.

Frank shook his head. *Cats.*

His father had moved easily. No left-side dragging. The stroke might as well have not happened. Except that it had. And it had brought with it a sense of mortality closing in.

It's not all bad—knowing how near death always is. We're here. Then we're not. And the world moves on—

Frank realized he'd missed something his father had said. "What?"

"Skeeter Hodges." Tom Kearney put the plates on the table. He pulled up a chair opposite Frank and sat. "Tell me about it," he said, cutting into a sausage. "Begin at the beginning."

"Hoser and I got the call . . . Friday night . . . about eight . . ."

Bayless Place . . . flashes of blue and red . . . the Orioles . . . Teasdale . . . isn't one bunch of gang-bangers, it's gonna be another . . . Pencil Crawfurd in the ICU . . . Marcus and Skeeter's mother . . .

His father listened, interrupting only to ask an occasional question. Frank finished. Tom Kearney sat quietly, somber, reflective. Frank remembered his father's days presiding in court.

"The seventies and eighties in this town were awful," Tom Kearney said. "I thought we were on the edge of anarchy. If it had been any other city but Washington, the place would have been under martial law. I thought things had gotten better. But they haven't. We've given birth to a lawless culture. It's passed on from generation to generation . . . like a family business. Brutal, unforgiving enterprise. You make a wrong decision and you get a nine-millimeter retirement or life in an eight-by-ten cell. The ones who succeed . . . who make it big . . . become even more deadly than their parents."

"Survival of the fittest," Frank mused. "Criminal Darwinism at work."

Tom Kearney shrugged and rolled one hand in a gesture of futility.

"Now, the numbers business doesn't surprise me. You let politicians play with numbers, it's turning the proverbial fox loose in the henhouse." He got up from his chair, unfolding slowly to stand. He reached for Frank's empty plate, stacked it on his own, and made his way to the sink.

"Fella with the lathe said he'd meet me at the flea market." Tom Kearney said. "He ought to be there by now."

Like so many mushrooms, the Georgetown flea market sprang up on Sunday mornings in a school parking lot on Wisconsin Avenue, just across from the Safeway. From Frank's house, it was a good walk: up Thirtieth to R Street, past Katharine Graham's home, Oak Hill Cemetery, Montrose Park, and Dumbarton Oaks.

At the market, his father went off to deal with the fella with the Shaker lathe, leaving Frank to wander through the aisles of vans. Canopies stretched out from them, over everything from honey, tomatoes, and home-baked breads to chandeliers, wicker chairs, and Bavarian beer steins.

He stopped to admire a bowling trophy awarded to one Norville "Splits" Casey in 1939. A nearby cigar box filled with marbles caught his eye. He picked out a marble and held it up, taken by a white ribbon twisting through the clear green glass.

"That there's a corkscrew." The speaker, a stocky older woman with short white hair, in red slacks and a Carolina Panthers T-shirt, held a Marlboro in the corner of her mouth.

"See how it cuts through the middle? That's why they call it an auger. Augers go through the middle of a marble. When the corkscrew is on the surface, they call it a snake."

"Akro Agate?" Frank asked.

The woman squinted at Frank through a cloud of cigarette smoke. "Yeah. Akro. You know marbles?"

"Some. How much for the box?"

. . .

He found his father, standing by the Shaker lathe, handing a check to a grizzled man in a red tank top.

Tom Kearney smiled. "Joe here's going to deliver it, aren't you, Joe?"

Joe nodded. "Wednesday, Judge?"

"Wednesday's fine." Tom Kearney stowed his checkbook away. He pointed to the cigar box under Frank's arm.

"What do you have there?"

"Marbles."

Tom Kearney acted as if it was the most natural thing in the world. He nodded approval. "Man can't have too many marbles. You ready to head home?"

For several blocks, the two men walked in silence.

"I've been thinking," Tom Kearney finally said.

"Marbles? Shaker lathes?"

"Hodges . . . the numbers. Fifteen hundred cold cases?"

"Yessir?"

Tom Kearney shook his head. "My years in court . . . for a while, a long while, I thought I'd seen it all. Took years for me to discover that all I'd actually seen was what had managed to get into court. And by the time it had gotten to court, it had been prettied up."

After another silence, Tom Kearney continued. "The stories were still pretty damn grim. But in court, they'd become just that . . . stories. Wasn't until later that I realized there was a lot of very nasty stuff that never got to court. That stayed out in the streets."

"Kate said it teaches a lot of people they can get away with murder."

Tom Kearney took that in, then asked, "Ever hear of the Plimsoll line?"

"A railroad?"

"No. In heavy seas, a ship that rolls over past a certain point isn't coming up again. Nothing you can do will bring it back. In the 1800s, a British member of Parliament, Samuel Plimsoll, demanded a safety limit, a load line marked on a ship to limit the weight of cargo."

"So you shouldn't go past the Plimsoll line?"

Tom Kearney nodded. "I've often wondered if our society doesn't have its Plimsoll line."

"Meaning?"

"Meaning fifteen hundred murders. Fifteen hundred unsolved murders loaded onto a society that isn't too stable in the best of times. How much more weight before we pass our own Plimsoll line? What if enough people—the people outside the courtrooms, the people in the streets—start believing the ship's going down?"

At home, Frank put the box of marbles down beside the answering machine in the kitchen. One message on the machine.

"Frank, I'm at home."

Frank checked his watch. José had called fifteen minutes earlier. His number rang twice before he answered. Sheresa Arrowsmith had called him from the Hospital Center. Pencil Crawfurd was groggy, but able to talk.

Don't know."

Frank stood on one side of the bed, José and Arrowsmith on the other. A mound of bandages covered Crawfurd's left shoulder, and dried saliva crusted around his mouth. The ICU was overly warm, the air heavy with the smells of ammonia, alcohol, and antiseptic soap.

"Come on, Pencil," Frank said in disbelief. "Somebody stood out in the street . . . right beside your car . . . opened up a shooting gallery . . . and you don't know who did it?"

"Don't know."

"What were you and Skeeter doing?"

"Sittin' there. Just sittin'."

"So you and Skeeter were just sitting on Bayless Place and somebody just walked up and just started shooting? And you don't know who and you don't know why?"

"Tha's it. Show me the muthafucka who did it, I take care a him."

"You got any guesses who?" José asked.

Crawfurd rolled his head to look venomously at José, then Frank. "You cops hard-headed? Or hard-hearing? Tol' you. Don't . . . know. We're sittin' there. Skeeter talkin' to me. All a sudden his face blows out. I don't remember hearin' anything. I don't remember seein' anything 'cept his face blowin' out at me."

"Come on," José prodded, "guess."

Crawfurd said nothing.

"You not a guessing man, Pencil? Nobody's name comes to mind? Nobody who'd want to take over the business you and Skeeter built up?"

Again, nothing.

José bent closer, bringing his face inches from Crawfurd's. "Let me ask it this way, Pencil. . . . Who you gonna watch out for when you get out? Who you gonna worry's out there, waiting for you?"

Crawfurd ran his tongue across cracked lips. "Take care a myself."

"Unh-hunh," José said, "like you and Skeeter took care of yourselves on Bayless Place. Somebody caught you two badasses like sittin' ducks."

Pencil Crawfurd's eyelids closed, then opened, then fluttered. "I'm tired," he murmured, and fell off the edge of consciousness.

In the hallway, Frank turned to Arrowsmith. "He still need to be in ICU?"

The doctor shook her head. "Not really. It's a precaution I take with all gunshot cases."

"You keep him there another couple of days?"

"I can. . . . Why?"

"Visitors have to sign in, don't they?"

Arrowsmith nodded. "And you want to know who?"

In the car, José settled into the passenger seat.

"Bad-nigga wannabe," he sighed.

"Scared bad-nigga wannabe," Frank amended.

"I could use some hash browns."

Frank started the car.

"With a couple eggs on top, sausage sides," José added.

"It's Sunday night."

José gave Frank his "So what?" look. "Get us a running start on the week's cholesterol quota."

NINE

Monday morning, Frank and José sat at their desks, facing each other, Eleanor's printout between them. Beside the desks, a battered institutional-green rolling file cabinet the size of a refrigerator held stacks of thick reddish-brown case folders.

"Dreamed about that, last night," José said. He stuck his lower lip out at the file cabinet. "Thing was suffocating me. Tried to get it off, but it was like a big octopus."

Yesterday at the flea market came back to Frank. His father . . . the Plimsoll line. He looked at the cabinet and wondered how much its files weighed. How many more could it take before everything tilted over, never to come upright again?

He took a deep breath. "Get started?"

Reluctantly, José stood, reached into the cabinet, and pulled out two folders. He offered one to Frank. "You think we'll know when we get to the last one?"

"The last one . . . ?" Frank was drawing a blank. "When we get to the bottom of that stack," he said, pointing to the cabinet.

"No," José said, "will we know when the last case comes our way—'This is it, we're hanging it up'?"

Frank thought about cabinets of case folders. The cases stretching back went a long way. The ones ahead didn't. Couldn't. There was a first case. There had to be a last one. He and José were damn sure closer to dealing with the last than they were to the first.

"I don't know," he told José. "What do you think?"

José studied the folder on his desk, then looked back at Frank. "Yeah . . . yeah, I sort of think we will."

"Why's that?"

"I think we're close."

"How's that?

José sat down and patted the folder. "We ever talk about it before? The last case? Our last case?"

"No."

José pointed a thick index finger at Frank. "*See?* Never talked about it before. Now . . . now we *are* talking about it."

Frank thought about that. A Kenny Rogers fragment ran through his head. *Time to get out of the game? Time to walk? Not yet. Soon, maybe. But not yet.*

He sat there, staring at the folder before him. *Alfonzo Betters.* Somewhere inside his memory, a relay tripped. A small door opened into a partially lit compartment. He and José had helped with the canvassing.

Betters. Was it '99? Maybe '98? He opened to the first page— the summary. *Alfonzo Betters, resident Orleans Place, NE, DOA Hospital Center, 25 July 1995.* Frank got a vague feeling of unease. *Couldn't have been almost six years ago. Seems like '99, '98 at most.* He looked through the rest of the folder—reports, inter- views, neighborhood canvassing notes. He looked across the desk to José.

"We get some music?" he asked.

José got up. The CD player was on a file cabinet behind him. Over on his side, Frank had the coffeemaker. They had a rule. Whoever complained about the coffee got the job of making it. The last switch had been seven years before, when Frank had muttered something about the coffee needing to be stronger.

"What you want?"

"Gould?"

José found the CD, and moments later, Glenn Gould's rendition of Bach's *Goldberg Variations* filled the small office.

Whenever he heard the *Variations,* Frank imagined Bach, maybe with a glass or two under his belt after dinner, sitting down to amuse himself, composing music that didn't have a beginning or an end. The musical equivalent of playing solitaire. Like Monet doodling or Rodin whittling. He looked at the Betters folder. It seemed to have gotten thicker.

"Know what I'm going to do when we retire?" he asked José.

"When we retire" was a game they played. They hadn't played it at the start, twenty-six years earlier, when they'd gotten out of the academy. They began eleven years later. After the hostage thing that had gone so badly wrong. In their game, they had ridden motorcycles through Mexico, taken flying lessons, run a deep-sea fishing charter out of Key Largo.

"What this time?" José asked, obviously not enthusiastic about digging through the papers.

Frank motioned toward the CD player. "There's what, thirty-some of those?"

José looked at the CD label on the jewel box. "Thirty-two."

"Well, I'm gonna memorize them. Get so I can say, 'That's number twenty-four.' "

"Sure. That'll win us a lotta bar bets."

Frank thought about it.

"Now, the Platters," José went on, "or Armstrong . . . if you could name everything they did . . ."

Frank nodded. "Yeah. In sequence."

Simultaneously both men knew the game was over. Their eyes met, then went to the folders in front of them.

Alfonzo Betters's folder lay opened to the first page, the Form 120. In the file cabinet, folders for Michael Darnal. Louis Fleming.

The names went on: Frederick Hankins. Ambrose Murray. Joseph Jameson. Deshawn Simkins. James Rivers. Eight cases. Eight out of the fifteen hundred in Eleanor's printout.

From his desk drawer, Frank took a wire-bound steno pad, the narrow kind used by reporters. He turned it lengthwise, opened it, and penciled a horizontal line from left to right across two pages.

He worked until ten, slogging through the Betters folder. Photographs, canvass questionnaires, sketches, phone records, the initial report, media clip files, the autopsy report, and investigator notes, notes, and more notes. Making sense out of other people's words—brutal going.

As he worked, he marked the line in the steno pad, ticking off events in Betters's life and in the investigation after his death. On pages following the timeline, Frank compiled a list of witnesses and others interviewed. Just after ten, he closed the folder and stretched to ease his tightened neck and back. He stared at the closed folder. Not quite seeing it as much as looking beyond it.

Picturing the killing of Alfonzo Betters. Imagining how the people, places, and times—like so many jigsaw pieces—fit together. He'd opened the folder and Betters was just another name.

Now Betters—Alfonzo David Betters—had shape and substance. It was as if he, Frank, had run time backward, like a reversed videotape.

He'd reassembled the disconnected body splayed out on the autopsy table. Reversed the trajectories of the four nine-millimeter slugs that had demolished heart and lungs. Ridden with Alfonzo as he drove his silver '93 Lexus along the Strip on Tuesday night, July 25, 1995.

Already weary, he turned to a fresh page in the steno pad and reached for Michael Darnal's folder.

. . .

Late-afternoon sun slanted through the window and onto the cork bulletin board with its yellowed clippings and curling Wanted posters. Paper plates and sandwich wrappings filled a deli carry-out box on the bookcase behind Frank.

He was opening his seventh folder. *James Charles Rivers . . . DOB 14 May 1973 . . . Resident Barry Farms . . . DOA 17 Sept 1996 . . . multiple gunshot wounds . . .*

He paused to leaf through the steno pad, reviewing the timelines. Frustration inside him was a voice screaming down an endless corridor of interwoven dates, places, names. The review board—Chief Noah Day's review board—had the authority to close cases administratively. Department Directive 304.1 spelled out the requirements.

And 304.1 let you close cases on stuff you'd never get into court—suppositions, conjectures, hearsay. Frank hated 304.1. You close a case that way, you feel greasy. You want to take a shower. He and José served once on the board. They'd balked so hard and so often and raised so much hell that Day had never picked them to serve again. And here Emerson had thrown them into this goddamn pit, and no matter how they got out, they were going to get dirty.

"I'll get it." José spoke before Frank even realized the phone had been ringing. José listened, then hung up.

"R.C.," he said.

Frank shook his head, trying to clear the brain-numbing fog of names, dates, and deadly-dull bureaucratic police prose.

"Says he's got something." Relief lightened José's voice.

Frank shut the Rivers file with a prayer of thanksgiving. You went when Renfro Calkins called. You did what Calkins said do. And in return, Calkins, the department's forensics magician, would make fibers, dust, blood spatters, and a thousand other minute things tell stories about where they'd been and what they'd seen.

Frank got up and followed José. He was at the door when he

stopped. He returned to his desk and rummaged through the center drawer till he found a small cardboard box, then slipped it into his jacket pocket.

Here." Renfro Calkins, a wiry man in a white lab jacket, stood at a counter, a clipboard with an aluminum cover under one arm.

In front of Calkins was a comparison microscope—actually two microscopes, side by side and joined at the hip with a single set of stereo eyepieces. Calkins motioned to the instrument and moved aside to make room.

José stepped to the microscope and began adjusting the eye-pieces.

Frank reached into his pocket and pulled out the cardboard box. He handed it to Calkins.

"What's this?"

"Found it at the flea market yesterday," Frank explained.

Calkins thumbed open a flap and shook a thimble into his palm. The overhead fluorescent flashed bars across the lenses of his steel-rimmed glasses. He turned the thimble to see the delicate carving around its base, and smiled in delight.

"Early-nineteenth-century scrimshaw," he declared, eyes still on the thimble. He rotated it once more, then focused on Frank.

"I thought it might have been plastic," Frank said.

Calkins grinned and shook his head. "Ivory, Frank, ivory." His eyes returned to the thimble. "Beautiful, beautiful," he whispered, half to himself, half to the thimble.

"It's yours," Frank said.

Calkins rewarded Frank with a kid's smile of surprise. He reached for his wallet. "How much . . . ?"

Frank shook his head. "Nothing. It was in with some marbles I bought."

"But . . ."

Frank waved him off. "Next time you buy a box of thimbles and find a marble . . ."

Calkins gave the thimble another once-over, put it back in the box, and slipped it into his jacket pocket.

"Got a match, here," José said, moving away from the microscope.

Frank stepped up and bent to the eyepieces.

A blur, silver and dark gray. He fiddled with the eyepieces. The focus sharpened. A vertical line split the image. On either side of the line, were horizontal lines like a compressed bar code. He adjusted a knob. The lines on the left moved down a fraction to match precisely those on the right. He was looking at two bullets. The horizontal lines—silver against dark gray—were the marks left by the grooves in a pistol's barrel as the bullet passed through.

Calkins's dry, matter-of-fact voice came in as Frank was still studying the comparisons.

"Slug on the right killed Skeeter Hodges, and . . ."

Frank looked up from the microscope.

". . . I sent it over to the Bureau to run it against Drugfire."

"Yeah?"

"They got a match." Calkins pointed to the microscope. "Like I said, the slug on the right killed Skeeter Friday night."

Calkins stopped to make certain he'd nailed this fact down with Frank and José, then dropped the other shoe.

"The one on the left killed Kevin Gentry."

"Gentry?" Frank asked. He wasn't certain he'd heard right. Then he was afraid he had.

"Gentry?" José echoed in the background.

"Gentry," Frank repeated. "Kevin Gentry . . . Capitol South Metro station . . . early 'ninety-nine. January? . . . February?"

"February," José said. "A real shitstorm."

"A very high-intensity shitstorm." Calkins, slipped into his classroom tutorial voice.

"They did a Three-oh-four-point-one, didn't they?" José asked.

Calkins nodded. "Administrative closure. Zelmer Austin ring a bell? Do you remember the grounds?"

Getting blank looks from José and Frank, Calkins frowned. He took the clipboard from under his arm, flipped open the aluminum cover and found a page. "Zelmer Darryl Austin . . ." he said. "Fifteen April 1999 . . . Eaton Road, Barry Farms . . . DOA, hit-and-run, Washington Hospital Center."

Calkins looked up from the clipboard. "Grounds for closing the case were Austin's track record, and testimony from an informant."

José nodded. "Yeah. Austin . . . one of Juan Brooks's enforcers. When Brooks got busted, Austin stayed on with Skeeter Hodges until they fell out."

Frank took that in, then glanced around the lab. He looked back at Calkins.

"So we have the weapon that killed Gentry showing up. Does that mean Austin didn't kill Gentry?"

"No," Calkins said. "All it tells us is that the weapon survived Zelmer Austin."

José shrugged. "Austin knew the business. You make a hit, you don't keep the weapon. You do, it's a go-to-jail card. So what we got is a scenario where Austin pops this guy Gentry. Austin dumps the weapon. Austin gets done in with a hit-and-run. Somebody inherits the piece, maybe it changes hands a couple a times. Two years later, somebody uses it to pop Skeeter and Pencil on Bayless Place. And the piece is still out there."

Calkins began smiling as he listened to José's story. "A precise summary, Detective Phelps. May I help you fill it out?" he asked, the smile turning slightly mischievous.

"Please do, Dr. Calkins. Be my guest."

"At some time or another, the weapon that killed Kevin Gentry and Skeeter Hodges was in Pencil Crawfurd's custody."

Calkins leaned against the edge of the lab counter and watched Frank and José exchange puzzled glances.

Frank sighed. "Okay, R.C. We give up."

Calkins motioned to another microscope, down the counter from the comparison instrument.

"Shell casing from Bayless Place. It had a print on it. A partial, but enough." He stopped.

"Damn it, R.C., you're gonna find your car towed, you keep this shit up," José said.

"The print, gentlemen," Calkins said archly, "is none other than that of Pencil Crawfurd."

"Pencil . . ." Frank said, trying to make sense of it.

"Pencil," Calkins echoed. "Unless he was a contortionist or a magician, he didn't do the shooting on Bayless Place, but he damn sure loaded the weapon that did the shooting."

José got a grip on it first. "Weapon kills Gentry, shows up two years later, kills Skeeter and wounds Pencil."

"And Pencil loaded it," Frank tagged on.

"Obviously," Calkins said, "the weapon got out of Pencil's possession sometime after he loaded it."

"So when'd Pencil load it?" José asked.

"Yes," Frank said, his voice on automatic while his mind tried to make sense of the ballistics. "If Pencil got the weapon after Gentry was killed and loaded it then, that's one thing. But if he loaded it before Gentry was killed . . ."

"Just might be," José finished, "that Pencil killed Gentry, then got shot two years later with his own weapon."

Over Calkins's shoulder, Frank contemplated the microscope, black and silver and mechanical, crouched smugly on the lab counter, silently mocking him with its riddle.

TEN

You two have a reverse Midas touch—everything you lay a finger on turns to shit."

Before the three men, on Emerson's desk, Kevin Walker Gentry's file.

Gentry's death had been one of those nightmare events every bureaucrat dreads: the murder of a politically connected victim in a politically symbolic setting. The staff director of the District of Columbia Appropriations Subcommittee, Gentry, had been gunned down virtually on the steps of the House of Representatives. For months, the heat had been intense, unrelenting: the *Post*, the *Times*, the *Blade*, and the *City Paper* had hounded Mayor Malcolm Burridge, the city council, and the department. Congress had held televised hearings. Clint Eastwood and Martin Sheen had come to town to testify.

"Milton saved Burridge and Emerson's asses," José was fond of saying. The Gentry flap had vanished overnight, when Milton had finally come up with Zelmer Austin.

Emerson scrubbed his face with both hands. He had the crestfallen expression of a bone-weary man who'd found out he had another hundred miles of rough going in front of him.

"So the Gentry case's biting us in the ass again." Emerson's lips pressed together into a tight, bloodless line. Viciously he slapped the desktop. *"Okay! Okay!"* He threw himself back into his chair.

For a long time, nobody spoke. Frank and José stood in front of the desk. Emerson sat in his chair in an angry, almost catatonic state, staring at the Gentry case jacket.

Frank took in Emerson's intense glare.

That case jacket's going to break into flame.

Finally Emerson took a deep breath and brought his hand up to massage the back of his neck. "We had that case closed."

"Yes." Frank shook his head, and spoke softly, as though saying it any other way might cause Emerson to shatter. "But . . . what's going to be in the papers—"

"What's that?" Emerson asked, a tight frown signaling that he knew what it was.

"—is that we may not have gotten the person who killed Kevin Gentry."

"It could still be that Austin killed Gentry." The hollow, mechanical way Emerson said it didn't sound like a man convinced. He pointed to Frank and José.

"Set up a task force."

"What?" Frank asked.

"Set up a task force," Emerson repeated, his voice suddenly brisk, energy returning with the prospect of bureaucratic ass-covering.

When in worry or in doubt, run in circles, scream and shout.

"Not us," Frank said.

"What?"

"He said, 'Not us,'" José repeated. "You get a crowd running all over the place, crossing each other's tracks. Contradicting each other in public. A real cluster-fuck."

"But the media . . ."

"Media's going to be on this any way you cut it," Frank said. "You form a task force and you just give the media a bigger target to home in on."

Clearly unhappy, Emerson shook his head and sat seeing nothing ahead but trouble.

Frank interrupted. "We got to look into the Gentry case."

"Yes."

"We could use some help . . . some manageable help."

"Bodies?"

"One'll do."

"Who? You want Milton?"

Frank and José shook their heads in unison.

"Rather have a fresh look," José said.

"Then who?"

"Janowitz isn't real busy."

A man thinking about the heat this's going to bring," José said outside Emerson's office.

"And thinking," Frank came back, "about how to pass the heat on down to us."

José shrugged. "What's new? How about call Bouchard? Give him a heads-up."

Ugly, ugly, ugly." Frank looked at the building.

FBI headquarters hulked over Pennsylvania Avenue, taking up the block between Ninth and Tenth Streets. Like dresser drawers left carelessly open, the top floors jutted out over the nine stories below. In a snit over the naming of the building after J. Edgar Hoover,

Congress had refused to pay for the granite facing called for in the original design. And so, precise rows of anchor points punctuated the dirty yellow poured-concrete walls, looking like bullet holes from the machine gun of a drive-by shooter.

"You should have gone into architecture," José said.

"Rather be in demolition."

Robin Bouchard stood just inside the Tenth Street entrance, near the visitor sign-in desk. He was a stocky, muscular man, and his Mediterranean heritage was marked by an olive complexion and coal-black hair nicely silvering at the temples.

"Welcome to the Ministry of Truth, Justice, and the American Way." Bouchard rolled it out in a baritone mellowed with traces of Cajun. He handed Frank and José visitor badges and escorted them past the sign-in desk toward an escalator bank.

"I feel like a priest or a proctologist. Only time you guys come through the door, you're bringing trouble."

José grunted. "Didn't want to come empty-handed."

The short escalator ride to the third floor gave them a look into the fishbowl that was the lab for DNA and materials. Bouchard led them down a long corridor decorated with movie posters from 1950s G-men films, charts and maps, and large iconic photographs of the FBI director, Louis Freeh, and the attorney general, John Ashcroft.

"You guys don't mind . . . when you said it was the Gentry case, I passed it upstairs." Bouchard said. "Brian Atkins wants to see you."

"*The* Brian Atkins?" José asked. "We're honored."

"He want to offer us a job?" Frank asked. "We'll take the Honolulu Field Office."

"He didn't tell me. I sent him an e-mail, said you'd be coming over for a fill-in on Hodges and Gentry. His secretary called down with a 'Be there.' I don't ask questions." Bouchard motioned to the elevators.

. . .

Brian Atkins's corner office was only four floors above the DNA lab, but another world away. Large windows framed views of the Capitol, the old post office, and, in the distance, the Potomac and the control tower at Reagan National. The deep-pile blue carpeting, the mahogany desk and bookcases, the antique conference table with its chairs upholstered in silk brocade—all put the office near the top of the heap. A place where voices were always subdued and neckties carefully dimpled and pulled snug against starched white collars.

Atkins, a man in his late fifties, had the casual grace and slender build of a sailor. A bachelor, he frequently showed up in the style-section coverage of Washington's black-tie galas. Silver hair, square jaw, and windburnt tan face.

He sat at the head of the conference table, Frank and Bouchard to his left, José to his right.

"Robin tells me Gentry's open again."

It came with a hint of Down East to it, a John Kennedy brogue— something to do with sea, sails, and salt air.

An assistant in a tailored dark blue suit brought in coffee. Atkins poured and passed around cups that Frank thought were Limoges or a pretty good imitation.

"How'd we get so lucky?" Atkins asked.

He sat silently, attentive, sipping coffee as Frank and José summarized Calkins's findings. When they were finished he smiled a thank you.

"I wanted to hear this from you. I've got a personal interest in the Gentry case. Kevin Gentry was a great help to us when I was at WFO." Atkins pronounced it "wif-oh"—Washington Field Office, the separate and subordinate FBI unit that did the Bureau's work in the District of Columbia.

"Juan Brooks." José filled in the silence.

Atkins got a tight, modest smile, the way a classy quarterback might smile when reminded of a winning touchdown pass in the last minutes of the Super Bowl.

"*We* busted Juan Brooks," he said. "It was a team effort. While Malcolm Burridge was mayor, he did everything he could to keep the Bureau off Brooks's back."

"There were family connections," José said. "Burridge's daddy and Brooks's daddy."

Atkins's brow furrowed. "I didn't know that," he said with a nod of appreciation. "Burridge was a problem. But then, Congressman Rhinelander and Kevin Gentry, who was his staff director at the time, came on the scene. Rhinelander had just taken over as subcommittee chairman and was looking for an issue."

"Crime in the District," Frank said.

Atkins smiled. "A rich social laboratory for any brave or foolish reformer, the District is. Anyway, Rhinelander and Gentry put the squeeze on Burridge. Burridge folded, and we finally bagged Brooks."

Frank and José exchanged glances.

"Were you working with Mr. Gentry when he was killed?" José asked.

"No," Atkins said regretfully. "By that time, they'd moved me up here"—he waved a hand to take in the office—"where I spend most of my time flying that desk. I've stayed in contact with Rhinelander. We talk occasionally. Kevin's death hit him hard. I'd hoped that Frederick could put this behind him when the case was closed. Now . . ." Atkins let it trail off.

"And now Skeeter Hodges," Frank said.

"Ah, yes," Atkins said. "Same weapon, two years apart. Maybe the same shooter. Maybe not." He looked at José and Frank. "You guys worked out a road map?"

Frank shook his head. "No maps yet. More like a compass direction."

Atkins nodded. Something on his desk gave a chirping sound. He listened, and when the sound came again, he stood, signaling an end to the session. He offered his hand to José, then to Frank. "Keep me in the loop," he told them, "anything we can do . . ." He smiled wistfully. "We all have our jobs to do in this, but I envy you two. Happiest years of my life were working the street."

Never fails, does it?" José asked as he started the car.

"What?"

"Oh, guys who've worked their butts off to get off the street and get into a big office telling you how much they miss the street."

That evening, Frank had a message on his answering machine from John McDonnell at Olsson's. The message, like McDonnell, was spare and abrupt. A book had come in, McDonnell was holding it for him.

John McDonnell, round-faced and in his seventies, leaned forward in the scarred wooden chair. His deep blue eyes and rimless bifocals gave him a priestly, bemused look—a beneficence conferred by a lifetime spent with books. Peering into the tiny green screen of an ancient Kaypro computer, he pecked at the keyboard.

Frank saw the screen flicker, but McDonnell's somber expression didn't change. Books surrounded him: books stacked on either side of the Kaypro, books on floor-to-ceiling shelves around him, three books in his lap.

Olsson's Books & Records, like McDonnell, was a cherished Georgetown landmark. A place where little old ladies could bring their dogs in. Only two windows wide, it had fronted Wisconsin Avenue for at least twenty years. Inside, the store extended back beyond sight. Immediately through the narrow door, an island of literary trade paperbacks. To the right of the island, a Ritz camera booth; to the left, three registers framed by racks of mass-market paperbacks. Farther on, the music section, with CDs, cassettes, and a curling black-and-white poster of Johnny Cash. The serious books were at the rear, where McDonnell and his Kaypro constantly inventoried the shop's backlist.

Foreclosure was in the air. Taxes go up. Leases run out. The chains open on every corner. An end of what had been. And what would be no more.

"Evening, John."

McDonnell didn't look up right away. He glanced at the computer screen, then opened a book in his lap and began easing an art gum eraser over the price penciled inside. That done, he closed the cover and looked up at Frank. The book, Frank saw, was Lartéguy's *The Centurions.*

"First British edition, the Xan Fielding translation," McDonnell said, fingertips caressing the dust jacket. He lifted the book, and the way he did it made Frank think of a priest offering the cup in communion. McDonnell held out the book, looking at it sadly.

"Here."

"How much?"

McDonnell shook his head. "Here. Take it."

"I can't. How much?"

McDonnell looked at Frank, then at the book, then back to Frank.

"You already have *The Praetorians.*" McDonnell thrust the book closer to Frank. "Please."

Frank took it. Tight binding. Only the slightest shelf wear at the jacket edges.

"I can't."

McDonnell had dropped his hand back into his lap. "Make a donation to the Salvation Army."

Frank thought about putting the book down on the stack by the Kaypro, then thought better of it.

"Thanks," he said. He felt uncomfortable. As if he'd witnessed a personal tragedy and knew he ought to say something comforting but couldn't find the words.

McDonnell broke the silence. "Haven't seen your dad."

"Moved back to the country."

McDonnell nodded approvingly.

On impulse, Frank asked, "What's the deal on Frederick Rhinelander?"

A woman came by, paused to browse over the books by the computer, and moved on. McDonnell watched her walk away, then looked up at Frank.

"Three-term congressman. Republican. New Hampshire." McDonnell recited the basics.

Like somebody had flipped a memory switch.

"Personals?"

"Personal? . . . A piss-ant." McDonnell said it dispassionately, without a trace of rancor. "All the nightmare insecurities of a little man who's got a lot of money he didn't earn."

"Piss-ant? A member of Congress?"

McDonnell smiled, shrugged, and went back to his inventory.

Frank held up *The Centurions*. "Thanks."

"You're still missing *Yellow Fever*," McDonnell said, eyes on the computer screen.

"You look for it?"

"Yes. But time's running out."

"And I pay."

"Sure."

"Closing a bookstore must be a lot like going to the gallows," Frank said. It had popped into his head and out of his mouth.

McDonnell, eyes still on the computer screen, gave no sign he'd heard.

Frank hesitated, and turned to leave. Then he heard McDonnell behind him.

"Life's pleasant, Frank. Death's peaceful. It's the transition that's troublesome."

Frank turned back.

McDonnell looked up from the computer and smiled a benediction.

ELEVEN

Milton, a white guy with a graying brush-cut, wore jeans and a khaki shirt. Yellow-lens shooting glasses and a pair of sound-suppressing earmuffs around his neck accented his high cheekbones and gave him the lean look of a hunter, which he had been once.

He sat on the bench between Frank and José, the Gentry case folder open in his lap. On the firing line, ten or so feet away, a single plainclothes—a female officer—practiced slow fire at a silhouette target. The peppery nitro odor of gunpowder hung in the air.

Milton ran his hand over the jacket. He looked at José, then Frank. "You say ballistics connect Gentry and Skeeter?"

Frank nodded.

"And Calkins did the analysis?"

"Yes."

Milton's eyes shifted into the distance, as he worked to pull together the implications of what Frank and José were saying.

"Tell us about your snitch, Milt."

"In so many words, the guy told me that Zelmer Austin got his head fucked up and decided to bag a honkie. He came back that night and told his woman he'd done it. Shot a guy at the Capitol South station."

"That's it?"

"Look," Milton said. "You guys know how it is. . . . It's a cold day in hell when a snitch comes to you with the whole story. All's you get are little pieces. This was this asshole's little piece. It wasn't the only piece."

"He say how he knew?"

"Said he got it from Austin's woman."

"You check?"

"We couldn't find her. You know how these bitches are. . . ." Milton turned to Frank, then José, seeking agreement.

Milton got a look as if things were crumbling inside him. He was silent for a long time, staring at the jacket. "I got a goddamn ulcer from that case. Everybody from the mayor on down was on my ass. Fucking Emerson was over me like flies on a manure pile."

"We remember," Frank said.

Milton looked at Frank. "I guess it's open again."

"Yeah," José said.

Giving no sign he'd heard José, Milton watched the shooter on the firing line squeeze off another round. "Same gun . . ." he whispered to himself. "Gentry and Skeeter Hodges."

Milton handed the folder back to Frank.

Frank took it, but Milton held on for a second or two. When he dropped his hand, his eyes met Frank's.

"Yeah?" Frank prompted.

Milton got up. He faced Frank and José. He motioned toward the folder. "I thought we had that case *good*, Frank. Wired. Or I wouldn't have let Emerson . . ."

"I'm sure you did."

"I mean *wired*."

. . .

Frank started the car. He heard gunfire in the distance.

Bam . . . bam . . . bam.

The single shooter on the range.

"I don't feel like going back to the office," he said.

"Me neither."

"Where to?"

"Long time since we been to the Smithsonian."

"National Gallery?"

"How about the Air and Space?" José pondered this, then nodded to himself. "Yeah. I feel like Air and Space. Something mechanical. You know, with wings and wheels and engines and shit like that."

The National Air and Space Museum is one of Washington's feature attractions. The busiest museum in the world pulls in more than nine million visitors a year. After flashing his credentials, Frank eased the Crown Vic down the ramp to the restricted underground garage.

A minute or two later, he and José stood in the elevator as the doors whooshed open onto the main entrance hall, the Milestones of Flight gallery.

Wow!

Frank felt a smile inside. No matter how many times he'd been to Air and Space, the sight touched off the same schoolboy reaction.

There stood *Friendship 7,* John Glenn's spacecraft, scorched and battered by its fiery reentry through Earth's atmosphere. High above Glenn's capsule, Lindbergh's *Spirit of St. Louis* flew in formation with the Wright Brothers' "flyer," a boxy kite of white muslin wings and brown ash struts.

For almost half an hour, the two men worked their way back through aviation history, from an Apollo lunar orbiter and Chuck Yeager's Bell X-1 to the old classics—a Douglas DC-3, a beautiful Beech Staggerwing.

They came to a stop in front of Otto Lilienthal's hang glider, suspended as if in flight. Frank stared up at the frail craft. A manikin dangled in a harness below the birdlike wings of the century-old glider. A placard explained that Lilienthal had died in a crash. Several years later, the Wright brothers had used his data to build their own powered machine and launch a revolution.

"Good choice, coming here."

"Yeah," José said. He was looking at the Lilienthal glider too. "Something about airplanes . . . you got to do them right. There's something clean about them. Bullshit and a fancy paint job can't make them fly. Basics—all comes down to basics."

Frank's mind skipped a groove or two. He'd been thinking about the glider; then he caught what José had said about basics. Skeeter popped up, and Frank connected basics to the killing.

"Same gun killed Skeeter that killed Gentry," he said.

José didn't respond.

Frank went on. "Question is, same person? Two years. Long time for a killer to hold the same weapon."

"Yeah." José sounded as though he were only half listening.

Frank looked at José's sad frown. "I know," Frank sighed. "I feel the same way."

"Milt shouldn't have folded like that."

"I know. But it must have seemed easy at the time to pin the rose on Austin. No red flags. After all, it wasn't like Austin was a choirboy. And the snitch did know the holdouts."

José didn't say anything, but the frown stayed put.

"Emerson's got to be sweating," Frank said.

José nodded. "Yeah. It gets out he pressured Milt . . ."

"You know," Frank ventured, "Milt always wanted that job running the range. Regular hours, no pressure. A good job to see him to retirement."

"You saying Emerson paid him off?"

"Whether he did or he didn't, that's what it'll look like. And Emerson knows it."

TWELVE

". . . Zelmer Austin . . . hit-and-run?" Kate asked.

Ahead on N Street, streetlamps cast pools of light on brick sidewalks laid before the Revolutionary War. Frank savored the feeling of well-being that came from sharing good food and wine with Kate. Earlier, while waiting for her at the bar, he had made a resolution to stay away from Gentry and Skeeter. The resolution held less than a minute after he and Kate had gotten seated. The rest of the dinner had been spent sifting through every nuance of the crowded day. Frank realized with a start that they'd had three coffees after dessert and that Cafe Milano was now packed with Washington's Euro-émigrés; as the night wore on here, the legs got longer and the skirts shorter.

"So Zelmer Austin didn't kill Kevin Gentry?"

They reached Thirtieth Street and walked south toward Olive.

"They found a pistol with him, but it was clean. No ballistics history. Zelmer himself was capable. Nasty piece of work. He'd been one of Juan Brooks's enforcers. Slipped one first-degree charge, two on manslaughter."

"That man has questionable intentions, young lady."

Frank and Kate turned toward the sound of the voice.

Charlie Whitmire walked down Thirtieth Street toward them, led by Murphy, a toffee-colored Wheaten terrier. Charlie, Frank's next-door neighbor, could wear anything and still come across as fastidious. Tonight he had on a pair of khaki shorts and a faded Gold's Gym sweatshirt. Short white hair and softly rounded features created the impression of an aging cherub, an impression destroyed by his roguish grin and floorwalker's discovering eyes. Charlie and his partner, Jack, had lived on Olive Street for nineteen years, and they had been the first to welcome Frank to the neighborhood.

"Hi, Charlie, Murph," Kate said, stooping to scratch Murphy's ears.

They all walked down Thirtieth toward Olive.

"Stopped by earlier," Charlie said. "You were out."

"Cafe Milano," Frank answered.

"The place to be, right, Murph?" Charlie turned to Frank: "You're going to be a busy boy."

"Always am, Charlie."

"Bus*ier*. I was talking with a friend on the news desk. She said the Gentry case is opening up again."

"You guys know already?"

"Frank," Charlie said in a reproachful tone, "this is a town full of spooks, investigators, and media monkeys like me. Secrets last only until the first phone call. Besides, you got something against freedom of the press?"

"Hell no, Charlie. Some of my best friends are reporters."

Charlie threw his head back in mock distaste. "I am *not* a reporter," he said with dignity. "I am a *columnist*. A sensitive, compassionate observer of life and living."

"You work for a newspaper," Frank said.

Charlie smiled big and slightly evil. "Newspapers! Thank God they exist, otherwise I couldn't find work in mainstream society."

"Gentry?" Kate made it a question.

"Oh," said Charlie. *"That.* That came in over the wire. Also that a congressman . . . Rhinelander? . . . is calling for an investigation of D.C. Homicide."

They turned the corner onto Olive Street.

"We're headed home," Frank said. "You and Murph want to come in for coffee or a drink?"

Charlie looked tempted, then held up an empty blue plastic bag, the kind newspapers came in. "You owe me. Murph hasn't gotten all her walk in yet."

Inside, Kate settled on the small sofa in the breakfast room. Frank stood at the kitchen counter and debated whether to take care of the coffeemaker or pay attention to the answering machine's insistently blinking red eye. He compromised and checked the caller ID.

"José," he said, punching the answering machine's Play button.

"Hey, Frank," came José's voice, "don't forget to pick me up, tomorrow—Savoy's. Oh . . . case you missed it, the Gentry thing's on the damn tube. Worsham at eight. Had an interview with Congressman Rhinelander." José's sigh filled the room. "Bend over . . ."

Frank punched the Off button. ". . . and kiss your ass good-bye," he finished. He stood staring at the machine, imagining how tomorrow would go.

"Come here, big boy," he heard Kate say.

He got a warm, sensual feeling in his stomach. He turned in time to see Monty spring lightly into Kate's lap.

She held Monty against her breast. The big cat purred, eyes closed, head resting on her shoulder.

Frank tried to freeze-frame the scene, knowing that he couldn't.

Life goes on. Any second she'll move and the picture'll be gone. Nothing stays the same. Memory's a blessing, he remembered his father saying once. Without it, there'd be no tomorrow, because there'd be no yesterday.

"What're you thinking about?" Kate looked up at him and the picture went away.

"Us," he said.

"What about us?"

"Just us," he said.

Penny." Kate's whisper came through the dark, warm and close to his ear.

Frank turned toward her and lined his body up against hers. "Ever play jackstraws?"

"Pick-up sticks? Not recently."

"Remember how you have to lift off one stick at a time without disturbing the others? If you lift off enough to get the black stick, you win?"

"Oh-*kay*?"

"Just thinking about the other players in the game."

"Emerson?"

"He's one. Him . . . the media . . . this congressman, Rhinelander."

"All after the black stick?"

"No. Not exactly."

"Not exactly?"

"They got different black sticks. Emerson's is a good set of numbers."

"So?"

"So he sets up a machine that gives him good numbers. You work for Emerson and you want an 'Attaboy,' you give him good numbers."

"You and José don't."

"No. We got to where we are before Emerson came on the scene. And we aren't going any further. Two old-timers who've vested retirement and who aren't sucking for promotion are bulletproof."

"But they're expendable."

"That too," Frank said.

"And the congressman . . . his black stick?"

"Rhinelander and the media will play off each other. He wants the publicity he's going to get if he investigates the department. The media knows law enforcement that works doesn't sell papers. So Mr. Rhinelander puts on a circus, shows that law enforcement's broken, and the media sells papers."

Kate put her hand on his neck. At the blood-warm crossroads of neck and shoulder. "And you and José, your stick is getting the killer. Simple as that?"

"It's good enough. The shooters have their way, they're going to sink the ship."

"And you and José stop enough of them, the ship doesn't sink?"

"Something like that."

"And the ship? Is it going to be a better ship?"

Frank felt his pulse beating against her hand and wanted her hand there forever.

"Not our job to make it better. Just to keep it floating."

THIRTEEN

Frank pulled off Florida Avenue at Tenth Street. In the middle of the third block, he turned into a lot full of cars and pickups in various stages of tear-down or build-up. A cinder-block building squatted on the back half of the lot. An ancient coat of white paint had been beaten threadbare by the weather, and you could barely read "Savoy" in an orange Coca-Cola script above the entrance.

The garage had the rich, organic man-smell of automobiles: grease mixed with motor oil, laced with slivers of solvent and brake fluid. From a hidden boom box Eric Clapton competed with the pneumatic hammering of impact wrenches. Frank found José in the last bay, head under an open hood, body bent over the front fender, peering into the engine compartment of a dark green convertible and in deep discussion with a mechanic beside him.

Frank and José had found the '65 Mustang in a Maryland barn after six months of weekend hunting. The top and upholstery had rotted, and generations of chickens had deposited layers of droppings on the paint. But the body hadn't rusted, and the frame had lined up true. And there were the plusses: 83,000 honest miles, no power-anything, a heavy-duty sports suspension, and a 271-horse V-8 harnessed to a Borg-Warner four-speed transmission.

"Getting rid of spare change?" Frank asked.

José backed out from under the hood.

"The Josephus Phelps foreign aid plan," he said, putting a hand on the mechanic's shoulder. A stocky dark-haired man straightened and showed a mouth full of white, even teeth.

"Meet Gustavo Montoya. I'm putting his kids through college."

Montoya winked at Frank. "Just my daughter at Harvard." He turned to José. "I have ready for you this afternoon. Six-thirty *máximo?*"

José nodded. *"Bueno."* He stood back and surveyed the car. "And they say houses are a money pit."

Frank let his eyes run along the Mustang's lines. "That's a classic. Classics are supposed to do that."

"You want a share of a classic?" José asked.

"I'll pass."

They left the garage and walked toward the car.

"I missed the late news last night . . . the interview? . . . the congressman?"

It took a moment to register.

"Oh . . ." José said, "the congressman . . . Richie Rich . . . hundred-dollar haircut, designer glasses with those little lenses."

"He say anything?"

"How he was outraged. How his subcommittee's going to get to the truth . . ." José sniffed. "The usual political shit."

Frank unlocked the car and opened his door. "You ready for more?" He asked across the top of the car to José.

"More what?"

"The usual political shit."

Chair cocked back, his feet on Frank's desk, Leon Janowitz was drinking coffee and reading the Gentry case file.

"Make yourself at home, Leon," Frank said.

Janowitz looked up and smiled. He swung his feet off the desk and levered forward in the chair. "I heard I'm working with you guys."

"José and I decided to do our part, keeping kids off the street."

Janowitz looked wounded. "I turn thirty next month."

Frank gestured to the coffeemaker. "Making coffee's my job."

"Mine is . . . ?"

"You," José said, "are our one-man task force."

"I'm honored."

"What do you know about the Gentry case?" Frank asked.

Janowitz tapped the file. "That Milton fucked it up and you guys got it on your plate."

"What's this 'you guys' shit?" José asked.

"*We* guys," Frank corrected. "We guys got Gentry *and* Skeeter. He pointed to the Gentry file. "Get into that. Deep as you can."

"And don't talk to Milton before you talk to us," José added.

"Why's that?"

José held up a finger. "One, because I said so, young man, and two"—he held up a second finger—"because like you say, Milt fucked it up. No sense you startin' from where Milt is . . . or was. Better you start from your present state of ignorance."

Janowitz nodded. "Okay." He drained his coffee, got up, and tucked the Gentry file under his arm. "You guys going to the press conference?"

José frowned and looked at Frank, who shrugged.

"Yeah," Janowitz said, "about the Gentry case. The mayor, Chief Day, and Emerson . . . front steps."

In the street, TV relay masts towered over mobile control vans. Headquarters doors opened. Three men clustered around microphones, with Mayor Tompkins, neat and bow-tie precise, in the middle.

"Father, Son, and Holy Ghost," José whispered.

He and Frank slipped through the crowd to get closer. Tompkins drew an index card from his pocket. Cameras clicked.

"I have a short statement. I'll be followed by Chief Day and then by Captain Emerson of Homicide." Tompkins paused and took a deep breath. "Yesterday, I learned that mistakes were made in the closing of a particularly tragic homicide case—"

"'Mistakes were made,'" José echoed. "They just *happen*. Nobody *does* anything."

"Bureaucratic immaculate conception," Frank whispered back.

"Accordingly," Tompkins was winding up, "we are reopening the investigation of Mr. Kevin Walker Gentry's homicide." The mayor stowed the index card in his pocket and turned to his right. "Chief Day?"

Noah Day, a big, hulking man, scowled as though, somewhere in front of him, the killer hid among the reporters and cameramen.

"Ladies and gentlemen"—his voice sounded like granite boulders grinding together. "I have some background information for you. . . ."

He cranked up what department insiders dubbed "Noah's Numerical Fog Machine"—an avalanche, a flood, a veritable tsunami of statistics and data. A rapid-fire chatter of numbers on everything that could be counted that had anything to do with crime and punishment.

José let the numbers flow through part of his consciousness while he thought about Skeeter Hodges, then found himself thinking about Edward Teasdale. Then he worked on making the connection back. Something, perhaps the inflection in Day's recitation, made him break off.

". . . but numbers don't tell the whole story," Day was saying as José surfaced and the meeting with Teasdale faded.

Day powered into his standard closing. "And performance isn't in the talking, it's in the *doing*." Like a bull eyeing a matador, he swung his big head back and forth, wanting to make certain the small brains in front of him had absorbed his wisdom.

Apparently satisfied, he stepped back, and Emerson came front and center.

"As Chief Day said"—Emerson smiled—"the performance isn't

in the talking, it's in the doing." He shot a suck-up glance toward Day, then looked out over the reporters. "Open for questions," he announced.

The gabbling and hand thrusting reminded Frank of third-graders trying to get the teacher's attention.

Emerson pointed into the crowd. "Ms. Lewis?"

Lewis went straight for the throat. "Two years ago, you held a press conference. You told us Zelmer Austin had killed Mr. Gentry. Are you telling us today that he didn't?"

Emerson pursed his lips and worked his jaw muscles. "That's not being said," he replied, erecting the passive-voice fortress of a seasoned bureaucratic warrior. "What's being said is that there is insufficient evidence to identify Austin as the killer." Emerson's eyes darted, searching for an escape route.

Like an intercepting hockey goalie, Lewis angled herself back into Emerson's line of sight.

"So you had evidence once . . . now you don't? Is *that* what you're saying?"

Emerson looked around desperately. No raised hands. Dozens of pairs of eyes watched him squirm.

"Is *that* what you're saying?" Lewis persisted.

Emerson coughed, started to bring his hand up to his tightly knotted necktie, then, apparently thinking better of it, dropped the hand. "There," he began slowly, "have been changes in . . . ah . . . the . . . um . . . evidentiary base."

"The evidentiary *base?*" Lewis repeated scornfully before she sprang the trap. "Isn't it a fact that you solved the Gentry case by a bureaucratic dodge? That you relied primarily on the testimony of an informant, and that then, on the basis of that testimony, you declared Austin the killer and the case closed?" She paused just long enough to gather momentum and not long enough to let Emerson reclaim the floor. She delivered high and hard. "And haven't you found that the weapon that was used to kill Skeeter Hodges was also used to kill Gentry?"

Emerson searched the chief's face, then the mayor's. Their blank expressions offered no refuge.

He knows she has the goods, Frank thought. He tries to dodge now, and the shit will get even deeper.

Emerson took a deep breath. "That has been found to be the case."

"And so Zelmer Austin didn't kill Kevin Gentry."

Emerson held up his hands in a "Halt there" gesture. "It may be that renewed efforts as described by Mayor Tompkins and Chief Day will produce proof that Austin was indeed the killer," he said. Then, quickly moving his head up as if to see farther back into the ring of reporters, he found a raised hand. "Next question? Yes? Hugh Worsham?"

"Oh, shit," José breathed.

Worsham, who made a living out of anarchy, confusion, and the failures of others, stood almost within arm's length of the two detectives.

"*What*"—Worsham chopped out a histrionic pause—"what are *you*, Captain Emerson, going to do about this imbroglio?"

Emerson winced. "Ah . . . Hugh . . . would you care to rephrase that?"

Worsham rolled his eyes and heaved a suffering sigh—*I have to put up with such fools.* "What, Captain Emerson, are you doing to make certain something like this doesn't happen again?"

Emerson decided to play. "*Cer*tain, Hugh? We can't be *certain* of achieving perfection, as much as we try." Emerson shot a sly smile at the mayor and Chief Day. "But we can reduce the probability of such errors."

"How?" Worsham followed up.

"One step we've already taken. I've ordered a thorough internal review of our evidence-handling process. And to ensure this is an un-prejudiced review, I am suspending the person who has been responsible for that process."

"This person have a name, Captain?"

Emerson paused. Frank thought he saw Emerson's eyes graze those of Chief Day. Emerson returned to Worsham.

"Yes, Hugh. He is the head of our forensic analysis. Dr. Renfro Calkins."

FOURTEEN

"Frank! . . . Goddamnit! . . . *Stop!*"

Grabbing his right arm and left shoulder, José spun his partner around, backing him against a parked patrol car.

"That son of a bitch." Frank heard the words come up from the murderous roaring inside his head and chest.

José clamped him into a bear hug and brought his mouth close to Frank's ear. "Let . . . it . . . go, brother."

The words came slow and deep, and Frank tensed as though to break José's grip.

"Let's get out of here," José said.

"I want to talk to that bastard."

"Not now." José tightened his grip on Frank. "You go in there now, all you're gonna do is get a ration of his shuck-and-jive bullshit. Then you'll get more pissed an' do something dumb."

A moment like a year finally passed and the roaring inside faded into the distance and he could breathe again and he felt José's arms loosen.

José squeezed the back of Frank's neck. "Let's go find R.C."

. . .

Renfro Calkins lived on T Street, NW, in the 1700 block, not far from Dupont Circle. The house was on the end of a group of four red-brick row houses in a diverse neighborhood at an intersection of Washington's black, white, gay, and Hispanic communities. A block west, the semiluxurious Washington Hilton, where Ronald Reagan had been shot. A block north, the beginnings of Adams-Morgan. A small brass plaque by the doorbell announced that the row houses, built in 1887, had been registered with the National Trust for Historic Preservation.

Frank rang the bell.

The door swung open.

"Yes?" The smile of surprise began before the question died away. "José! Frank!" Elsa Calkins pulled the two men through the doorway and into the living room. Petite and fine-boned, Elsa stood on tiptoe to kiss each of them on the cheek. She smelled of vanilla and nutmeg, and her dark curly hair glistened in the light.

"How's he doing, Elsa?" José asked.

Tears welled in her eyes. "He's better than I am. Come on." She led them down a hallway lined with framed displays of exotic seashells. "Almost twenty years," she said, her voice bitter. "Now this. They throw him out. Shut the gate."

"It's only a suspension, Elsa."

She stopped at a closed door and turned to face Frank and José. "It's a travesty." She glared at them, then turned, knocked once, and opened the door.

Shelves and bookcases covered the walls. An antique walnut desk in the center of the room faced French doors leading to a small walled-in garden.

Renfro Calkins, seated at the desk, swiveled around. Surprise flickered across his face, followed by a look of withdrawing caution, as though he'd pulled himself back into a protective shell. He stood, one hand on the back of his chair, the other resting on a large ledger open on the desk. Several smaller notebooks also lay open. He followed Frank's and Jose's gazes.

"Updating my journal. If I don't capture my thoughts right away, they just fly off."

José nodded. "What happened, R.C.?" he asked in a voice heavy with concern.

Calkins gestured toward a couple of chairs. He and Elsa exchanged a wordless message, and she left, shutting the door behind her. The sound of the door had a finality to it, and the three men sat as though time had stopped.

José broke the silence, asking again, softly, "What happened, R.C.?"

Calkins thought about how he might describe it, then lifted a piece of paper out of the clutter on his desk.

"Two gentlemen from IAD walked in, served me with this."

He handed the paper to José.

José studied it, then handed it to Frank. It bore the Internal Affairs Division letterhead.

"It says IAD's investigating procedural compliance," José said.

"It also says," Calkins added, "I'm suspended."

"With pay."

"Nice of them."

"Internal Affairs," Frank asked, "they say anything?"

"I asked. They just pointed to that." Calkins gestured to the letter.

"Then what?" José asked.

"Then they sealed my files, my computer, my office door. Then they escorted me out of the building." Calkins's eyes moved to middle distance, reliving the scene. "In front of all my people . . . they escorted me out of the building," he said in wonderment, as though he couldn't believe it had happened. He brought his eyes back to focus on Frank and José, then smiled ruefully. "At least they didn't cuff me."

Frank felt a vicarious flush of embarrassment and stole a glance into the garden. A sparrow fluttered in a lichen-covered birdbath, and Frank searched for something to say. José got there first.

"How you doin', R.C.?"

Calkins frowned at José like a man who'd been asked an impertinent question. "Doing? Why, I'm updating my journal." He motioned to his desktop. "Later, I'll be cataloguing additions to my stamp collection. . . ."

"That's not what we mean, R.C.," Frank put in. "Inside . . . you okay?"

That brought Calkins to a halt. He pondered that for a moment, then ventured out. "Am I disturbed?" Another second's thinking. "Yes. Certainly, I'm disturbed."

A pause.

"Am I angry? Yes . . . I suppose so . . . somewhat."

Another pause, then, "But am I despondent?" Calkins shook his head emphatically. "No. Definitely not. Evidence will out, Frank, evidence will out. We run a responsible and professional shop. And *that's* what's going to be found out when the evidence is in."

Frank found part of himself cheered at Calkins's certainty, another part worried about the same certainty. He tried to shut out the worry side.

"I'm sure it will, R.C."

Italian sausage, Muhammad."

"José?"

"Steak supreme."

Muhammad scratched out the orders and handed Frank and José their numbered call slips.

Mon Cheri Cafe was open six a.m. to three a.m. Sunday through Thursday, and twenty-four hours a day Friday and Saturday. Gleaming white ceiling with bright fluorescents, scrubbed floors of large black and white square tiles. Muhammad or one of his brothers was always there. So was a steady stream of police, laborers, taxi drivers, and old-time Georgetown residents.

Frank and José took a table at the back along the wall. At a table toward the front, an old man sat by himself, drinking coffee and reading a newspaper.

"This is a clean and pleasant café," Frank said. "It is well lighted."

José squinted at Frank. "You been reading Hemingway again?"

Frank smiled. "Can't help myself." He watched the old man get up and take his cup to the front for a refill. "You know, don't you, how IAD's going to go after R.C.?"

José nodded. "But R.C.'s a man with faith in the system."

"Let's hope he's not disappointed."

Muhammad called their numbers. Frank added a Diet Coke to his tray, José picked out a cranberry juice. For several minutes they ate in silence, concentrating on keeping their overstuffed sandwiches together.

"I'm full." José put down the last of his sandwich and wrung out a paper napkin. He wadded the napkin and dropped it on the table. "R.C.," he began experimentally, "you don't think there's a chance IAD can tag him with something? Anything? I mean, Emerson needs a scapegoat bad."

Frank shrugged. "I think there's always a *chance*. But do I think there's any *probability*?" He shook his head, answering his own question. "Slim and none. R.C.'s too meticulous."

"Yeah." José nodded.

"So?"

"So maybe we ought to talk to Milt some more." After a second thought, José finished off his sandwich.

The two men locked eyes.

"IAD investigation's under way," Frank cautioned. "Milt's a material witness."

"Unh-hunh."

"We go talking to Milt, that could bring down a load of shit."

"Unh-hunh," José agreed. "Sure could."

.   .   .

First the sleek sound of precision-milled metal turning. Then light breaking the darkness, framing a man in a doorway. The figure flicked a wall switch. Nothing. A muttered curse. The man closed the door behind him and made his way through the dark. A table lamp suddenly snapped on. The light caught Milton in the middle of the living room, keys still in his right hand.

"Evening, Milt," Frank said.

"Hi, Milt," José chimed in.

"What the fuck?"

Frank motioned to the sofa. "Why don't you sit down, Milt? We'd like to talk."

Surprise kept Milton rooted in the middle of the room.

"Renfro Calkins," José rumbled. "Frank and I think a good man's being railroaded to save Emerson's ass."

"So? So why the fuck does that give you the right to bust in here?"

"Sit down, Milt," Frank said pleasantly.

Milton paused, as though weighing what to do.

"Sit down, Milt," Frank repeated, this time not so pleasantly.

Milton took a seat on the sofa, both feet on the floor, hands guarding his crotch, fingers interlaced.

"We'd like to understand better how you came to close the Gentry case. You had to rely on this snitch."

"Yeah."

"The snitch told you that Zelmer Austin's woman said that Austin did Gentry."

"Right."

"The snitch have a name, Milt?"

Milton mumbled something.

"I didn't hear you," Frank said.

"Cookie."

"He have a last name?"

"Yeah, but he wouldn't give it to me. Real hard on that. Like he was scared. And look, Frank, José, the guy knew the hold-out details. He knew stuff he couldn't a read in the papers or see on the tube . . . how many times Gentry was shot, what time it was, no money taken."

"You find him, Milt?" José asked. "Or did he find you?"

Milton took a deep breath of resignation. "He called me. We met."

He looked at Frank and José, pleading with his eyes. "Emerson and the chief put the squeeze on me. I didn't want to close the case on the snitch alone. But before I could say anything, they were out with a press release saying we'd found the killer."

"You didn't say anything to Emerson?" José asked. "Like hold up on the release?"

Milton's face clouded. "I . . ." He began, then stopped.

His chin dropped a fraction, his shoulders sagged. "Emerson called me in," Milton whispered hoarsely. "Asked me how I was doing. I told him we had good poop from the snitch . . . about how the guy knew the hold-out details. Emerson damn near danced around that desk of his. I told him I wanted more before signing off on the Three-oh-four-point-one. But he waved me off. Said he'd already told the chief, the chief had already called the mayor."

"Essentially, Emerson told you to shut it down." Frank said.

Milton looked at Frank, then at the ground. "Not exactly . . . not so many words . . . but I knew what it was he wanted."

Frank looked at José, who was staring at his shoes with the embarrassed expression of a man who'd stumbled on another man's private weakness.

We've all been there, Frank wanted to tell Milton. *Maybe we didn't make your mistake. But we know what it was like . . . how close we came.*

The three men sat silently, all aware of what had happened, none wanting to say any more about it.

. . .

José started the car and checked the rearview. "You've had a hot day," he told Frank. "Gave your blood pressure a workout."

Frank slumped in the passenger seat. His anger gone, in its place a debilitating fatigue.

"Emerson really got to him," José said, pulling out into the evening traffic.

"One thing about Cookie what's-his-name . . ."

José nodded. "About getting the story from Austin's woman?"

"Funny that Austin would tell her the hold-out details."

"Ha-ha?"

"No," Frank said, gazing at the headlights of the oncoming cars. "Not ha-ha funny."

José was quiet for a block or two. "You think this is just a case of Emerson covering his ass?"

Frank looked at him. "Or?"

"Or something else?"

You got it made," Frank said.

Monty sat on a nearby chair, giving Frank the look that said he wanted dinner, not conversation.

Frank mixed a half-cup of shredded chicken with some puréed pumpkin and banana, and put the result in a bowl by Monty's door. The big gray cat pondered whether to make the effort, then leaped, achieving a cushioned four-point landing on the floor. He sent a cool glance to Frank, then began working on his dinner.

Frank turned to the refrigerator. He foraged listlessly through the freezer compartment. The sausage sandwich from lunch was still with him, dulling his appetite. Nothing in the emergency cache of Lean Cuisine appealed. Two beers would have worked. But you didn't drink dinner. You ate at the end of a day, even a day as shitty as this one.

Groping at the back of the freezer, he found a plastic container. He brushed the frost off and held it to the light. It came to him—the last of a batch of his father's chili.

He bounced the container in his palm. Nothing else came to mind. "What the hell," he muttered, and started the microwave.

Monty glanced up, then nosed back into his dinner.

Frank watched the microwave timer on its countdown. A restless pulse hit him.

Call Kate?

He stopped his hand halfway to the phone.

And we'll talk about . . . what?

His hand detoured to the TV remote on the counter.

For a fractured moment, the story on Channel 9 rocked him back to another time: *A helicopter crash in Vietnam—seven GIs killed?* Not his war. Not this time. Days ago, not 1968. A few days ago, seven Americans died searching for remains of other Americans killed thirty-some years before. And so, in 2001, Americans continued to die in Vietnam.

Channel 7 dissected a report that Michael Jordan would return to the NBA to play for the Washington Wizards.

They used to be the Washington Bullets. Then D.C. earned the title of "America's Murder Capital," and sensitive souls changed the team name to Wizards, and they never had a season worth a damn after that.

Frank flicked over to Channel 4. A file clip of Chief Noah Day's face filled the screen. Then the camera switched to Jim Vance. Barely concealing a smile, Vance reported a congressional investigation into obscene e-mails being sent among DCMPD patrol cars.

"Send in the clowns," Frank whispered, keying the TV off. Without replying, Monty nosed his door open and disappeared.

Frank was reconsidering calling Kate when the microwave timer chimed.

. . .

He sat up in bed reading until after midnight. It was his second time through Martin Cruz Smith's *Havana Bay*. The Russian detective, Arkady Renko, had just regained consciousness after having been beaten by a thug with a baseball bat.

Frank closed the book and turned out the light. "G'night, Arkady," he said. "Don't worry, you'll get your guy."

He lay staring at the ceiling through the darkness. Smith had told a good story. He'd put Renko behind the curve, kept the pressure on, bombarded the Russian detective with bits and pieces of stuff from every direction, stuff that could be something or nothing at all.

Arkady Renko understood: Connecting dots was easy . . . a two-dimensional problem. But try a puzzle where the pieces constantly change shape, no one piece remaining the same.

Monty had come in from the night, and he settled into his place on the pillow beside Frank, who drifted off into a turbulent sleep.

And the scrambled pieces swirled in the darkness.

. . . Renfro Calkins . . .

Robin Bouchard . . . Brian Atkins at FBI—you have a road map?

Chief Day, fiddling with un-PC e-mails among bored cops on the night shift while the cold cases rise up out of their file cabinet graves, angry and accusing and demanding . . . demanding . . . what?

FIFTEEN

Frank parked on Second Street, SE, then walked down C Street toward South Capitol. He passed the Cannon House Office Building, the first of the three House of Representatives office buildings. Cannon, completed in 1908, was his favorite. The grand old building's Doric columns and rotunda shouted out its Beaux Arts lineage. The Longworth building was next, its neoclassical style a product of the restraint of the Depression era. Last, the huge Rayburn building, finished in 1965, an H-shaped monstrosity of pink granite and white marble, reflecting the Texan grandiosity of its namesake, Speaker Sam Rayburn.

Leon Janowitz stood at the corner of C and South Capitol, nose deep in *The Wall Street Journal*.

"Running with the bulls?"

The young detective looked up. "Long as they're running. Trick's to know when to jump out. José not coming?"

"His turn for paperwork. Where's Susan?"

"Said she'd meet us at the top of the horseshoe." Janowitz motioned up the block. He folded his paper and stuck it in a beat-up

L. L. Bean canvas briefcase. "By the way," he said, "thanks for asking for me."

Frank nodded and waited for the follow-up that was in Janowitz's voice.

"Question?" Janowitz asked.

"Yeah?"

"Why me? I mean, next month, I'm outta here."

"Maybe we'll get it done by then."

Janowitz grinned. "And pigs'll fly."

Frank ignored him. "You've got a nose for digging. You can follow a paper trail."

Janowitz shrugged. "Paper's paper."

"You did good on the Keegan case."

Another shrug. "Tracking credit cards? Utility bills?"

The walking was uphill. The effort warmed Frank's legs and lungs, and he wanted to keep going.

He looked at Janowitz. "Easy for you, hard for others. You've got intuition. Other people see a piece of paper or a computer file, you see connections."

Janowitz lowered his eyes modestly, then looked back at Frank. "Long's you know I'm outta here next month."

"Question?" It was Frank's turn. "Why'd a nice boy like you want to be a cop?"

"You mean, a nice Jewish boy?"

"Jew, schmoo. Why did Leon Janowitz want to be a cop?"

"Oh . . . I love cities."

"Love cities." Frank echoed.

"Yeah." Janowitz had the intense look of someone thinking through a cosmic riddle. "I'm a city kid. My family, all the way back to Warsaw . . . city people. I love cities."

"You love cities, you became a cop. Something in between?"

"I got fed up with what these schmucks have done to our cities. They fucked up our schools. They fucked up our streets. They fucked up everything."

"Leon Janowitz, unfucker of America's cities?"

"I just wanted to get my licks in."

The two men turned to go up the horseshoe-shaped drive leading to the Rayburn Building.

"So you got your licks in, and now you're getting out."

"So I haven't. And *that's* why I'm getting out."

"After this case," Frank added.

"Next month," Janowitz corrected. "No matter what."

Frank sorted through the knot of people standing under the portico. "Where's Susan?"

Practically all organizations in Washington with a phone number have go-betweens who know their way around Capitol Hill. Susan Liberman's business card read "Legislative Counsel, District of Columbia Metropolitan Police Department," a large title for the diminutive dark-haired woman whom Frank finally spotted.

"Big," Janowitz said, looking up at the massive building.

"Two million, three hundred square feet of office space," Liberman recited. "A gym, cafeterias, recording studio, its own subway system to the Capitol."

"Real big," Janowitz amended.

"And fireproof," Liberman added.

"Too bad," Frank said.

"Next life"—Janowitz motioned to Frank—"he wants to come back as a wrecking ball."

They pushed through the tall glass-and-steel doors. Inside, the security checkpoint. Liberman shepherded the two detectives through the metal detector and a credentials check, and signed them in at the Capitol police desk.

Once out of the cavernous foyer, Rayburn shrank to human size. There were marble floors, but the hallways were plain, utilitarian, and filled with staff and visitors.

"The D.C. subcommittee?" Janowitz asked.

"Thirteen members of Congress," Liberman answered. "Five Democrats, eight Republicans."

"Why're they in our knickers?"

"Two reasons. The subcommittee writes the checks that make the D.C. government work. There's no way city hall could run on local taxes alone."

"You said two."

Liberman smiled cynically. "Publicity, silly boy. Democrat or Republican, don't ever get between any of them and a camera or microphone. And Frederick Rhinelander's no exception. Kevin Gentry was his chief of staff. Gentry's replacement is Alessandro Salvani. Aka Al. Newark, New Jersey. Professional Italian-American, professional Democrat. Everybody says he's related to Dean Martin. He never denies it. Looks like him too. One of those yummy Italian men who never age."

"I thought he was dead," Janowitz said. "Dean Martin."

"He *is* dead, sweetie," Liberman replied. She nodded toward the door on their right. A bronze plaque read "Subcommittee on District of Columbia Appropriations."

Yes, Ms. Harman. . . . No, Ms. Harman. . . . Consider the alternatives, Ms. Harman." The patient voice came in a bourboned baritone. Tanned, toothy, and flat-bellied, Al Salvani stood behind an ornately carved walnut desk, one manicured hand folded around the telephone, the other hooked in a suspender strap. Frank saw that the suspenders were embroidered with clowns. Salvani rocked back and forth slightly as he talked, a man in perpetual motion. A man who owned the ground he stood on.

Salvani's office had the requisite view of the Capitol across Independence Avenue. Autographed photos covered the walls: Salvani with presidents, sports celebrities, Hollywood stars. Salvani with Pope John Paul II, and next to that, Salvani with Yasser Arafat. These clustered around a larger photo of Salvani standing shoulder to shoulder with Joe DiMaggio in Yankee Stadium.

"... of course, I'll talk to the chairman about it, Ms. Harman."

Salvani hung up and looked curiously at Frank, Janowitz, and Liberman as though they'd materialized out of thin air.

"Susan Liberman," Liberman said, "Metropolitan Police Dep—"

"Oh, yes." Salvani shifted gears. He shot a scowl at Frank and Janowitz, and dropped with a pneumatic gust into a leather swivel chair. "Sit, sit."

Liberman made the introductions. "Detectives Kearney and Janowitz."

Salvani took them in with a sour look that said he was having a difficult time somewhere in his lower digestive tract.

"How," he asked, "could such a screw-up like this come about?"

"We—"

Salvani held up an impatient hand, then rooted among the papers and pamphlets littering his desk. He came up with a thick bound document in a tan official-looking paper cover. He thumbed through several paper-clipped sections. Finally he nodded and stuck an index finger on one page.

" 'Forensics,' " he read, " 'in which the sharing of responsibilities among agencies increases the possibility of evidentiary mishaps resulting from lapses in coordination.' "

Salvani closed the report and held it up. "A two-hundred-page study on the criminal justice process." He looked at the book with respect, then at Frank, Janowitz, and Liberman in accusation. "The General Accounting Office did that report. Just last month." He swung his big head sadly. "Lapses in coordination," he intoned, dirgelike. "Lapses in coordination . . ."

He let it trail off, then his eyes flashed. "And we had your chief up here when we published the report," he snapped. "And your chief, Chief Noah . . . Alton . . . Day"—he rolled out the name—"your chief threw out a bunch of stats and as much as told us we were full of shit."

"Excuse me, Mr. Salvani," Frank said, "you've got a beef. But we"—his gesture took in Liberman and Janowitz—"we're just trying to find out who killed Kevin Gentry."

Salvani paused a beat to bank that. "Okay," he said. Apparently deciding he'd played enough hardass to set the newcomers' impression of him, he settled back and asked, "How're you going to do that?"

"We start with establishing Mr. Gentry's timeline."

"That was done, I remember—"

"I want it done again," Frank cut in, playing hardass himself. He indicated Janowitz. "With a new set of eyes."

Salvani studied Frank and the others.

Frank was about to say something when Salvani sighed. "People here thought that was all over. You gonna be flicking scabs off old wounds."

"Wounds?"

Salvani laughed. "No shortage of walking wounded around here. This place's a zoo of prima donnas. Each one, they look in the mirror in the morning, they see the next president of the United States. They eat breakfast, they plan how to get a leg up on the others. They elbow in the aisles, they backstab in the cloakrooms."

"Nice place to work," Janowitz said.

Salvani laughed again. "Hey! It's the distilled essence of the human race, American politics is." His smile went away.

"You replaced Gentry," Janowitz said.

"Yes."

"You weren't aware of anything that could have made him a target?"

"Sometimes just walking down a sidewalk in this town's enough to make you a target."

"I don't think it was walking down a sidewalk did it," Janowitz said.

"Oh?"

Janowitz ignored the question. "Any subcommittee business?"

Salvani slapped his fingertips lightly on the edge of his desk. "Like I told your fellas two years ago, we were gearing up for the District's annual budget hearings."

"You make it sound like an everyday thing."

"Annual event. Bills have to be paid, pork has to be handed out. Hearings are part of the process."

"Mr. Gentry was in charge of the hearing?" Frank asked. "What'd that involve?"

"Kevin and a couple of his assistants would do research . . . define the issues, sell the members on them. Then they'd line up witnesses, schedule the hearing, work out the press releases"—Salvani spoke dismissively—"that sort of thing. Standard stuff."

"He kept Congressman Rhinelander informed?"

"Of course." Salvani said it with care. "I suspect he didn't come in often. Word was, he was a good staffer. You got to remember, at the time the subcommittee was up to its collective ass in alligators with the Waco investigation." A sour look again crossed Salvani's face. "What a godawful mess that was."

"The hearings took place?" Frank asked. "After Mr. Gentry was killed?"

Salvani nodded. "Pro forma . . . nothing sexy."

"Gentry's files?" Janowitz asked. "The background research and all? You've kept them?"

Salvani made a show of checking the wall clock. "Not here."

"Where?"

"Procedure is they archive the stuff . . . over at the library." He pointed in the general direction of the Library of Congress.

"We'll be wanting to go back over everything . . . correspondence, calendars, e-mail."

Salvani frowned.

Anticipating resistance, Frank said, "This's getting high on the flagpole."

Salvani's frown stayed. "I'll have to clear everything with Mr. Rhinelander."

"When . . . ?"

"I'll talk to him this afternoon."

Salvani stood, followed by the three visitors.

"If it's not an imposition, I'll call you," Janowitz said.

Salvani eyed Janowitz, adding another dimension to his earlier measurement.

"No imposition at all." Salvani drew his words out, making it clear he thought it was. He didn't offer to shake hands, but sat down and pulled a sheaf of papers from an overflowing in-box.

He waited until they were in the doorway. "Kearney?"

Frank turned.

"You any relation to Judge Tom Kearney?"

"His son."

Salvani nodded, a small curtsy. "His son," he echoed.

SIXTEEN

Just as he started the car, Frank's phone chirped.

"Frank? Where're you?"

"Second and C, Hoser. What's up?"

"Arrowsmith called 'bout Pencil."

"What about him?"

"Didn't say. Just said she was having trouble and get my ass down there."

"Where're you?" Frank asked.

"Gettin' in my car."

"Meet you there," Frank said, switching on lights and siren.

Sheresa Arrowsmith thrust her hands deep into the side pockets of her white jacket and glared at the empty ICU bed. The sheets had been stripped, and an orderly was stowing away the IV. A nurse stood nearby, a clinical chart under his arm.

"Stupid, stupid man," Arrowsmith said, shaking her head, still looking at the offending bed.

"What happened?" José asked.

"David?" Arrowsmith beckoned the nurse over. "This's David West," she said. "He was here. David, you tell the officers what happened."

West glanced at the clinical chart, ran his index finger down to an entry, then looked up. "It was ten-fifteen. We needed another blood sample. I came in. Mr. Crawfurd was watching TV."

West pointed to a small wall-mounted TV. The Fox noon news, muted, was just coming on.

"I told him the lab wanted another sample. He said something obscene. Something about being bled to death."

West hesitated and looked from José to Frank as though worried about his performance.

"Go on, David," Frank said.

"Well, I was thumping his vein . . . to bring it up to stick . . . and the local news came on. It was the press conference . . . the mayor, the chief of police . . . ?"

"We know the one," José said.

"I'm just getting ready to stick him. All of a sudden he hollers . . . sits up. Jerks so I almost stuck myself. Mr. Crawfurd's really upset. Yells for me to get out."

"And?"

"Nothing else I could do. I got Dr. Arrowsmith."

Arrowsmith picked up: "It took a few minutes. I was with another patient. We got back, he was gone. Tore out the IV and split."

"Clothes?" José asked.

"They were in the closet," West said, pointing to an open door.

"When he hollered . . . why you think he did that?" Frank asked.

"It was the TV. That part where the reporter was questioning about that murder case . . . Gantry?"

"Gentry," Frank absently corrected. "What'd he say?"

" 'Shit!' He said, 'Shit!' Then he told me, 'Get out, motherfucker.' "

"You a pretty big guy," José said.

West's mouth tightened. "Hospital doesn't pay me to restrain patients," he said. "I got out."

"What was Crawfurd's state of mind?" Frank asked. "He angry, scared . . . what?"

"Scared." West made a vague gesture that took in the small room. "He wanted out of here in the world's worst way."

"How's he physically, Sheresa?" José asked.

"He's going to be hurting, but what he's got isn't going to kill him," Arrowsmith said.

Frank punched the play button.

". . . *changes in . . . ah . . . the . . . um . . . evidentiary base.*" In the replay, Emerson's voice came across as even more tentative.

"Sounds like he was caught with his hand in the cookie jar," José said.

". . . *weapon that was used to kill Skeeter Hodges was also used to kill Gentry?*"

Frank watched as the reporter did a number on Emerson. "Woman's got a good source."

Frank clicked the power off. The reporter's image faded.

For moments, he and José sat slouched in their chairs, staring at the blank screen. Finally José got up, stretched, and went over to the coffeemaker.

"It's burnt," Frank warned.

José filled his mug anyway and returned to his desk. "Man on the run," he said, settling into his chair. He sipped the coffee and made a face. "Shit's burnt," he muttered. "Pencil worried more about Skeeter? Or was there something about Gentry got him spun up?"

"Maybe he's worried that the same person who killed Gentry and Skeeter is coming after him."

"That means some kind of connection between Gentry and Skeeter."

José watched Frank think about that.

"Figure it this way," José offered. "Pencil was okay about Skeeter gettin' waxed. . . . I mean, Pencil wasn't exactly tearing out IVs and beatin' feet just because of Skeeter. It wasn't until that reporter hooked Skeeter to Gentry that Pencil went apeshit."

"More than that, Hoser. We know that Pencil had his hands on that weapon sometime before he and Skeeter got shot with it."

"Yeah."

"It just might be that what got him up and gone was the realization that the weapon that he loaded . . . and that was used . . . to kill Gentry was the one that killed Skeeter and wounded him."

"I guess we better talk with Pencil," José said.

Frank stood up and pulled on his jacket. "I guess we better *find* him first."

SEVENTEEN

Dinner had started with a simple salad, lemon vinaigrette dressing. A garlic-marinated hanger steak had followed, accompanied by a Frog's Leap Merlot and Brussels sprouts sautéed in sweet butter. Tom Kearney had helped Judith Barnes clear the table and bring in cognac and dessert—a strawberry tart.

Barnes circled the dining room table, pouring dense black coffee from an antique silvered copper pot with a beaklike spout.

"*Qahveh,*" she explained, filling Kate's demitasse cup, then Frank's. "The Turks pave their streets with it when they run out of asphalt."

Frank sipped the thick, pungent coffee. "I'm surprised anybody in the country ever sleeps."

"Lower caffeine than the stuff you manufacture," Tom Kearney said. He pushed his chair back from the table. "So your survivor jumped ship."

Frank stirred his coffee. "Gone."

"You've set the dogs out for him?" Barnes asked. "Or whatever it is you do?"

"I wish we could. No charges on him unless the Hospital Center claims he skipped payment."

"But it shouldn't be too hard to find him."

"Not as easy as you think. Look at all those kids they put on milk cartons. Pencil's got money, and he's got what's left of Skeeter's outfit to run interference."

"Then what do you do?"

Frank rolled a hand over and back. "Go out, talk to people on the street."

Easier said than done. Crawfurd's house had turned up cold. And then they'd spent a long afternoon, touching the bases, passing the word. Show enough that people know you're interested; don't show so much that they think you're desperate.

You seen Pencil? We got something he might want to know. He could help us, we could help him.

Barnes leaned forward. "Snitches?" she whispered, eyes bright with excitement. She suddenly looked worried. "That *is* what they call them, isn't it?"

The little-girl way she said it made Frank smile.

"Well, isn't it?" she insisted.

"Yes, Judith, that's what they call them. There's also sources."

"The difference is . . . ?"

"Motive. You always have to be looking for the snitch's motive. He's telling you something to get something for himself."

"Like money."

"If the motive's money, that's at least straightforward. When it isn't money, things get more complicated."

Tom Kearney cut in: "Sometimes a snitch wants to settle a score. Or he gets manipulated by a cop. I saw cases where a snitch was cutting a deal for a reduced sentence for his own crime. Fingering some poor bastard to get a few years off his own time."

Barnes looked at Frank and Tom in frustration. "Then why listen to them?"

"Because," Frank said, "you have to. You get a piece of information from a snitch. You know it might not be straight. Even so, it might help you if you can figure out the motive . . . understand what's behind it."

"Double-think?"

"Double- and triple-think. Like somebody said about the spy business . . . it's a wilderness of mirrors."

Barnes asked. "And you can get the truth out of this . . . this *mess*?"

"Sometimes." Tom Kearney sipped his cognac. "Sometimes," he repeated. He turned to Frank. "You wanted to know about Al Salvani?"

"Yes."

"He was a junior staffer in the Senate when I was counsel on the Judiciary Committee."

Kate cocked her head. "I didn't know you'd been on the Hill."

"Just two years," Tom Kearney said. "After I left private practice and before I joined the bench. A tour of the sausage factory . . . a necessary pit stop in the education of a cynic. If the outside of big government frightens you, the inside will scare the hell out of you, once you see how it works. I can recall one day—"

"Al Salvani?" Judith prompted softly.

Tom Kearney pulled up abruptly and gave her a small smile of embarrassment. "So many good stories, so little time . . . Al Salvani . . . I was old man for a Senate staffer . . . fifty-four, fifty-five. Al was much younger—"

"He's sixty-two now," Frank said.

"Damn kid. Anyway, Al was already a fixture on the Hill. One of those guys goes up to the Hill and stays. When I signed on, he'd been there ten years or so. New Jersey. Heavy-duty Catholic. Old-line Democrat down to his bones. He knows the two basics of Hill politics."

"Which were?" Kate asked.

"Which *are*," Tom Kearney corrected. "Which are: Know who's with you, and know who's agin you."

"Pretty basic," Frank said.

"Wasn't for me." Tom Kearney smiled ruefully. "Sides shift minute to minute up there on the Hill. Being a judge was more my line. Truth's not as slippery in the courtroom."

"I don't think I'm going to have an easy time with him."

"What do you have to do?"

"See if Kevin Gentry was into anything that'd make somebody want him dead."

"And Al isn't happy about that."

"No."

"You can't blame him. You're an outsider. You want to come digging. And on the Hill, there're things buried that people want to stay buried."

"But Tom," Judith protested, "they're looking for a killer."

"Like I say, kiddo, bodies aren't the only things some people want to keep buried." He turned to Frank. "Free advice?"

"I'm afraid to hear what it is."

"Don't underestimate the importance of staffers like Al. Guys like him run the Hill."

"Senators and congressmen don't?" Kate asked with a touch of sarcasm.

Tom Kearney took another sip of cognac. "They've been hoisted on their own political petards. The pols have made government so damn big that they have to rely on their staffs to find out what's going on and to draft legislation. There's just too much going on for a congressman or senator to get their hands on. Hell, when I was on the Hill over twenty years ago, the senator I worked for got two to three thousand letters a week from his constituents. It's probably gotten worse, what with e-mail."

"You aren't going after us poor Democrats, are you?" Judith asked.

Tom Kearney laughed. "Republicans grow government almost as much as the Democrats—they just don't advertise it as much."

"And Salvani in all this?" Frank asked.

"He's a major player. He knows how to make himself indispensable to those with the elected egos. At the same time, he makes certain they get the credit. He stays offstage."

"The invisible man."

Tom Kearney drained the last of his cognac, looked thoughtfully at the empty snifter and reluctantly set it down on the table. "The invisible man," he said, trying out the description, and finally nodded, as though deciding he liked it. "He can help you a lot, or he can hurt you a lot. Either way, he can do it without leaving any tracks. You want, I can give him a call."

Frank turned that over, then shook his head. "Maybe later."

Kate and Frank stood for a moment on Judith Barnes's steps. Across Thirty-second Street, a "For Sale" sign hung from a wrought-iron standard in front of a small red-brick row house. Above the sign, another one read "Under Contract."

Frank remembered the first time he'd been in that house. Last October, an autumn morning with a blue sky that went out to forever. That morning, the house had smelled cleanly of tomato and fennel and garlic and its owner had been found dead in a neighboring park by a woman walking her dog.

Kate took his arm and they started down the steps. "You think the new owners know?"

"Probably," Frank said. "A thing like that . . . Georgetown's too small for people not to know."

As they walked the block over to Wisconsin Avenue, Frank wondered if Mary Keegan's ghost lived in the neat Federal-era house. He hoped she did. A nice ghost to have watching over you.

Kate slipped her hand down his arm and interlaced her fingers with his. "I watched you and your father tonight."

"Oh?"

"You love him very much."

"Well . . . yes . . ." he answered, struck by her saying it. "What brought that on?"

"Oh, I don't know . . ."

"Sure you do."

Kate looked at him, and he could tell she was trying to sort it out, the way she narrowed her eyes and bit her lower lip.

"Maybe it was the wine and the candlelight," she said, "but I suddenly saw the two of you as you and an older you. There was a . . . a . . . a *connectivity.* . . ."

Kate squeezed his hand. "Like I say, maybe it was the wine and the candlelight."

Frank felt his face warm, and he squeezed back.

"Looks like we're going to have fun on the Hill."

Kate said nothing, then nodded, as though agreeing with a thought she had had. "You have your hands full."

"Juggling."

"More like threads," Kate said. "You have to pull hard enough to unravel, but not so hard that you break them."

"Gentry, Skeeter."

"They're two."

Wisconsin Avenue was still bright with lights and evening traffic. And no taxis in sight.

"We could go to my place, get my car," Frank said.

Kate shook her head. "You had more wine than I did, and I wouldn't drive."

Frank knew better than to argue, first because it was Kate, and second, because Kate was right. After three attempts, he semaphored a cab over to the curb. He opened the back door and held it open once Kate had settled in.

"Rashid," he told the driver, picking the name off the laminated license over the visor, "take this lady home." At the same time, he flashed his badge and let his jacket fall away to let Rashid get a good look at his shoulder holster.

He watched the cab disappear down Wisconsin Avenue, then began walking south. A display in an antique store caught his eye. He stopped to look over a simple pine chest. He imagined a French carpenter, needing something to keep his tools in, throwing together the chest in an afternoon, little knowing—or caring—that it would bring a four-figure price in an upscale shop in an American village a century later.

As he continued down Wisconsin, he considered dropping into Billy Martin's for a decaf. He glanced at his watch and decided to head home instead. As it was, Monty would be sulking about being fed late.

He crossed Wisconsin and turned down N Street.

Threads.

Who killed Gentry?

Who killed Skeeter Hodges?

Connections?

How? Where? What? When? Who?

Ancient maples along the sidewalks formed a leafy tunnel over Olive Street. Frank hadn't left the outside light on, and the houses on either side of his were dark. He held his key ring up to catch the dim light from the corner streetlamp.

As he did so, he heard behind him the slight rasp of a shoe on the brick sidewalk. He switched his keys to his left hand and turned toward the sound, silently cursing his vulnerability.

"Good evening, Detective Kearney," came the BBC announcer's plummy voice.

"Good . . . evening, Waverly."

The big Nigerian's eyes widened as he noticed Frank's right hand, armpit high inside his jacket. "I am sorry. . . . I have given you a turn."

"That's all right, Waverly, I've been given worse."

"I came by. There was no light. But I thought you would return. And so I decided to wait."

Ngame motioned behind him toward the cars parked across the street. One of them was a black Cadillac with someone in the driver's seat.

"Come in?"

Ngame shook his head. "Thank you, no." He paused, weighing a matter of some delicacy. "I regret that I was not open for business today, when you and Detective Phelps were making . . . ah . . . inquiries."

"I'm sorry we missed you, Waverly."

"Pardon my inquisitiveness," Ngame said, "but have you had success in locating Mr. Crawfurd?"

"Not yet."

Ngame pursed his lips and paused as he did another weighing of another delicate matter.

"I have two things. They are not much, but . . ." He paused apologetically. ". . . they are some*thing*." He came in heavy on the last syllable.

"Yes, Waverly?"

"The two things—one, Skeeter Hodges had insurance, and two, there are eyes on you and Detective Phelps."

EIGHTEEN

Skeeter had insurance?" José scoffed. "Didn't get his money's worth."

"Maybe he didn't keep up the premiums."

"Names?"

"I asked Waverly who he heard it from—"

"Yeah?"

"He heard two guys he didn't know jiving about it while they were looking for a watch."

"And the eyes business?"

"Same guys . . . 'eyes on you and Detective Phelps.'"

"He'd recognize them if he saw them again?"

Frank shook his head. "Two black males, late twenties, early thirties. Medium build. Shorter than Waverly."

"Big help." José tilted back in his chair and gazed out the window. The Weather Channel had predicted rain. Not a cloud in the sky. His eyes came back to Frank. "They had our names? I mean, Waverly said . . . ?"

"Yeah, he did. He said they said our names—Kearney and Phelps."

The two men sat thinking about it, neither moving. Finally José broke the silence. "Two calls this morning. Salvani and Gideon."

"Oh?"

"Salvani wasn't happy."

"Unh-hunh?"

"He talked with Congressman Rhinelander."

"And?"

"Just that the congressman didn't want us digging in the subcommittee files, and was talking about calling Emerson about us."

"Oh, shit."

Emerson's face . . . first, the wide eyes as he realized he really had heard what he thought he'd heard. Then the shattered look of disbelief. Finally the angry flush of betrayal. Get yelled at by Chief Day or, God forbid, the mayor.

"Salvani said he did some damage control."

"Oh? Rhinelander just going to shoot us outright? No drawing and quartering?"

"We got a command performance with the congressman today."

"We? You and me?"

"Yeah. I figure we're gonna get a lecture, but we'll get in. Otherwise Rhinelander'd be talking with Emerson."

"Time?"

"TBD . . ." José said. "Sometime this afternoon."

"Gideon . . . ?"

"He wants us to drop by."

"He didn't say why?"

José shook his head. "Maybe he and Waverly been listening in on the same party line."

"Why don't you take that? I want to do a little digging on Congressman Rhinelander."

"Where you going to dig?"

"The Dragon Lady," Frank said, reaching for the phone.

José nodded. He stood and gathered his cell phone and pager. He got the look of a man who had remembered something.

"Frank . . . ?"

Phone at his ear, Frank looked up.

"Those guys with our names . . . they said Kearney *and* Phelps?"

"That's what Waverly said."

José smiled. "Tell me, brother, how'd you get top billing?"

NINETEEN

Commuters jammed the incoming lanes of the Fourteenth Street bridge. José eyed the bumper-to-bumper traffic as he drove past the Jefferson Memorial toward northern Virginia. He glanced at his watch.

Ten o'clock. Where the hell do all these people work, coming in this hour? Next life, I'm gonna get me a job like that—come in late, leave early, and nobody shoots at you.

Across the bridge, he swung off a ramp to his right, circled beneath the bridge, and headed south to Reagan National. Taking the left lane on the racetrack that routed cars by the terminals, he turned off into the hourly parking garage for US Airways. He drove slowly down one lane then the next until he'd covered the ground level, then took the ramp up and repeated the process on the second level.

As he came off the ramp onto the third level, he spotted the dark blue Ford Econoline van. He drove past the van and pulled into a slot two rows away. The early-morning flurry of passengers for the New York and Boston shuttles had subsided. The garage, filled with waiting automobiles, was still.

José got out and looked around over the tops of the cars. Terry Quinn had died in a garage like this. Shots and screeching tires had filled the semidarkness, and Terry's brains had been splattered over the grease-stained floor. After the shooting, there'd been the cold silence, a weeping emptiness that came from an adrenaline hangover and the losing struggle to deny the in-your-bones knowledge of loss.

In the middle distance, the roar of engines on the runways.

His footsteps made hollow cupping sounds on the concrete as he approached the van. He reached inside his jacket and loosened his pistol in its holster. Coming up on the van from the right rear, he made out someone in the passenger seat, then circled around behind the vehicle. He walked to the driver's side and tapped on the window.

The window lowered with a whine.

"Morning, Gideon."

"Josephus."

Weaver touched a button, and the cargo door slid open. José climbed into the van and settled in the backseat.

"This's Cookie." Weaver motioned to the passenger seat.

Cookie didn't turn around. He had lowered his visor so that its mirror gave him a bank shot of José. All José saw in the mirror was a pair of wraparound Oakleys eyeballing him.

I paid that much for shades like that, I'd have Internal Affairs down on me in no damn time.

"Cookie? There a last name?"

"Cookie's good enough."

The voice was young and sullen, and José thought he sensed an undercurrent of fear.

"Cookie," Weaver said gently, "tell your story."

"I don't answer no questions I don't want to."

"Your call, Cookie," José said.

Cookie sat immobile and silent.

"Cookie." This time Weaver had a warning note in his voice.

"Skeeter wanted Z-Bug dead because Z-Bug killed that whitey what brought down all the shit." Cookie spewed it out and fell silent.

Z-Bug? Zelmer Austin? . . . Whitey? Gentry? Where's this shit coming from?

As if he'd read José's mind, Weaver said in a whisper, "Tell us where you got this, Cookie."

"TV sayin' Z-Bug didn't kill that whitey, so why you give a shit?" Cookie asked.

"Just want to know where you heard it, Cookie."

Cookie glanced out the side window, then started in a low, nearly inaudible voice. "Pencil tol' me. Me 'n' him was partyin' one day and he got to braggin' 'bout how big his balls was."

José nodded. "Pencil tell you why Z-bug did the whitey?"

"Said Z-Bug was feelin' like poppin' a cap on some whitebread mu'fucka."

"Watch your mouth," Gideon cut in. "God don't like ugly."

Cookie gave an almost imperceptible nod to show he'd heard. "He did the whitey."

José detected excitement in Cookie's voice.

Cookie hesitated, as though making certain his audience was still with him.

Once a snitch gets on about his story, he keeps on to the end.

"Yeah," José urged, "go."

"Z-Bug was partyin' at his girlfriend's house. They drank up all the Stoly. Z-Bug's woman blasted him a couple times. Pencil said Z-Bug started yellin' . . . screamin' how he wanted to kill him a white man."

"Unh-hunh," José whispered.

"Z-Bug went out. Did it."

"Killed the white man?"

"Yeah!" Cookie said in a tight, excited voice. "Oh, yeah!"

"What night was this?"

"Long time ago."

"When'd you hear this?"

Cookie thought. "Year, maybe more."

"You tell this to any police?"

In the rearview, José got a long look from Cookie through the Oakleys.

"It could help," José added.

Cookie said nothing, but bobbed his head trying to figure out how much the truth might cost, then, "Yeah. A plainclothes name Milton."

Not wanting to seem eager, or let Cookie know it was important, José took a couple of breaths before asking, "Those real Oakleys, Cookie?"

Cookie almost turned around. "Course they real."

"Thought so. Good-lookin' shades."

"That all you want?"

"Yeah. Thanks."

Cookie shifted, ready to open the door.

"By the way," José asked, "you tell this cop Milton you heard the story from Pencil? Or from Z-Bug's woman?"

Cookie sat still, as though somebody had thrown a switch and turned him off. In a sudden motion, he opened his door and got out. He looked back into the van at José.

"I tol' you how it was, an' I tol' you how I tol' that cop," he said, voice rising, "You start givin' me that 'this or that' shit." He slammed the door, and walked away toward the entrance to the Metro.

José knew not to ask Weaver for Cookie's real name. Weaver wouldn't tell him, but Weaver could find him again.

Weaver sighed. "Young ones . . . they want to fly like eagles, but then they wear their pants down around their buttocks."

Frank bought a copy of the *Post* from a vending machine at the corner of Sixteenth and H, and walked into Lafayette Square. The Secret Service had closed off Pennsylvania Avenue after the Oklahoma City bombing, and you could see straight through the square to the White House without having traffic block your view. That part he liked. The other part, though, he didn't. Adding more locks to your doors didn't mean you were any safer. Only that you were more isolated. Bearing right, he found his favorite bench and sat down. For a moment, he gazed across Jackson Place at Stephen Decatur's home.

Swashbuckling naval hero of the War of 1812. Conqueror of the Barbary pirates. Dead at forty-one, killed in a duel. Back in Decatur's day, you could walk up to the White House, knock on the door, and ask to speak to the president.

Frank opened the *Post.*

The chemical industry was fighting the EPA over a report on dioxin. China had finally released the crew of the American EP-3 intelligence plane. A survey had counted 12,850 homeless in the Washington metro area. And forty-three people had died in a South African soccer stadium stampede.

"Good morning, Lieutenant. Any good news?"

Frank looked up. "I thought you'd know."

Jessica Talbot was small—barely five feet—a delicately rounded face punctuated by dark eyes and framed by a halo of dark hair swept into a bun on the top of her head.

The first time Frank saw her, he figured Seven Sisters, Washington A-list, Kennedy Center patron, National Cathedral altar guild— quintessential bleeding-heart, little-pinky liberal.

He'd figured wrong. The only girl in a Pittsburgh steel family of five boys, a scholarship to Penn State. Ten years as an Associated Press stringer in Laos, Botswana, Nicaragua, and a dozen other pestilential-fever swamps whose major exports were malaria, dysentery, and plague. Jessica Talbot—never, *ever* Jess—had started at the bottom when the top management of the *Post* was known as the HBC—Harvard Boys' Club—and had demolished several glass ceilings before the term had been coined. Along the way she picked up a Pulitzer and turned out several generations of reporters who wrote simple declarative sentences in plain English.

"I don't do good news," Talbot said, sitting down next to Frank. "Just the bad stuff. The kind that sells papers."

Frank folded the newspaper and put it beside him on the bench.

Talbot pulled a pack of unfiltered Camels from her purse, along with a battered Zippo lighter. She stuck a cigarette in the corner of her mouth. "Tell me"—she fired up the Zippo—"tell me what was behind the Calkins firing."

"I thought you were on the foreign desk. Aren't you supposed to worry about France and Bangladesh?"

"I live *here*, Lieutenant. Not Bangladesh, *which*, I might add, is safer than the District."

"That's because judges in Bangladesh don't let killers out of jail."

Talbot sailed a plume of smoke skyward. "Touché, Lieutenant. And speaking of judges who don't let killers out, how's your dad?"

"In love."

Talbot nodded approvingly. "That'll either kill him right away or add another twenty years."

"I think add another twenty."

Another drag on the Camel, and Talbot turned to business. "Okay, now . . . Calkins?"

"He was suspended, not fired."

Talbot shrugged. "Whatever . . . hung out to dry."

"Emerson covering his ass."

"Washington's favorite pastime. Calkins screw up?"

"I don't think so."

"You want to know about Frederick Rhinelander. He a suspect?"

"He's a congressman."

"As Twain said, a member of America's only criminal class."

"He was Kevin Gentry's boss."

Talbot reached into her purse and brought out an envelope. "Clips," she explained, handing it to Frank.

He weighed the thick envelope in his palm, then put it in a pocket inside his jacket. "You said you knew him personally."

"Him and his wife. She's on the board of directors."

"Of the *Post*?"

"It *is* a publicly traded company. And she—her family—owns a big chunk of our stock." Talbot paused like a diver at the edge of a high board. She gave Frank a severe look. "This is background," she warned. "This gets out, you're dog meat."

"Go."

"Tom and Daisy Buchanan," Talbot said cryptically.

"I'm sorry?"

"The couple in *The Great Gatsby*."

"That's Rhinelander and . . ."

"His wife, Gloria . . . Gloria Principi Rhinelander," Talbot said. She took a drag deep into her lungs and Frank remembered how good a cigarette could taste. "Fitzgerald described Tom and Daisy as 'careless people.' He must have known Frederick and Gloria Rhinelander."

"Sloppy careless?"

"No. Careless in the sense that they didn't care about the consequences of their behavior. They never had to as kids. They've never had to as adults."

"Entitled."

Talbot blew a near-perfect smoke ring and watched as it dissipated. "Old-money people are interesting. Especially the men. A frightened bunch."

"What's scary if you got more money than God?"

"Losing it. A market crash. Somebody taking it from you. You see, they know deep inside that the money is what makes everything possible for them. It buys them through life. It buys things, influence. Even buys them friends. They know they wouldn't be who they are without it. And because they inherited the money . . . because they didn't earn it . . . they don't have the foggiest idea how to make more if they lose what they have."

"And so?"

"And so they see danger around every corner. Everyone they meet is out to rip them off. They have a terrible sense of vulnerability."

"Where'd the money come from . . . originally?"

"His from four generations of Boston banking and shipping. Hers from a father who set up a chain of pizza parlors, then sold out and got lucky in the market."

An old man in a yarmulke came down the path. He took a seat at a table opposite Frank and Talbot. From a pocket of his frayed overcoat he pulled out chess pieces and arranged them on the board set into the tabletop.

"So his old money was older than her old money," Frank said.

"Problem is, his ran out."

"Oh?"

"The Rhinelander fortune hit the rocks with a succession of bad mergers. A bunch of Greeks stripped the family down to its monogrammed boxer shorts. Young Frederick snagged Gloria just in time."

"She brought the money to the party, he brought the ancestors."

Talbot stubbed out her cigarette and stood up. "You do good with a few words, Lieutenant. Want a job?"

Frank shook his head. "Your work's too dangerous."

Talbot walked a few steps, then turned around. "You owe me," she said. "First dibs on this Calkins and Gentry thing."

Frank watched her walk away. He knew there had once been a Mr. Talbot, and he wondered if the guy had ever won an argument. He patted his jacket pocket where he'd put the envelope of clippings, and got up.

The old man in the yarmulke and overcoat was working out chess moves by himself.

Frank walked over.

"You used to play here with a black kid," Frank said.

The old man didn't look up. "Karim," he replied. "He's dead."

The old man moved white king's bishop on f1 to b5. He stared at the empty seat opposite as though waiting for his invisible adversary to make his move. He was still waiting when Frank left the park.

TWENTY

Frank finished off the cheeseburger and the cole slaw. He considered the fries against two additional miles in the morning. He pushed the plate away and reran José's meeting with Cookie.

"Cookie says he got it from Pencil. But Milt says Cookie told him he got it from Austin's woman."

José pulled Frank's plate over and picked out a French fry.

"I think we got it as straight as Cookie could give it . . . that he got it from Pencil, and not Austin's woman like he told Milt."

"So Pencil was either ratting out Austin two years ago for actually killing Gentry, or he was trying to frame Austin to cover for somebody else killing Gentry."

José dipped the fry in a puddle of ketchup.

"Whatever . . . Milt bought it."

"And Milt made it more credible, claiming that Cookie got it directly from Austin's woman rather than Pencil."

"Worse than the used-car business," Frank said.

They sat on the terrace of Potowmack Landing, a marina restaurant. The lunch-hour crowd filled the place. Lanyards and pocket clips carried ID badges from the Pentagon and Reagan National, a mile or two up the GW Parkway.

José dropped his chin to his chest and watched a 737 over the Potomac, wheels and flaps down for a landing at Reagan National.

"Rhinelander?" he asked Frank.

"We got an appointment with him at four. Janowitz'll meet us there."

"What'd the Dragon Lady have to say about him?"

"Nothing complimentary."

José finished the French fry and studied the check.

"Even split?"

"But you ate my fries," Frank protested.

José shot him his narrow-lidded Mike Tyson look.

"Even split," Frank said.

Back in the office, Frank fired up the coffeemaker and José switched on the CD player. Frank spread out the clippings while José picked up Zelmer Austin's case jacket. The coffee was ready just as Ahmad Jamal was wrapping up "Poinciana." The two men settled into reading and making notes. Jamal moved on to "Ole Devil Moon."

"You about through?" José asked an hour later.

Frank checked his notes. "Frederick Dumay Rhinelander the Third, born with a silver spoon in each hand." He passed an *Architectural Digest* clipping to José. "The homes of Frederick Rhinelander."

Frank watched José's eyes widen.

A 23,000-square-foot lodge in Aspen, complete with its own mountain and helicopter hangar.

A palace in northern Virginia: 40,000 square feet fronting the Potomac, just upriver from a Saudi prince.

An apartment in Paris: gilt, mirrors, and Louis XVI furniture overlooking the Place Vendôme.

José handed the article back. "Must be tough," he said with a roll of the eyes, "camping out in Paris."

"Yeah. Life's unfair. A lousy three thousand square feet . . . cramped accommodations."

"Guy makes . . . what?"

"Congressional salary? Hundred fifty, sixty. Somewhere in the neighborhood."

"Chump change. Think he even notices it come in?"

"Don't think he balances his own checkbook, Hoser." Frank took a cautious first sip of his coffee. "Our boy Zelmer?" he asked José.

José picked up his notebook. "Found in the middle of Eaton Road, ten forty-five Thursday night, April 15, 1999. M.E. report: Death by multiple trauma, manner of death automobile impact."

"What'd he have on his sheet?"

"Assault with deadly weapon. Assault, intent to maim. Vehicular manslaughter. Burglary. Breaking, entering. Grand theft auto."

"Time?"

"He and Skeeter and Pencil came from the same neighborhood. The three of them hand in hand to Lorton in 'eighty-seven. Skeeter met up with one of Juan Brooks's top boys doing time. All three get out in 'eighty-eight. Now they're back, business gets big. Then our FBI man Atkins busts Brooks in 'ninety-two. Skeeter takes over. Goes low-profile. Stealth operator. Narcotics knows he's up to his ass in the business, but nobody can lay a finger on them. Austin is a hanger-on. One of Skeeter's gofers."

"Until he kills Gentry."

"According to the story as told by Cookie as supposedly told to Cookie by Pencil Crawfurd." Frank tossed his pencil onto his desk in frustration. "We got zip. We got absolutely . . . positively . . . *zip*."

"One thing we got."

"What?"

José gestured to the clock. "An appointment to meet the MFWIC of the Subcommittee on D.C. Appropriations. You think he'll introduce us to his real estate agent?"

. . .

There he is," Frank said.

Janowitz stood in the hallway opposite the door to the Subcommittee on D.C. Appropriations.

"You're on time."

"You're surprised?" José asked.

"On time for what?" Frank asked.

With an index finger, Janowitz pushed his glasses back so they touched the bridge of his nose. "Nothing definite," he said. "Al . . . Mr. Salvani . . . said Rhinelander wasn't happy about me digging in the files."

"You didn't talk to Rhinelander yourself?"

Janowitz shook his head.

"You getting stonewalled?"

"No. Al's been helpful. Had one of his staffers show me around. Got me a parking pass and a building badge, a cubicle and a computer. But"—Janowitz held up two empty hands—"no files until Rhinelander approves."

"Almost four." Frank gestured toward the subcommittee doorway.

Janowitz pushed through the door. Frank and José followed him in. At a desk in the middle of the room, a largish formidable woman looked up at them. She wore a worried frown, and held a pencil frozen in midair over an appointments register.

Janowitz walked up to the desk. "Marge, Detectives Kearney and Phelps have an appointment with Congressman Rhinelander at four."

She eyed Frank and José, then brought her pencil down and moved it over the register. The pencil stopped. She bent closer, as though to make certain of the entry, then looked up.

"Have a seat." She aimed the pencil at an L-shaped leather sofa. Janowitz settled down, pulled a Palm Pilot from a jacket pocket, and began tapping with a stylus. José picked out a *Reader's Digest* from a nearby magazine rack, while Frank found an issue of *People*.

"These guys must get their reading material from my dentist." José said. Marge rewarded him with an acid look.

By four-thirty, Janowitz had finished tapping the Palm Pilot, but he held it anyway, apparently unsure what to do with it. Frank dozed, his chin dropped to his chest, the *People* open in his lap to a spread on Madonna. José sat with his eyes fixed glassily on a seemingly paralyzed wall clock.

Suddenly Frank awoke, snapping his head up, momentarily confused about where he was. His head cleared. "Why don't we come back tomorrow?" he asked Janowitz.

"Rhinelander won't be here."

"What?"

"He'll be back in his district," Janowitz explained. "Congress usually breaks for the weekend Thursday evenings."

"Come back Monday, then."

Janowitz shook his head. "They usually don't start up again until Tuesday morning."

"Tuesday, Wednesday, Thursday," José said in wonderment. "How'd I ever miss out on something like that?"

"You live in the District," Janowitz said. "Foreigners, felons, and D.C. residents can't be elected members of Congress."

"I guess we wait," José said unhappily.

Another half-hour passed. The hands on the clock had slowly, almost painfully, crawled toward five.

Marge's phone chirped once. She answered, listened, and eyed Frank, José, and Janowitz.

"Yes," she said, "they're still here."

The Rayburn Building's architect had attempted to graft the ornate nineteenth-century decor of the Capitol onto Frederick Rhinelander's mid-twentieth-century office. The expensive operation had failed. Heavy velvet drapes, patterned carpets, and faux plaster crown moldings clashed with modern windows, fluorescent lighting, and government-bland pseudo-Danish teak furniture.

Frederick Rhinelander sat at his desk, the only genuine antique in the room, a massive piece with a sweeping, flaring grain that looked crafted from a solid block of oak. On the desk, a richly embossed leather-trimmed blotter, a Cross pen-and-pencil set, and a brass banker's lamp with a green glass shade.

Rhinelander, a man of medium build, wore his dark hair short and neatly combed. He had on a well-tailored dark blue pin-striped suit, a snowy white shirt with an English spread collar, and a silver-gray silk tie.

Frank's first thought was that Rhinelander looked younger than in his photographs. But that wasn't it. In some indefinable way, Rhinelander looked more *juvenile*. As though he didn't quite fit into the adult costume he was wearing. And there was an alertness about him, as though he was constantly sniffing the air for danger.

Al Salvani sat in an armchair to the side of his desk.

"Congressman Rhinelander," Frank said, "I'm Detective Kearney, and this's my partner, Detective Phelps. Detective Janowitz is working with us on the Gentry case."

Frank and José offered their credentials. Rhinelander took them, examined them, then handed them back. He pointed to three chairs that had been drawn up in front of his desk.

"Please, gentlemen."

Rhinelander spoke with a studied, careful enunciation. His New England accent carried a foppish nasal overlay of Old England.

"Please don't think me brusque," he said, "but there's going to be a vote on the floor any moment. If so, there's no telling when I shall return. So . . . shall we cut to the chase?" He touched his fingertips together, making a tent of his hands. "Detective Janowitz has already had access to Kevin Gentry's appointments calendar."

"Yes," Frank said.

"But now he wants to go fishing in the subcommittee's financial records." Rhinelander spoke as though Janowitz weren't in the room. "This line of investigation is presumptive of a motive for Mr. Gentry's death arising from the subcommittee's activities."

José got through Rhinelander's bureaucratese before Frank did.

"Nobody's presuming anything, Congressman. We want to know what Mr. Gentry was doing and why he was doing it. If we know that, we might find out who killed him. We'd appreciate your help to establish what Kevin Gentry was doing before he was killed."

Rhinelander smiled condescendingly. "Very well put, Detective Phelps. And that means precisely . . . what?"

"It means we want to find out who he was dealing with and what the dealing was about."

Rhinelander's smile disappeared. "And *that* means . . . ?"

Irritated over Rhinelander's none-too-subtle baiting, Frank cut in: "*That* means we need access to people and records so we can build a timeline for Gentry's activities."

"You don't believe that it was a case of Kevin being unlucky?" Rhinelander persisted. "Someone with a gun looking for any available target?"

"That's only one possibility," José said.

Rhinelander, his face a flat, expressionless mask, stared steadily at José. "I am the first to appreciate the value of *good* police work," he said, with a righteous air. "Some of my colleagues complain to me that they've seen too little of it here in Washington. But I support your efforts fully. I'm inclined to have the subcommittee assist you. I hope you appreciate that."

Rhinelander looked expectantly at Frank, José, and Janowitz.

"Well?" he asked. "Do you?"

"I'm sorry," Frank said. "Do I . . . what?"

"I didn't hear you say that you appreciated it . . . that I'd have the subcommittee assist you."

It took Frank a moment to realize what Rhinelander wanted. "Yes. Of course, Congressman, we appreciate it."

Rhinelander almost purred. "Good," he said. "That's good."

"If you have a moment?" José asked.

"Yes?"

"Mr. Gentry . . . could you describe your relationship with him? He was your staff director for, what, four years?"

"Not exactly."

"Oh?"

"It was less than four years," Rhinelander said emphatically. "Three months less. And a couple of days."

"Okay. How was the relationship?"

Rhinelander cleared his throat. "If it had been anything but excellent, Detective Phelps, Kevin wouldn't have stayed on as staff director. He was very industrious . . . and *very* loyal."

"What was the social relationship?" Frank asked.

"Socially?" Rhinelander asked. "We weren't social . . . friends." He leaned forward. "We had a splendid working relationship. I'm *certain* Kevin had friends. But I never met them."

"In an interview after his death," Frank continued, "you said that you saw him a little less than an hour before he was shot."

"Yes."

"Did he seem worried? Distracted?"

"Worried—no. Preoccupied—yes. We were getting ready for the annual District budget hearings. He had a lot on his plate."

"The preoccupation . . . do you think it was about getting the work done? Or something to do with what he'd found out?"

Rhinelander held up a hand in a "Stop" motion. "That is so speculative that it's ridiculous. I'm not going to answer."

"I know the difference between fact and speculation, sir," Frank said, feeling his face warming. "What someone like you thinks can be of help. That's what I'm asking."

Rhinelander stiffened slightly, then put on a small, patient smile. "Very well, Detective Kearney, my best *speculation* is that Kevin was harried by the amount of work. That's not unusual. If a staffer isn't overworked, he isn't doing his job."

A hidden loudspeaker buzzed angrily. Rhinelander's eyes jumped to the clock on his wall.

"Ten minutes to get to the floor, gentlemen," he said, standing, and shooting out his shirtsleeves so that his heavy gold cuff links shone in the late-afternoon light. "If you'll excuse me . . ."

. . .

José's mouth tightened. "Mr. Congressman Rhinelander's used to talking down."

"Don't you appreciate that?" Frank bantered.

"Appreciate my ass," José said sourly. "Like he was holding up a doggy bone and wanting us to roll over. Did you get the impression he was trying to put some air between Gentry and himself?"

"The bit about 'three months less'?"

"Yeah. And when you asked him about a personal relationship with Gentry . . . he acted like you'd asked him if he sat in the back of the bus."

"Or drank California wine."

"A place for everybody, and everybody in their place."

"You guys finished up here?" Janowitz asked. "I'll get to my cubicle and start."

Frank shook his head. "Are for now. Wish we were for good. Hoser and I have a dinner date."

"Sexy chicks?"

"Not our luck, Leon," José said. "Two hairy-legged guys from the Bureau."

TWENTY-ONE

Robin Bouchard met Frank and José at the corner of Ninth and D, across from Bureau headquarters.

"When he heard about Pencil skipping, Atkins asked me if there was anything we could do to help," Bouchard explained. "I suggested he have you guys over, he could ask you himself."

"And so dinner," Frank said.

"And so dinner." Bouchard motioned to a nearby doorway.

José did a double-take. "The Caucus Room? I can't float a second mortgage."

Bouchard shrugged. "Atkins has a slush fund, and the Bureau cafeteria has rats."

"Nice of him to worry about us," José said.

Bouchard did his wise-guy grin. "Atkins isn't doing a Dudley Do-Right."

"He getting heat?" Frank asked.

"Probably."

"You don't know?"

Bouchard shook his head. "I'm not on his share-my-soul list." He paused at the door. "Matter of fact, this is the first time I've been here." He pulled the door open.

Inside, a hostess in something very Italian and very expensive smiled as though greeting an afternoon lover. Bouchard mentioned Atkins's name. The hostess's smile grew wider.

"The Roosevelt Room, gentlemen," she purred.

She led the three down a lushly carpeted corridor past larger dining rooms, to a mahogany door with heavy brass fittings.

José whistled softly.

"I'm impressed," Frank said.

The private room resembled a Victorian library: leather-bound volumes in walnut bookcases, green shaded reading lamps beside morocco-leather club chairs, a massive globe in a bronze cradle near a coal fireplace. Oil portraits of the Roosevelts, Theodore and Franklin, bracketed the fireplace.

Near a set of double doors that apparently led into the kitchen, a slender white man in a severe dark suit whispered to a young black waiter. Frank couldn't hear what was going on, but from the body language, he guessed the two were getting their signals straight for the coming dinner crowd. The waiter's eyes shifted to Robin, Frank, and José, and the suit turned around.

"Gentlemen?"

"Here for dinner with Mr. Atkins," Robin said.

The man came closer, and Frank could read his silver name tag: "Thurmond."

Thurmond then led them to a table closest to the window.

"Mr. Atkins," Thurmond said, "likes to sit facing the door." With that, he walked to the waiters' station and returned with three menus. "Dobbs will take your orders when you're ready."

Bouchard took a seat that covered the door, with Frank and José opposite. "A menu for Mr. Atkins?"

Thurmond tilted his chin upward and smiled. "I know what he wants."

"Oh? What's that?"

"Baked scrod, new potatoes and spinach, iced tea."

"Scrod a house specialty?" Bouchard asked.

"Ah . . . no." Thurmond said it as though concerned he was revealing a secret. His voice dropped to the confiding whisper of a Frenchman offering dirty postcards. "Beef . . . and coconut cake."

Bouchard grinned. "Helluva combination, Mr. Thurmond."

Thurmond returned a conspiratorial smile. "A combination to die for." He paused, then turned and disappeared through the swinging doors into the kitchen.

"We got a choice," Bouchard said. "We suck up to Atkins and order scrod, or we go with the house."

"Scrod taste better than it sounds?" José asked.

"Has to, Hoser," Bouchard said.

A moment's silence as the three men looked over their menus. Frank glanced up from his and found José and Bouchard, their menus closed, eyes on him.

Bouchard signaled to Dobbs, who came over and took their orders. Then he turned to Frank and José. "So what's new?"

José told him about the meeting with Cookie, how Pencil had been fingering Zelmer Austin for Gentry's killing.

Bouchard listened intently for a few moments before he raised one hand an inch off the table and nodded toward the door.

From behind Frank and José came Brian Atkins's voice. "I invite you to dinner and I'm late."

Bouchard, Frank, and José started to get up, but Atkins waved them down.

"You guys looked at the menu?"

Bouchard nodded. "We've ordered."

Atkins grinned. "Hope you went with the beef. My cholesterol's got me stuck with the scrod." He made a face. "An acquired taste."

Bouchard gestured toward José. "We were just catching up."

"I was telling Robin about a meeting," José said.

Atkins nodded. "Go on."

José backtracked, working his way through the meeting with

Cookie. In the middle of it, Dobbs brought Atkins's scrod, New York strip steaks for Frank and Bouchard, and a Delmonico for José.

Atkins looked longingly at the steaks, then sipped his iced tea. "So Pencil dropped the dime on Zelmer Austin? That Austin did Kevin Gentry?"

"And now, Pencil's split," Frank said.

"You think it spooked him, hearing that the same weapon that killed Skeeter killed Gentry?"

"It's a possibility."

"Where does that lead?" Robin asked. "Is Pencil afraid that the same guy who did Skeeter is going to come after him?"

"You've got to remember," José said, "two years ago, Pencil was pushing the story that Zelmer Austin killed Gentry. Now Pencil finds out it isn't so . . . or that other people know it isn't so."

Frank cut in. "Then again, we don't know for sure that Zelmer *didn't* do it. Just that the admin case against him doesn't hold up."

"I'm getting an overload," Bouchard said. "What all this boils down to is . . . what?"

"Finding Pencil," Atkins answered. He turned to Frank and José. "I know you guys are already working that. Could we help?"

Frank paused. He felt José's shoe nudge his.

"Emerson wanted to set up a task force," Frank said, searching for a graceful out, "but José and I wanted to keep it small. It's just us and another detective."

Atkins nodded emphatically. "I think you were right. I wasn't envisioning a bureau pile-on. No publicity. Just one person." At "person," Atkins put his hand on Bouchard's shoulder.

Frank and José exchanged glances. Both nodded.

"Deal," said José.

Neither Frank nor José said anything until they were on the sidewalk.

"What about that?" Frank asked.

"Great coconut cake," José replied.

"No . . . What Atkins was up to?"

"They want in," José said. "Atkins was nice about it. But we'd said no, he would have gone to Emerson. . . ."

"Who'd have folded like a cheap suitcase . . ."

"And probably gone ahead with that brain-fart of his about a task force. At least we got Robin and no publicity."

"We got Robin," Frank amended, "but I'm not betting on no publicity." He paused, playing out possibilities in his head. "Yesterday afternoon, Rhinelander calls Atkins. Whines about having us on his ass . . ."

José picked up. ". . . Atkins sees an opportunity to get the Bureau in on the case . . ."

". . . and score points with Rhinelander at the same time," Frank finished.

Ahead, down Pennsylvania Avenue, windows shone on the Capitol's West Front, and the dome glowed white against a dark velvet-blue sky.

Nothing in this town works along a straight line. Everything moves along a curve just in front of you. And you can never see around the curve.

Frank pointed toward the Capitol. "Tomorrow morning, why don't we drop up and see how Janowitz's doing?"

TWENTY-TWO

Gentry's personnel file . . . nothing in it but his résumé, pay records, and a couple of letters of commendation."

Leon Janowitz pushed the folder across the table to Frank and José. Meeting in Janowitz's cramped cubicle was impossible. It was Friday, the cavernous subcommittee hearing room wasn't being used, and so the three men huddled at the witness table. Before them, a semicircle of raised seats from which subcommittee members could look down on those testifying and into the cameras. Centered on a low wall below the seats, the crest of the House of Representatives marked where Frederick Dumay Rhinelander would preside.

Looking up at the crest, Frank remembered a vacation in Rome when he and Kate had toured the Colosseum. He had stood in the arena and had looked up toward where, with a roll of the hand, emperors had once decreed who would live and who would die for the entertainment of the crowd.

"ROTC at UCLA," he heard José reading off the résumé. "Lieutenant, Southern Command . . ."

"I've asked for his service records," Janowitz said. "They have to send off to St. Louis."

"Law school, NYU," José picked up. "Then State Department, Western Hemisphere Affairs . . ."

"I've had a few of those," Janowitz murmured.

"Those . . . what?" José asked.

"Affairs in the western hemisphere," Janowitz cracked.

José frowned and lowered his eyelids and gave Janowitz his "Down, boy" look, then continued. "Four years at State, then staff of Senator Patterson, New York, then here."

"Interesting background," Frank said. "Anything else?"

"Just this."

Janowitz passed over a sheet of paper.

"Character references," he explained. "Gentry gave them when Rhinelander interviewed him for the job."

TWENTY-THREE

Trees! Yes, damn it! I said, *trees!*"

All six feet, six inches of Senator Daniel Dugan Patterson stood behind his desk, phone at his ear. He listened for a moment. What he heard evidently met with his approval—his almost feminine lips pulled into a smug smile.

He hung up and, with his hand still on the phone, gazed out the window at the panoramic view down Pennsylvania Avenue toward the Treasury and the White House. The man's lean body didn't fit a round face made even rounder by large horn-rimmed glasses. The glasses, the unruly silver hair, the rumpled blue seersucker suit, and the yellow paisley bow tie gave him the air of a slightly distracted college professor, which he had been at Harvard between stints in the administrations of four presidents.

"Pennsylvania Avenue," he whispered to himself. "America's main street. And the silly bastards complain about the cost of a few dozen trees."

He shook his large head as though to clear it of silly bastards, then turned and regarded Frank and José with the perplexed look of a man finding a stranger using his toothbrush.

"And who are you?"

"Ah . . . police," Frank said. "District Homicide."

Patterson's bewilderment hung on for another moment.

He fished in his jacket pockets until he came up with a pack of three-by-five cards, then shuffled through them until he found one that seemed to satisfy him. Holding it high in front of his face, he studied it, his mouth slightly open. He nodded and tucked the cards away.

"Yes. About Kevin." He pointed to Frank. "You are . . ."

"Frank Kearney."

"And you?" Patterson swung the finger around to José.

"José Phelps."

Patterson nodded. "Very good, gentlemen. Please sit." He gestured to a leather sofa and took a nearby chair for himself.

"So," he said, "you didn't catch Kevin's killer."

"No, sir, we didn't," Frank said.

"But you're going to do so now." Patterson spoke it kindly, but with a flat irony.

"Takes being lucky and being good, Senator," José said. "We're good. But we still need luck."

Patterson's expression softened. Leaning forward in his chair, he rested his hands on his knees and thrust his head at Frank and José.

"How can I help?"

"Mr. Gentry—"

"Kevin." Patterson whispered the correction.

Frank nodded and began again. "Kevin . . . came here from the State Department in 1991. He stayed seven years . . . tell us about him."

With a sad smile, Patterson shook his head. "Neither you nor I have enough time for me to tell you all I remember. Suffice it to say I was lucky to have him here. The office was lucky to have him. The single most exciting thing you encounter in government is competence, because it is so rare. Kevin was a bright fellow who could run easily ahead of the rest while devoting time to those who struggled at the back."

"Why'd he leave?" José asked.

"Staff work on Capitol Hill is repetitive," Patterson said. "After a while, a job here resembles riding a carousel . . . one moves, but 'round and 'round through the same scenery. Kevin needed to move in a different direction."

"And the job with Congressman Rhinelander offered that?"

Patterson's lips parted as though he was preparing to speak; then something happened behind his eyes, a flicker like a camera shutter. He hesitated, then said, "Rhinelander offered a different challenge from what Kevin could find here."

"What was that?" José asked.

"Why," Patterson said quickly, "the challenge of the District of Columbia, of course."

"Of course?" Frank raised his eyebrows.

Patterson looked at Frank, and José as if at students in a seminar.

"This country," he began, "is coming apart." He flung his arms out dramatically. "Coming apart!"

He aimed a questioning look at Frank and then José as though trying to detect a hint of ignorance or disagreement.

Finding none, he continued. "The District is a microcosm of our disintegrating society . . . the proverbial miner's canary. Understand what ails the District and perhaps . . . *just* perhaps . . . we might be able to save ourselves. And if not ourselves, pray to God, we might be able to salvage the next generation, or perhaps the one after that."

For a moment, no one spoke. Then José said, "That's a pretty bad picture."

Patterson tilted his head back and laughed. Light danced across his glasses.

"Actually, Mr. Phelps, it's quite optimistic. I used to think salvation out of reach."

"So we haven't passed the Plimsoll line." The thought had struck

Frank while Patterson was talking, and he was surprised that it just came out.

"The Plimsoll line," Patterson repeated thoughtfully, turning it over in his mind. "Yes," he said, drawing it out. *Yessss.* "Yes! Samuel Plimsoll!" he said, with a catch of excitement. "That's good. That's *very* good."

"My father made the connection."

Patterson grinned mischievously. "Fathers manage to do that, sometimes . . . commit a modest bit of wisdom."

"When was the last time you talked with Kevin?" José asked.

Patterson's face clouded. "The day he was killed. We had lunch."

"What'd you talk about?"

"Cabbages and kings. Our lunches were always a dog's breakfast . . . odds and ends of this and that. The smallest of details, the largest of pictures."

"Anything in particular?"

"Insofar as the details were concerned, Kevin was absorbed in the upcoming hearings on the District appropriations."

"Do you remember any of those details?"

Patterson shook his head. "Oh . . . the procedural worries . . . witness lists, staff coaching of the subcommittee members, publicity . . . that sort of thing."

"And the big pictures?"

"When we got to that, it was always the same. . . . Bits and pieces might change, but essentially we always ended up talking about numbers and levers."

Patterson took in Frank's and José's expectant looks.

"Numbers," Patterson explained, "the statistics . . . the harbingers of society's tomorrow . . . crime, illiteracy, disease, divorce, children born out of wedlock." He paused as though somewhere in his head a tape was bringing in the latest figures.

"And the levers?" Frank prompted.

"The levers," Patterson said, "yes, the levers. The means by which we might shape society's tomorrows. From Archimedes . . . 'Give me a lever and a place to stand and I will move the earth.' "

"And Kevin's place to stand was on Rhinelander's subcommittee."

Patterson nodded.

"And the lever?"

"He was still searching."

Frank glanced at the antique wall clock, now getting on to six.

"Last question . . . Did Kevin ever mention anyone who might have a motive to kill him?"

"No. But I never believed his killing was a random act."

"Oh?"

Patterson's chin dropped to his chest, and he looked at Frank and José over the tops of his glasses. "The fates don't allow such a man to die at the whim of another."

With that, Patterson's attention seemed to drift away. Frank and José stood.

"Thank you for your time," Frank said.

Patterson continued staring off into the distance, or perhaps into another time. Without acknowledging Frank and José, he took off his glasses and wiped his eyes.

"There's no use being Irish," he said to himself, "unless you know the world is going to break your heart."

Look!" José pointed with theatrical alarm. "Someone's been in our office! And there he is . . . in your chair!"

"You're right, Papa Bear," Frank said. "And I bet he ate up all our porridge too."

In what was becoming his trademark position, Leon Janowitz was cocked back in Frank's chair, feet on the edge of his desk. Arms extended, he was reading from an accordion-folded computer printout.

Still holding the printout, still cocked back in Frank's chair, he turned to face Frank and José.

"You guys get a bigger office, a hardworking fella like me wouldn't have to borrow a place to sit."

"Hardworkin' fella like you, Leon, shouldn't be sittin'," José said. "Oughta be out savin' the world."

Frank nodded toward the printout. "What you got there?"

Janowitz folded the printout, tossed it onto the desk, and dropped his feet to the floor, righting himself in a controlled crash.

"Subcommittee financials." Janowitz tapped the printout with his fingertips. "And xeroxes of Gentry's appointment calendar."

"Why the frown?" Frank asked.

Janowitz stared for a moment at the printout and the sheaf of xeroxes as though searching for the answer, then looked at Frank and José.

"You know how sometimes you know there's something right under your nose? But you really aren't seeing it?" He turned to the paperwork on the desk and shook his head.

"Sometimes," José suggested, "you're lookin' too hard."

"Or too long," Frank added. "TGIF. There's something called weekend. We do get one every month or so."

Janowitz smiled. "I haven't forgotten." He reached down to a shopping bag on the floor and pulled out a bottle of champagne.

"Mumm demi-sec," he said, gazing lovingly at the label. "Mrs. Janowitz and I will be in New York tomorrow night. We will be ensconced in the Plaza Hotel, drinking champagne, fucking ourselves absolutely silly, and forgetting there's any such thing as crime and punishment."

Frank felt suddenly tired and at the same time envious. "You figure out how to do the last, let Hoser and me know."

A few minutes later, on the sidewalk outside headquarters, Frank and José watched Janowitz head toward his car, shopping bag in hand.

"We ever that young?" José asked.

Frank took in Janowitz's bounding stride. "We ever that smart?" he asked back.

Both men stood quietly, until José broke the silence. "Bothers you, doesn't it . . . him leaving the force."

Frank didn't say anything immediately. Then, feeling a sense of loss, he said, "It's like watching a priest walk away from the Church."

Janowitz started his car. The headlights flashed on.

"Helluva church we're in," José said.

Frank watched Janowitz back out of his parking place and drive down the block. He watched until the taillights disappeared around the corner.

"Wonder if there's another room at the Plaza?"

TWENTY-FOUR

"What're you doing?" Kate asked, her eyes still shut.

Frank trailed a fingertip down her cheek toward the corner of her mouth. "How'd you know I'm doing anything?"

"I can just tell."

"I was watching you breathe."

"Exciting?"

"Very."

She opened her eyes and turned to face him.

"A good weekend," she smiled.

The Caps had beaten the Penguins in the playoff opener Friday night; on Saturday, Renée Zellweger had been hilarious in *Bridget Jones's Diary*; and Sunday had been spent sleeping late, with breakfast at Clyde's, antique browsing in Kensington, and dinner at Saigonnais.

"A very good weekend."

Kate sighed. "Too bad they're only two days long."

"You're a lawyer."

"Yes?"

Frank traced down her cheek again. "Get a law passed. Make weekends forever."

Kate turned slightly and nipped at his finger. "Nobody'd get any work done."

"Getting work done is the source of all mischief."

"Profound."

"You want profound on a Monday morning early?"

"I'll tell you what I want on a Monday morning early," she said.

A light rain stacked up the morning traffic along Pennsylvania Avenue to Washington Circle. Twenty-third Street thinned out, and Frank found a semilegal parking spot behind the Federal Reserve. José was waiting under the C Street entrance at State. Frank paused to take in the boxlike building.

He and Hoser had been here . . . what . . . six months before? A montage of mental images . . . a once beautiful woman dead in a Georgetown park, the statue at Hains Point with its defiled cargo, and, of course, here, David Trevor.

"Good weekend?" Frank asked.

"Almost forgot how to do weekends."

"Think Leon survived the Plaza?"

"No doubt," José said. "Kid sets a fine example. Who we seeing here?"

Frank checked his notebook.

"Bureau of Western Hemisphere Affairs. Guy by the name of Khron . . . Sidney Khron."

Sidney Khron, a spare, balding man with rimless glasses, stared into his computer screen. He rapped his keyboard, clicked his mouse, stared some more. Then he turned to Frank and José.

"We don't have those records."

"Kevin Gentry?" Frank asked. "Kevin Walker Gentry wasn't in the State Department? Not in Western Hemisphere Affairs?"

Khron took a deep breath and studied the ceiling, then made eye contact with Frank.

"No. I mean . . . yes. Yes, he was in the bureau. No, we don't have his records."

"We were told," José said patiently, "that you had access to the personnel records of everybody who's been assigned to Western Hemisphere."

"There are . . . *exceptions*," Khron said primly.

"Exceptions for what?" José asked.

"For many things."

"Such as?"

Khron's face resembled a lifeless mask. "I'm not authorized to say more."

"But Gentry's one of those exceptions?" Frank asked.

Khron thought about the question and decided to duck. "I'm not authorized to say more," he repeated.

"Why?" Frank persisted, knowing as he asked that he wouldn't find out.

"Because I'm not," Khron replied. "There are privacy issues concerned."

"Privacy? Gentry's dead."

Khron dropped his hands into his lap. "Nevertheless," he said with finality.

Frank stood, then José.

"Who do we have to see?" Frank asked.

Randolph Emerson's face darkened the longer he listened. When Frank and José had finished, he stared wordlessly at the two men.

"The State Department's general counsel?" he finally asked.

"That's who we have to see," Frank said.

Emerson got an aggrieved look. "First, we'd have to see the chief. Then go to the mayor."

"Mayor wouldn't have to do it," José said, "the U.S. attorney—"

Emerson cut him off with a slicing motion of his hand and launched into a death spiral of calamity. "Still, we'd have to go to the chief, then the mayor. That'd stir up some shit. U.S. Attorney's Office is a bunch of Republicans. They'd leak it. Then the papers'd get a hold of it . . . more shit."

Emerson picked up velocity. "And do we know what we'd get for it?" He jabbed the air with an angry fist. "I mean, we go to the mayor, we spin him up, we get the papers down on our asses, then we get nothing. We look like fools."

As though disaster had already struck, as though his career had been carpet-bombed, Emerson collapsed into his chair and glared accusingly at Frank and José. "We could go through all that and get nothing."

"Even nothing's something sometimes," José said.

"We've got to check it out, Randolph," Frank said.

Emerson's lips thinned. "No we don't," he grated.

Frank turned to look at José and found José was looking at him, silently signaling a question. Frank nodded a yes.

"We," José said, "Frank and me . . . we're running the investigation. We're responsible."

Emerson tensed, knowing he wasn't going to like what he was going to hear.

"Either we go after Gentry's records," José said evenly, "or you find somebody else."

"You mean—"

"We mean," Frank said, "we're off the case."

"You can't do that."

"You don't want to bet," José said.

"Maybe you could get somebody else, Randolph," Frank suggested. "Like . . . Milton?"

Emerson gave Frank a dead-fish look, then started a slow smile. "Okay, we'll ask. We'll ask our pals at the Bureau. They wanted in on this case. Let them bend their pick."

. . . **A**nd this guy Chrome at State said there were 'other considerations'?" Brian Atkins asked.

Frank, José, and Robin Bouchard were at a small conference table in Atkins's office. Atkins sat at the head of the table, listening carefully, jotting in a small leather notebook.

"Khron," Frank corrected. "The go-to guy at State to get the records released is the general counsel."

"General counsel." Atkins paused, then nodded. "That's Tommy del Gado." He fastened Frank with a look. "Your department wants us to deal with State?" He spoke like he was putting Frank on record.

"We'd appreciate it." Frank said, feeling his gut tighten.

"How about Pencil Crawfurd?" Atkins asked.

"Still hanging out with Elvis," Frank said. "But we'll find him."

"Any idea what spooked him?"

Frank shook his head. "No, not really."

"Okay." Atkins got up and tucked the notebook in an inner suit jacket pocket. "You guys find Elvis and Pencil, we'll rattle State Department's cage."

Well, your basic good news, bad news," José said outside on Pennsylvania Avenue.

"Good news?"

"The Bureau gets to handle the pussies at State."

"And . . . ?"

"We had to get the Bureau to—"

"—handle the pussies at State," Frank finished. José was right. It did rankle, Randolph Emerson passing the buck to Atkins and the Bureau. Emerson making José and him come down, hat in hand, asking the big boys for help. It was a bush-league play.

"At least Atkins didn't rub it in," José said. "Now we can concentrate on finding Elvis."

TWENTY-FIVE

I could ride to town on your lower lip," Frank said.

Leon Janowitz threw his hands up. "Well, shit," he said, "there goes my piece of the action."

José fired the remote at the stereo. Dexter Gordon's cut of "Don't Explain" came on, all soft sax and cabaret piano.

"Atkins is just doing battle with the suits at State. You keep tracking Gentry on the Hill." Frank tilted back in his chair and inspected Janowitz with a narrow-lidded look. "I thought a weekend at the Plaza'd mellow you out."

"It did," Janowitz said, pulling on his jacket and picking up his briefcase. "City's gotten its act together."

"Didn't just happen," José said.

Janowitz stood at the door, turning that over. "A message there, Hoser?"

"Just that it took work."

"And some balls," Janowitz snapped. He took the edge off with a smile. "I got a meeting with the subcommittee's finance clerk," he said, opening the door. "Thought about some leads over the weekend."

Frank raised an eyebrow.

Janowitz caught the question, and his smile turned roguish. "You got to think sometime, even with Mrs. Janowitz in the Plaza."

And like the Cheshire Cat, Janowitz left, leaving his smile hanging in the air.

Frank and José regarded the closed door.

José broke the silence. "Kid wants to kick some ass."

"Most cops do, starting out. Then they lose it."

Frank was still thinking about Janowitz's goofy smile when he realized his phone was ringing.

"This is Detective Kearney."

For a moment silence, and Frank started to hang up. Then the woman's voice came, unsteady, uncertain.

"I want to talk to Detective Kearney or Detective Phelps."

Frank repeated softly, "Miss, this is Detective Kearney."

Another silence followed. Frank heard vague office noise in the background, muted voices, canned music, doors opening and closing.

Then a sharp intake of breath and, "I heard you want to know about Tobias Crawfurd."

"Yes." Frank played the call gently. "Yes, we do."

Yet more silence. The office sounds disappeared as though a hand had closed over the mouthpiece.

Oh, shit, she's going to hang up!

He forced himself to speak slowly, softly. "Miss . . . if you want to talk, we can meet you anywhere. Anytime. You name it."

Glass-and-stainless-steel buildings surrounded a pocket square that had been turned into a park. A handful of small trees broke up the concrete sameness, and repro nineteenth-century park benches offered islands where office workers ate lunches of deli sandwiches or salads brought from home in Tupperware and brown bags. It was midafternoon, the park empty except for a man on a cell phone, and farther off, two women sitting together, smoking and talking.

"Sure this the place?" José asked, eyeing the unfamiliar buildings.

"Beautiful downtown Rosslyn, Virginia," Frank said, pointing to a corner bench from which they could cover the approaches into the park.

European settlers in the late seventeenth century built the first houses in Rosslyn, just across the Potomac from the tobacco port that was Georgetown. But Rosslyn's notorious growth came later, when the District of Columbia outlawed usury and handguns. Pawnshop owners and gun dealers crossed the river and set up shop in Rosslyn where enterprising criminals could rearm and fence their loot on the same block.

In 1899, the District of Columbia again spurred growth in Rosslyn, this time by passing the Heights of Building Act, which prohibited private structures in the District higher than the Capitol "or other significant government edifices."

Fortune 500 companies that wanted to do business with the government also wanted imposing offices, and in Rosslyn they could reach skyward with glass and stainless steel. The resulting skyline was a pimple compared with New York, but it towered over the low-lying District buildings across the river. And thus the banks and defense contractors drove out the pawnshops and gun dealers.

"Bet that's her." José watched a young black woman cross the street. She stopped at a curbside vendor's.

Frank noticed her survey the park as she paid for a bottle of water. She wore a modest dark brown skirt and a flowered blouse.

"More women ought to dress that way," Frank said.

The woman entered the park and walked straight to Frank and José. Both men stood.

"You're Detective Phelps," she said to José, then, turning to Frank, "and you're Detective Kearney."

José reached for his badge case.

"I know who you are." The woman's voice matched the voice on the phone, but was now confident, as though, decision made, she wasn't going back.

"And you're . . . ?" José asked.

Water bottle in her left hand, she brushed her right hand over her bottom, smoothing her skirt, and sat down on the L-shaped bench.

"Does it matter?" she asked, looking up at the two detectives.

Frank and José sat.

José nodded. "It's comforting to know who you're talking to. You do. We don't."

The woman considered this while twisting the bottle cap.

"Alta Rae," she said, unscrewing the cap.

"Alta Rae what?" José asked.

She frowned. "Walsh."

Frank anted first. "Pencil Crawfurd."

Walsh frowned again. "Tobias," she corrected. "What do you want to know?"

"Where he is."

"You been by his place."

"He hadn't been there since he left the hospital. You got any ideas?"

"Don't know." Walsh said. "Don't care."

"Well," Frank said, "I guess what we want to know is what you want to tell us."

"We were . . . we lived together for seven years." The telephone uncertainty crept back into Walsh's voice.

"Tell us about it," José said gently, "we're not in a hurry."

Walsh glanced at her watch.

"Met him," she began, "I'd just graduated . . . 1992. I knew he'd been in jail. Knew he and Skeeter were into dealing. But he treated me respectful. Mama warned me, but . . ." Walsh shrugged.

"Him and Skeeter," José said, "how'd that work?"

"They were close. Almost like brothers. I asked Tobias once, how it was Skeeter, being younger, Tobias went along. Tobias said Skeeter did the thinking, he did the doing."

"What kind of doing?" José asked.

Walsh sipped at her water. "He called it persuadin'."

José exchanged a glance with Frank. Frank eyed a no, so José followed up.

"But it wasn't persuading, was it?" José said.

"No." Walsh's voice came in low and slow.

"Tobias killed people."

Walsh looked around the park with a trapped expression, and Frank was certain she was going to bug out.

"He did, didn't he?" José asked, quietly but firmly. "Kill people?"

Walsh nodded. She didn't say anything for a while. Then, "Skeeter did too," she whispered defiantly.

Very carefully, Frank probed. "He . . . Tobias . . . ever talk about it . . . ? Details?"

"I didn't want to know," she said. She hugged herself, bending forward as though in pain. The words came out in a rush. "I was goin' to have his baby, we needed money, and I didn't ask."

José waited a moment, then took over. "The dealing . . . Tobias talk about that? What he was doing and all?"

"Some." Walsh ran her hand over her hair, captured a strand and twisted it nervously with her fingertips. "He'd come in all excited. Tell me how he and Skeeter took over somebody's territory . . . how many street dealers he had workin' for him . . . his travelin'."

"Travel? Where to?"

"South America. Skeeter and him."

"You know where in South America?"

Walsh shook her head. "I told you, I didn't want to know. He'd come back, tell me how he was gonna take me with him down there." She paused. Her lips pulled into a thin disapproving line. "Never did, though. Shuckin' and jivin'. Just shuckin' and jivin'."

José backtracked. "You said you didn't want to know about Tobias killing anybody."

"Yes."

"How'd you know that was going on?"

"He'd brag on it. Like the travelin'. I'd tell him I didn't want to hear. He'd brag anyway. Like it got him a rush."

José's voice dropped almost to a whisper. "Tobias say any names?"

Walsh closed her eyes so tightly that her mouth pursed. Her face put Frank in mind of a child squenching up its face to shut out something scary.

"Zelmer Austin?" José tried.

"I don't remember," she said without hesitation, and Frank knew she was lying.

"You don't remember if Tobias said any names?" José persisted. "Or you don't remember the names?"

Eyes still closed, Walsh shook her head. "I don't know," she said in a rising tone, "and I don't want to talk any more about it."

The three sat without speaking.

Walsh opened her eyes. "He left me and Samuel. He left his boy. Just . . . walked out." She said it to no one else, just to herself.

Frank had to strain to hear, and he realized that what she'd come to tell was a story about a woman and a man and love and betrayal.

He led her on. "When was that?"

"Two years ago."

"He helping out?" José asked.

Walsh lost her wistfulness. "I don't need his money," she said sharply to José. "I used to think money was important. Don't want it. Not what Samuel needs . . . he needs a father. Boy growing up needs a man around. Money . . ." She curled her lip in contempt.

"Did you ever worry about him going back to jail?" Frank asked.

"All the time. 'Specially after I had Samuel. First time I said something, he laughed at me. Told me not to worry. I couldn't help but worry. Tobias and Skeeter . . . all the money. I knew they had to be dealin' bigger. I kept worryin'. We'd fight about my worryin'."

"He ever tell you why not to worry?" José asked.

Walsh nodded. "He said he and Skeeter had insurance. That nobody'd come down on them."

"He tell you why?"

Frank listened as José asked the question. He was holding his breath as Walsh took it in and thought about it.

"He said he saw a meeting Skeeter had."

José hesitated, then asked, "A meeting?"

"Unh-hunh."

"What'd he say about the meeting?"

"He said one day Skeeter told him he had a meeting. A big deal. He wanted Tobias to make sure he wasn't bein' set up."

"How'd Tobias do that?"

"He said he went out before . . . to watch the meetin' place. He watched to make sure it wasn't a setup . . . you know, a trap or something. Then he call Skeeter on his cell. Tell him it was clear."

"Where was the meeting place?" José asked.

"Golf course."

José did a slow take. "Golf . . . course?"

"That one down at Hains Point."

"Skeeter played golf?"

For the first time, she smiled. "No. The man Skeeter was to meet parked in the lot and waited. When Skeeter came, the man got in Skeeter's car."

José did the eye-exchange again with Frank. This time Frank gave him a nod. José sat back as Frank leaned forward ever so slightly.

"When was this, Alta Rae?" Frank said.

"The same time he and I . . . Tobias and I . . . same time we met."

"That'd be June 1992?"

"Yes."

"He say who it was, Skeeter met?"

Walsh shook her head.

Frank looked at José and gave it back over.

"Last question," José said.

"Yes?"

"Why'd you call us?"

Walsh eyed the two detectives.

"You thinkin' it's because I'm angry at him."

"You certainly got grounds," José said.

Walsh shook her head.

"Because a my boy." Her jaw tightened and lines hardened around her mouth. "I'm gonna shut the door on all that shit his daddy got into and didn't know how to get out of. That shit's gonna kill his daddy. It's not gonna kill Samuel."

She checked her watch. "I gotta be back."

"Where's that?" José asked.

She pointed to the tall, silvery airfoil-shaped building that was the home of *USA Today*.

"I'm the senior receptionist," she said proudly. "I got benefits and they're payin' for school."

"School?"

"American University," she said, the tilt of pride still in her voice. "Finish up in June. Gonna be a paralegal."

Frank and José watched her walk away.

"Good luck, lady," José breathed. "You don't have to see the whole staircase, just take the first step."

In high heels and carrying two-year-old Samuel, Alta Rae Walsh managed to stay on the treadmill until the man in the suit threw a massive switch and the treadmill picked up speed and Alta Rae stumbled once, then twice, and holding her son with one hand reached out for support and came up with empty air and the treadmill sped on. . . .

"No!"

Frank bolted upright.

The telephone was ringing and Monty was looking up from the pillow beside him and the clock was saying two-seventeen a.m.

TWENTY-SIX

"I came up here to smoke," the slender nut-brown man named Alem said.

"Up here" was the rooftop of McKinney's Auto Storage, a grim four-story garage of time-stained raw concrete on Half Street, just down from the DMV inspection station.

"You see, the manager will not let us smoke in the office." Alem said it almost apologetically. "So I came up here to smoke, and then I notice . . ." The man paused delicately, as though worried he might offend. "I notice," he repeated, "the odor."

A dust-covered Trans Am squatted in the headlights of a squad car. Off to the side, a Forensics van and a meat wagon from the M.E.'s Office. The slightest wisp of breeze carried a pungent rotten sweetness to Frank and he noticed that the techs and the uniformed officers were standing upwind from the car.

"I then call nine-one-one." Alem looked at Frank and José anxiously. "I hope I do the right thing."

José took a breath and exhaled loudly. "You did, Mr. Alem. How long's the car been here?"

"It will be on the ticket . . . under the windshield wiper. I smell *that*"—he pointed to the Trans Am—"I do not touch the car. I do not touch it anywhere." His anxious look returned. "I do right? Yes?"

"Yes," José said. "Nobody notice it before? Anybody say anything? About the smell?"

Alem shook his head. "Up here is long-term storage. There is no elevator, so . . ."

"Thank you, Mr. Alem," José said.

"Blessingame answered the nine-one-one," Frank explained to José as the two walked toward the Trans Am, "ran the tag through DMV."

Two forensic techs were going over a checklist on a clipboard placed on the hood of the Trans Am. The older of the two looked up as Frank and José approached.

"We've done the outside," the tech said. "Considerable latents. Picked up soil samples out of the fenders, off the tires. Tread casts made."

"You satisfied?" Frank asked, knowing what was next and not really wanting to know.

"I said we're done," the tech answered crossly.

"Okay," Frank told Blessingame, "open it up."

With screeching sideways motions, Blessingame worked the edge of the pry bar deep under the trunk lid. He paused to gather strength, then with a massive effort heaved downward on the pry bar.

With a metallic protest, the trunk popped open.

The death smell rolled across the rooftop—thick and putrid, violating the night air, instantaneously filling the lungs with dread.

A collective gasp from the techs and the cops. Mixed curses . . . "Jesus Christ" along with "motherfucker."

It was the smell of just beyond. Of that which waited around the corner. You came on it, you knew it. Even the first time, you knew it for what it was. The inevitable. The end.

The Trans Am's alarm warbled, then climbed into a satanic screeching.

"Mornin', Pencil," Frank heard José saying.

Crawfurd lay faceup, legs drawn up, knees to chest. His throat had been cut ear to ear. His tongue had been pulled through the opening, and it hung obscenely down his chest.

The digital clock in the autopsy suite said four forty-seven a.m. when Tony Upton snapped off his latex gloves and tossed them into the waste receptacle. Pencil Crawfurd lay on a stainless-steel table. The noisy overhead hood was working hard, but it failed to pull the odor away. Frank found himself wishing he hadn't given up cigarettes.

"Time of death?" Upton surveyed the corpse before him. "Preliminary estimate based on putrefaction, blowfly larvae, staphylinidae . . . I'd say about three days. Looks like somebody worked him over before. Be able to give you a better fix after the examination. You staying?"

Frank exchanged glances with José. He turned back to Upton. "No. Hoser and I are going to check out his place."

"I could send out for ribs after," Upton offered a damper of disappointment in his voice.

José shook his head disbelievingly. "Don't see how it is—"

"How it is I can be hungry?" Upton interrupted.

José laughed.

"How it is, Tony, you always ordering ribs. Never any pizza?"

The sky hinted dawn soon, with rain later. A breeze had blown advertising flyers, scraps of paper, and miscellaneous bits of street trash against the front door. A dim light came from a second-floor window.

José knocked, waited, then knocked again. Several blocks away, a truck ground through its gears. Down the darkened street, a dog barked once, twice, then fell silent.

Look around back?" José said.

Accompanied by sounds of scratchy scurrying and glimpses of retreating rats, Frank and José made their way down the litter-strewn alley behind the row of houses.

Crawfurd's back door opened onto a small porch on which stood two plastic garbage cans and a plastic carton emblazoned "DC Recycles!" Frank climbed the three steps. He stopped right before knocking and played his flashlight on the door.

"Hoser."

José joined him.

"Window."

Frank's flashlight beam focused on a missing pane in the door, the pane nearest the deadbolt. Stepping forward, he angled the light through the opening.

The broken pane lay inside on the floor. Duct tape held the glass shards together.

As the two detectives slipped on latex gloves, José said the necessary words. "Indications of felony breaking and entering."

Before José finished, Frank had turned the knob and swung the door open. He eased his pistol out of its shoulder holster. Without looking, he knew that José had switched his flashlight to his left hand and had his Glock in his right. Frank stepped through, into the kitchen.

Drawers had been dumped, cabinet shelves swept clean. Scattered across the floor were knives, forks, and spoons, pots, pans, and broken crockery.

The wreckage conveyed a savage intensity, not the mindless, universal destructive energy of a tornado, but the focused precision of a human hunter.

Avoiding as much of the debris as possible, Frank and José picked their way across the kitchen. Near the doorway into the hall, they switched off their flashlights and stood stone still.

Frank felt his pulse beating in his throat, then his stomach contracting.

At first he thought it might be something off his clothes, a leftover from the garage rooftop or Upton's autopsy suite. Then he knew it wasn't. Leaning close to José, he whispered, "Smell that?"

In the dimness he saw José nod. The two stood quietly another few seconds, then switched on their flashlights. Down the hallway toward the stairs, they passed the living room, with its furniture turned over, upholstery slit, stuffings spilling like the intestines of some gutted animal. At the end of the hallway, Frank ran his flashlight beam up the stairs.

Again the scratching sounds of small scurrying feet. The flashlight stopped on a hand frozen in the act of reaching out over the top of the stairway.

TWENTY-SEVEN

Frank watched as Randolph Emerson, nose wrinkled in distaste, looked around the upstairs room. Along one wall, a neatly kept workbench with speakers, wiring, and circuit boards. In contrast to the orderly workbench, an adjacent wall cabinet had been ripped apart: expensive sound and video components hung by their wire guts and lay strewn across the floor.

Past Emerson, through the open doorway, in the hall, the woman's body lay sprawled on the landing.

"Jesus . . . two in one night."

"Tony Upton says it was about the same time somebody did Pencil, two, maybe three days after he'd gotten back on the street," Frank said.

"All this . . . that . . . that *mess* downstairs . . ." Emerson began, "who . . ."

"Skeeter left a big business," Frank said. "Maybe somebody didn't want Pencil to inherit it."

"Or maybe somebody thought that Pencil had something they wanted," José added.

"Or both," Frank said.

"Okay," Emerson said impatiently. "So we got two rotting bodies and a tossed house. You got me out of bed and down here for that?"

"We got you out of bed," Frank said calmly, "so you could call Renfro Calkins and put him back to work."

"*What?*" Emerson looked as if someone had waved a snake in his face. "*What?*" he repeated.

"We need him," José said. "We need him now . . . here."

Emerson's anger was edging out his incredulity.

"Calkins was put on suspension because . . ."

"Because, Randolph," Frank finished quietly, "you were covering your ass."

Emerson's eyes narrowed. He worked his mouth but then stopped, as though something inside him had sounded a warning.

"We had a heart-to-heart with Milton," José explained.

Frank bore in. "You pressured him into making that admin closure on Gentry."

"You can't prove that."

Emerson said it coolly, but Frank detected a deep uncertainty beneath.

"If IAD squeezes Milton," Frank said, "he'll recite chapter and verse." He saw in Emerson's eyes that he knew it was so.

"Look, Randolph," Frank continued reasonably, "these two on top of Skeeter and Gentry are gonna cause all kinds of shit to roll downhill. You know how good Renfro is. We can't afford to keep him out of this."

Emerson shut his eyes as though to blank out what was around him. He opened them and everything was still there.

"And if you don't get him back," he said bitterly, "you two will make sure the shit ends up on me."

Frank and José said nothing; both gave Emerson a poker player's "Don't call my hand" look.

Emerson surrendered. His shoulders sagged and his mouth drew up in a grimace.

"You two are bastards, you know," he gritted, "real bastards."

José teased him with a smile. "Aw, but we're *your* bastards, Randolph."

Frank had his cell phone out. He punched in some numbers and waited until someone answered.

"R.C.?" he said. "Wake up. Captain Emerson wants to talk with you."

And he handed the phone to Emerson.

Two hours later, Renfro Calkins told Frank and José, "I'm releasing the body."

Nobody had said anything when Calkins walked in. But Frank had sensed a ripple of discipline that spread among the techs, notes on a piano striking now with more authority, with greater certainty.

José motioned up the stairs with his chin. Toward where the woman's body lay and where the room had been ripped apart.

"How long's it gonna take to get through this?"

Calkins gave José a disapproving look. "Long's it takes, Hoser. Long's it takes."

"Nice havin' you back, R.C.," José said.

Calkins shot José another shaft of disapproval, then turned and made for the stairs. At the same time, the front door swung open. Blessingame stuck his head through.

"Frank, Hoser, you got a visitor."

At the police line set up across the front walk, Brian Atkins chatted easily with one of the uniformed patrol officers. Atkins wore a raincoat against a mist that was off and on turning into real rain. He saw Frank and José, and half waved, half saluted.

"Crappy morning," he said, glancing skyward. "Robin called. Said you'd found Pencil and this . . ." he gestured toward the house.

Frank waved him in.

Atkins took in the destroyed living room.

"Guy did a job."

José pointed to the stairs. "If you want to see, M.E.'s gonna take the body away."

The three men climbed the stairs in single file, watching their footing, keeping to one side.

At the top of the stairs, the stench hovered over the corpse like an invisible predator guarding its kill. Frank had been in the house for hours now, but the odor still caused a trembling in the back of his throat.

"Shot twice," José said. "Once through the shoulder, in the room back there. She makes it out here. Shooter follows. Hits her in the back of the head before she gets to the stairs."

"Any idea about the weapon?" Atkins asked.

Frank shook his head. "Have to wait for the M.E. report."

"No cartridge cases?"

"Nothing yet."

Frank led the way into the room.

"Combination office and electronics hobby shop," Atkins observed, looking around, stepping carefully to avoid a patch of dried blood.

Frank nodded.

"Think whoever it was found what he was looking for?"

"No way of telling, but I've got a hunch he didn't."

"Why?"

"The mess downstairs," Frank said. "If he was looking for something, he started here."

Following Frank's logic, Atkins nodded. "So if he'd found it up here—"

"He wouldn't have tossed downstairs," José finished.

Calkins appeared in the doorway with one of his crew. When he saw Atkins, Frank, and José, he frowned.

"R.C.," José said, "this's Brian Atkins from the Bureau."

Calkins nodded curtly and scanned the room as if to assure himself it hadn't been disturbed.

"Good to know you're back," Atkins said.

"Thank you," Calkins replied perfunctorily. "You goin' to be up here long?" he asked Frank and José, obviously anxious to have them gone.

Frank suppressed a smile. "Just leaving."

At the foot of the stairs, Atkins paused. Up above, the indistinct sound of Calkins and his tech talking.

"Never knew a good forensics man who didn't think he owned the crime scene," Atkins said, looking back in the direction of the body.

"You'll never know a better one than R.C.," José said.

The front door was open, and Frank gratefully pulled in the fresh air. A spitting rain was falling outside. At the curb, a government black Mercury Grand Marquis waited, its windshield wipers flapping a metronome beat. Atkins looked past Frank and José, back into the house, then focused on the two men.

"I hear somebody put a Colombian necktie on Pencil."

"Yeah," Frank said, and he took another breath, as if it would flush away the image of what had been done to Pencil before he'd been stuffed in the trunk of his car.

"Filthy bastards," Atkins muttered. "Fits," he said.

"Fits?" Frank asked. "Fits what?"

"We finally broke the code at State."

Frank had trouble connecting. He glanced at José, who was also running slow this morning.

"State?"

Atkins looked at Frank, then at José. "Kevin Gentry," he said. Seeing he'd gotten the detectives' attention, he continued. "That State Department job of his was a cover."

"Cover?" Frank said, irritated at himself for not catching on and at Atkins for making it more difficult than it had to be.

Atkins nodded. "Kevin Gentry was CIA. State Department had him listed as a political officer, but actually he was the deputy chief of station in Bogotá."

. . .

A Colombian connection?" Kate asked.

Frank felt his bullshit detector twitch and didn't know why, but registered it anyway.

"Gentry's time in the agency . . . the way somebody did Pencil. Not much there."

After dinner at Tahoga, they'd walked down Thirtieth Street to the river and found a bench along the walk in front of Harbor Place. A 737, landing lights on, wheels and flaps down, passed overhead, then banked to starboard to line up its approach to Reagan National. At the same time, a cabin cruiser, steering between the red and green buoy lights, made its way up the Potomac.

"There's the time gap," Kate said uncertainly, as though the thought had suddenly appeared.

Frank shifted on the bench, bringing his shoulder and thigh into contact with her. Dragging itself through the long day's fatigue from door-to-door canvassing, the thought unreeled slowly, then more rapidly. *Yes, the time gap. If there was a connection, why did the person who did Gentry wait two years to do Skeeter and Pencil?*

Kate continued circling the riddle. "Maybe the Agency," she mused to herself as much as to him, "maybe Gentry was still Agency and they had him working the Hill undercover."

The cabin cruiser had now cleared Roosevelt Bridge, and the 737 had disappeared behind the finger of trees, marking its last turn into Reagan.

Frank added another "What if?" to the conjecture pile. "Or did he use his old Agency connections to go into business with Skeeter and Pencil?"

"You mean Gentry was their 'insurance'?"

"Skeeter met with somebody in June 'ninety-two. Gentry was working on the Hill at that time for the New York senator. He quit to move to Rhinelander's subcommittee in January 'ninety-eight."

"Which could have put him in a better position to be Skeeter's insurance," Kate finished.

Frank's mind replayed the garage rooftop, the Trans Am and the Ethiopian attendant, then Pencil's house and the dead woman at the top of the stairs. And that brought him to something he'd said to Emerson.

"What?" Kate's voice seemed to come from a long way off.

"What?" Frank echoed.

"What you just said," Kate persisted, "quote, Skeeter left a big business, unquote."

"Oh." It took him a moment to register. He shrugged, too tired to follow further. "Just something that came back to me from this morning." He felt himself drop into mental overload. He reached for Kate's hand.

They sat without talking. Music, soft and indistinct, carried across the water from the cabin cruiser. Finally Kate squeezed his hand. "You're down."

"Just tired."

"It's more than that."

He started to shake his head but then realized she was right. He probed, trying to sense the outlines of something lying hidden in the underbrush.

"It's a feeling. A feeling more than a thought."

"And the feeling's like . . . ?"

He probed some more. "It's like the dropping feeling in your gut," he added slowly, "like when you sense you're on a losing team."

"Losing? Why?"

"Emerson's face this morning . . . He sees all this as something he just wants to go away. He tried to sweep it under the carpet once. He'd try again, if he got the chance."

Kate thought about that, then shook her head. "But he can't," she said, "it's gotten too big."

Frank drew in the night air and exhaled in a sigh. "Yes, he can.

For precisely that reason . . . that it's gotten too big. He can pass it off to the Bureau."

"What makes you think that's probable?"

"Knowing Emerson for twenty-five years."

"In a perfect world," Kate challenged, "why'd it make any difference? If the Bureau could solve it, or the department?"

"In a perfect world it wouldn't make any difference. In the real world it does. It makes a real difference, who closes the case."

"Why?"

"If the Bureau takes this over, it sends a message to everybody on the street. It tells them DCMPD can't do its job. We're already catching a load of crap because of the cold cases. Now we throw our hands up because this's just too hard?"

He felt anger rising in his throat. "It's not up to the FBI or the CIA to keep the peace on the streets. That's our job."

"And you don't want your job taken away?"

"I don't want somebody saying I can't do it. Especially somebody like Emerson."

"And there's Atkins," Kate said simply.

He had the eerie feeling she'd read his mind.

"This morning"—Frank drifted, putting his thoughts together for the first time—"we were standing in the door at Pencil's. There Atkins was, wearing a raincoat that must have cost what I pay for a suit. Hell, *two* suits. He's got a driver waiting in a big black car to take him back to an office that's like the Taj Mahal. Beside him, Hoser and I come off looking like poor cousins . . . a pair of ragpickers."

Kate squeezed his hand again. "Envy . . . a deadly sin," she teased.

"No. I don't want anything he's got. He earned it . . . putting down Juan Brooks. He stuck his neck out on that one."

"You and José have done a lot of that. But nobody's given you two a Taj Mahal office."

"I may not be happy all the time, but I'm content . . . where I am, what I'm doing. I think Hoser is too. Anyway, neither one of us was cut out to work in a Taj Mahal. What does bug me, though, is a system that rewards the dodgers . . . the Emersons."

"I think he's good for you and José," Kate said, a provocative lilt in her voice.

"Night air's corroding your brain."

"No . . . think about it. You and José define your own rewards. One of those is getting the job done despite the Emersons. It's almost perverse. . . . Sometimes, I think, the worse he is, the better you two get. So maybe the system works?" Kate said it as though she were saying "Checkmate."

"It works because Hoser and I are dinosaurs," Frank came back. "We remember how it used to be. New talent comes in, they're isolated. They didn't know the old-timers . . . the Terry Quinns . . . the guys who were leaders, not managers. The dodger culture rewards risk aversion. The good ones get out—"

Kate finished the thought. "Like Janowitz?"

"Or sell out, like Milton." Frank watched as the cabin cruiser dropped anchor off Teddy Roosevelt Island and another 737 swung in from the north just over Key Bridge.

Kate reached across and put her hand on his forearm.

"You and Monty have room for a visitor tonight?"

TWENTY-EIGHT

The faintest of sounds . . . a slap, a slide, a thump.

Frank opened his eyes. The alarm said just before six a.m. He looked over to Kate. Monty was curled on the pillow above her head. Kate was still asleep, but the way the tiny muscles tightened around her eyes told him she was floating up toward waking.

"Paper," he whispered.

Kate breathed something in acknowledgment and her face relaxed as she drifted off again.

Frank shut his eyes. Somewhere down the street a dog barked; he wondered if it was Murph. He felt Monty get up and make his way toward the foot of the bed. He opened his eyes in time to see the big cat stretch, then jump to the floor, landing with a cushioned thump. Frank gave up the thought of going back to sleep and instead lazily gazed at the ceiling, listening to Monty at work at his water dish.

After a second or two, he sat up and swung his feet to the floor. He snagged a pair of running shorts out of the bureau, and went downstairs, Monty following.

The *Post* lay where it had skidded across the sidewalk and caromed off the front door. He picked up the paper, and stood, still half asleep, sorting out the sky.

Soft blue. Rain-washed blue. There was another word. A better word. What was it? Cerulean? Yes . . . cerulean. Cerulean blue. A good spring day in the making. With a cerulean-blue sky.

He shifted his gaze from the sky to the paper in his hand.

Papers come in plastic bags now. Even when it's not raining. Condoms for newspapers? Come to think of it, not a bad idea.

In the kitchen, first things first. Monty to be fed. Then the coffee. Frank ground it extrafine and, while the maker gurgled and wheezed, stood absorbed in thinking about absolutely nothing but the coffee filling the carafe.

He'd finally sat at the table with a full mug and taken the *Post* out of its plastic sheath when Kate, wearing one of his shirts, entered and came over to the table and tousled his hair.

He slipped his hand under the hem of the shirt.

Kate swatted his hand. "Let's not get started."

That made him want even more to play around under the shirt.

"Why not?"

"*Be*cause," Kate said, twisting away and walking to the cabinet for a mug, "I don't like burnt coffee."

With a sigh, he let his early-morning fantasy fade and opened the paper. Like a magnet, the headline drew his eye. His chest tightened.

"Holy . . . *shit!*"

Carafe in one hand, mug in the other, Kate turned.

Frank held the paper up, pointing to the headline.

"Subcommittee Chairman to Investigate District Drug Crimes."

He read the subhead aloud: " 'Rhinelander says recent deaths connect to Gentry murder.' "

Before he read any further, the phone on the wall, his pager, and his cell phone interrupted with a medley of electronic beeps, chirps, and whistles.

. . .

Mayor Seth Tompkins wore a pale-yellow shirt with antique gold cuff links, charcoal-gray trousers held up with burgundy-and-dark-blue suspenders, and his trademark bow tie, today a carefully knotted silk accent that matched the blue in the suspenders.

"Not only do we learn that Congressman Frederick Rhinelander is going to open hearings on crime and punishment in the District," Tompkins said in a deceptively quiet voice, "we find that the good editors of *The Washington Post*"—here his irritation cracked through the veneer of calm—"recommend that the congressman expand the hearings to investigate the overall performance of my administration."

Frank's first impression was of a spare, neat man, a man who shaved each morning, lathering with a brush, using his grandfather's straight razor, and splashing his face with bay rum after.

The morning's *Post* lay at Tompkins's place at the head of the long conference table. On his right, Chief Noah Day; on his left, Randolph Emerson. Frank and José sat on Emerson's side. Across from them was Tompkins's press guy, John Norden, a stocky red-haired man with rimless glasses. Beside Norden, a young woman, presumably one of Tompkins's aides, prepared to take notes on a yellow legal pad.

Tompkins lightly ironed out the *Post*, running the palms of both hands across it. The hands came back together, fingers interlocked over the Rhinelander article.

Composure recaptured, he asked, "So, what have we here?"

Chief Day hulked in his armchair, large head forward, looking disappointed and petulant, like a bullfrog whose fly had gotten away.

"What we have," Day rumbled, "is a pile a shit."

Tompkins shut his eyes briefly and moved his lips as if saying a prayer or counting to ten. He turned to Randolph Emerson.

"What we have," Emerson glided in smoothly, "is an investigation that started as an everyday street shooting and is escalating into a political witch-hunt."

Tompkins looked weary. "An . . . every . . . day . . . street shooting," he recited, wringing out all the meaning from Emerson's words. He thought about that for a moment, then cocked his head and regarded Emerson. "Tell me, Captain Emerson, where are the witches in this everyday street shooting?"

"I'm sorry?"

"What pitfalls do you see?

"Gentry," Emerson said. "Congress didn't care whether Skeeter Hodges or Pencil Crawfurd lived, died, or flew to the moon. But connect them with the killing of a . . . a . . ."

Emerson ground clumsily to a stop. Frank watched a touch of color rise in his cheeks.

"The killing of a white congressional staffer?" Tompkins supplied.

Emerson added, "Who'd been with the Agency in Colombia."

"And," Tompkins added, "whose killer wasn't caught even though we said he'd been."

Emerson winced slightly, but recovered with an ingratiating smile. "The District's a punching bag for Congress, Mayor," he said. "We don't get a vote. So we're a safe target for any politician who has an itch to scratch."

Frank could tell from Tompkins's stony expression that he wasn't buying into the victimization line that had always worked for Emerson with Malcolm Burridge, the former mayor.

"Tell me something new and different," Tompkins said dryly. "But while you're at it, tell me how the *Post* learns these things before I do."

"You know how the leaking game's played, Mayor," Emerson said, scrambling for firmer ground. "Anybody who's got a beef with the establishment, anybody who comes out on the losing side of an argument . . . all they have to do is make a phone call."

"A phone call," Tompkins said softly to himself. Then he regarded Emerson. "So now we have a Colombian connection because the *Post* says we do? Is that it?"

"It is a possibility," Emerson said.

"I read it in the *Post* and therefore it must be so," Tompkins mused. His eyes shifted down the table to Frank and José.

"And you, gentlemen? You're on the ground floor. What connections do you see?"

Frank looked at José. With a nod, José passed the lead to Frank.

"We see four dead people who are connected to each other. That's the basics."

Holding up both hands, Tompkins interrupted. "Four? There's Hodges, Crawfurd, Gentry . . . who's the fourth?"

"Chantara Wilkerson, the woman in Crawfurd's house, Your Honor."

Tompkins's shoulders dropped—yet another weight added to the burden on his back.

"Four dead people," he said in a hollow voice. "And you say there's a Colombian connection?"

José cleared his throat. "We say we don't know."

Tompkins turned a questioning glance toward Emerson.

"But it's a potential," Emerson persisted.

"Life's full of 'potentials,' Captain," Tompkins said. "We can't chase them all down."

"I'm only saying," Emerson came back, "all's you need is a hint of a Colombian connection and Rhinelander will be adding that to his campaign against home rule."

"I appreciate your political acuity, Captain," Tompkins said, with exquisite precision. "What you're telling me is that this case might be too big for you to handle." Tompkins fixed Emerson with a prosecutor's look. "Is that it?"

Frank had the feeling he was standing on the rim of a bottomless canyon.

"Is that it?" Tompkins repeated very softly.

Emerson jiggled on his tightrope. "I'm only saying, Your Honor, that our jurisdiction and assets are limited."

Tompkins affected sudden enlightenment. "Ah . . . I see, your forte is taking care of local crime."

Frank looked over to José and got a quarter-wink. If Emerson caught the irony, he didn't show it.

"That's right, Your Honor. We get into the international arena, it's a different ball game."

"And that's a game in which we should not play?"

Emerson made a show of thinking about it, then clasped his hands together on the conference table. "I'd like to talk to our liaison at the Bureau and explore passing the investigation to them."

Tompkins remained impassive. He turned to Noah Day.

"Chief Day, you have anything to say?"

A large, black Buddha, Day sat with his hands laced across his paunch. "Like I said, this's a pile a shit. I'm backing Captain Emerson."

Tompkins turned toward Frank and José. Frank knew what he'd have to say if Tompkins asked, and part of him wanted Tompkins to ask and another part didn't.

Tompkins studied the two detectives for a long moment, then turned back to Emerson.

"For now, Captain, let's keep this in house."

"Liaison can just talk to the Bureau . . ." Emerson began.

Tompkins shook his head. "Once you put something on the table, you have to address it. And I'm not ready for that." He looked sternly at Emerson. "Not yet, Captain."

He pushed his chair back and stood. "Thank you all, gentlemen. At least I know some of what I don't know." A wry smile wrinkled across his face. "Problem is, I don't know all that I don't know."

Well, what about that?" Frank asked, as soon as they were alone in the hallway outside Tompkins's office.

José checked over his shoulder. "Emerson's selling."

"Tompkins isn't buying."

"Isn't buying *yet*," José amended. "And Emerson hasn't finished selling."

Hi, guys," Leon Janowitz said. Cocked back in Frank's chair, he held up the *Post* front page. "You seen this?" he asked brightly.

"Little man, all spick-and-span," José chanted, "where were you when the shit hit the fan?"

Janowitz gave up Frank's chair.

"Which fan was this?" he asked.

"The one in the mayor's office," Frank said.

"Brutal?"

"Emerson tried to give the case away to the Bureau," José said. "Mayor held off."

"Sounds like a full-court press."

"Meaning?" Frank asked.

"Meaning that I just came from Al Salvani's office. He says Rhinelander wants to talk with you and José. Off the record."

"About?"

"Salvani wouldn't say. Maybe he didn't know."

"When?"

"He'll call."

"I guess we hold our breath," José said.

"But wait!" Janowitz said, imitating a TV pitchman. "There's more!" He unzipped his canvas briefcase and held up a slender folder. "Army records center finally came through. Copies of Kevin Gentry's Two-oh-one file, evaluation reports, discharge physical."

TWENTY-NINE

Gentry's military files in his lap, Frank rested his head back against the passenger seat. The trail to CIA and Colombia was there—UCLA political science, Army commission into Military Police, Ranger school, and service in the Army Attaché Office, Bogotá. Outstanding efficiency reports, top-notch physicals.

A man on paper . . . a paper man . . . two-dimensional . . . black-and-white.

He put Gentry out of his mind and, half drowsing, took in the trees and the river. He liked the GW Parkway. An endangered species in an age of interstate takeovers. Built in the 1930s, it had become a commuter freeway, but it still kept its original character as an extended park along the Potomac, from Great Falls in the north to Mount Vernon in the south.

"What you thinking about?" José asked.

It took him a moment to realize José was talking to him.

"Why you think I'm thinking?"

José took his eyes off the road long enough to shoot Frank a look that said, "Come *on.*"

Frank sorted through the jumbled thoughts and images.

"We got us a first-class fur ball, Hoser. One day, everybody's got the same picture down cold. Then somebody pops Skeeter. All of a sudden, it's like somebody took the picture apart like a jigsaw puzzle and tossed all the pieces up in the air. We don't know who did Gentry . . . or why. We don't know how Gentry fits. Hell, we don't really *know* Gentry. And we don't know why Pencil's dead along with his woman."

"And," José added, "we don't know about the cartels."

Frank motioned toward the roadside sign indicating Chain Bridge Road.

"And to finish out our day, Congressman Richie Rich demands our presence."

José slowed and stopped at the top of the ramp, then turned east on Chain Bridge Road.

Less than a mile down the road, Frank pointed to a "Private Road" marker beside a drive that disappeared into a thick stand of trees.

"I think that's it."

The winding drive led through the trees to a low hilltop and a massive gate between two stone columns. A chain-link fence Frank estimated to be at least nine feet high ran from the columns into the dense woods on either side.

"Welcome to Fort Knox," José grunted. He stopped the car, lowered his window, and reached out to punch a button on a pedestal-mounted squawk box.

A short static burst, and a disembodied voice followed, asking for name and identification. José held his badge case out to the camera lens set in beside the loudspeaker. A moment's pause and the gate slid silently open.

For fifty or so yards through more trees, the drive dipped, then rose again. The trees dropped away with a final turn.

"Jesus, Mary, and Joseph," Frank breathed.

The house crested the highest ground of Arlington Ridge, the basalt granite promontory channeling the Potomac into the rapids below. Three stories of pristine white wide-plank siding, a mantle of greened copper roof with ornamental cupolas and weathervanes. A rolling lawn impeccably trimmed, magnolias towering over the two-story columned portico, a raked gravel drive. The scene echoed with the sounds of horse's hoofs and carriage wheels.

José laughed. "Reckon Miz Scarlett's home, Massa Rhett?"

A large-boned blonde woman in a severe black dress answered the door. She wore no makeup, and her hair was pulled back to a tight bun. She took Frank's and José's cards, muttered a "Please wait" that sounded like a command, and closed and locked the door.

José made an exhaling sound over his lips. "Wouldn't want to mess with that," he whispered.

Frank nodded. "Woman looks like she might have a collection of tattooed lampshades at home."

A moment later came the sound of a bolt being drawn back, and the door opened.

"Good afternoon, gentlemen, I'm Cornell, the house manager."

Cornell spoke with an English accent and carried himself with the muscular poise of a gymnast. His dark brown hair had been meticulously bleached at the tips, and he wore gray slacks and a dark blue Lacoste knit shirt. On first glance, Frank judged him to be in his late twenties or early thirties, but another look revealed lines etched around the eyes and mouth; lines that came with an understanding of the capriciousness of life.

"We're here to see—" Frank began.

"Yes," Cornell said with a professionally pleasant modulated voice, "this way." He turned and led them inside.

Large black and white square tiles paved a foyer Frank imagined he could fit his row house in and still have room for a basketball court. The curving ebony arms of a dual marble staircase swept down from a mezzanine encrusted with crystal chandeliers.

Frank realized that he and José had stopped to gawk, when Cornell turned around.

"It *is*, isn't it?"

"It certainly is," Frank said, recovering.

"Mrs. Rhinelander found it in Alabama," Cornell said in a passive tone.

Puzzled, Frank asked, "The staircase?"

"No." Cornell smiled with the mischievous delight of an amateur magician enjoying his audience's mystification. "The house. She had it disassembled and brought here."

Cornell led them toward a door between the two staircases.

Frank felt a whispering gust of air in his face as Cornell swung the heavy door open. Muted lighting and dove-gray walls blurred the dimensions of the gallery, drawing the eye to paintings that seemed to float magically in a mist.

A critic might have called the collection eclectic. Frank found it jarring. A Madonna and Child icon gave way to an oil of two wrestlers, their side-lit bodies twisted and straining against a dark background.

"George Bellows." Cornell gazed thoughtfully at the wrestlers. "Magnificent muscular definition, don't you think?" he asked, without expecting an answer.

Halfway down the gallery, a low bench along the left wall faced a still life hung on the wall opposite. The painting looked familiar. Frank stopped to examine it more closely.

Cornell put on a tiny condescending smile, almost a smirk.

"It looks like a Cézanne," Frank ventured.

"It *is* a Cézanne. *Still Life with Apples and Peaches*, circa 1905."

"Unh-hunh," Frank said, now more certain. "I've seen it before." He turned to Cornell. "The National Gallery?"

Cornell grudgingly awarded Frank a passing grade. "Mrs. Rhinelander lent it to them. We've just gotten it back."

As they continued down the gallery, Frank thought he recognized a Chagall and something that looked authentically old Dutch—

certainly not a Vermeer?—but by now he wouldn't have been surprised to see *Guernica* or the Mona Lisa.

They reached the end of the gallery, and Frank looked back, taking it all in.

"Very nice."

"The same contractor who built the Pompidou Center," Cornell said with a burble of proprietary pride in his voice. "Separate climate control keeps the humidity and temperature constant. The light is concentrated in three spectral bands. Brings out the color and depth but doesn't damage the paintings."

Without knocking, he opened the door into the library.

Directly ahead, a waist-to-ceiling window stretched across the room, framing sky, forest, and the boiling, churning falls of the river below. Floor-to-ceiling bookcases lined the walls on right and left. An oak Victorian partner's desk at least seven feet wide sat angled so its occupant could see the river as well as a semicircle of leather-upholstered chairs.

Cornell gestured to the chairs.

"Please sit. I shall fetch him."

José watched the door close. He leaned close to Frank " '*Fetch him?*' " he repeated in a mock English accent.

Several minutes passed. Finding himself drifting off, Frank got up, stretched, and walked over to the bookcases behind the desk. One shelf contained a matched set of large, folio-size volumes, gold-edged pages bound in burgundy leather. Using his restaurant French to translate the titles, Frank guessed them to be something about—or by—Voltaire. Elsewhere on the shelves, Melville's *Billy Budd* led to Thackeray's *Vanity Fair*, Dostoevsky's *The Idiot*, Fielding's *Tom Jones*, Balzac's *Old Goriot*, Darwin's *Voyage of the Beagle*—all, to judge from the bindings, first editions in what John McDonnell at Olsson's would describe as "fine/fine" condition.

"You're a reader, Lieutenant Kearney?"

Frederick Rhinelander stood at the desk. Behind him, a section of the bookcase was closing with a pneumatic sigh. Rhinelander glanced back at the meticulously crafted door, then at his visitors. He wore a bright, childlike smile.

"I *love* that thing," he said, and pointed to the now closed door. "It always creates *such* a stir. Please . . . sit," he told Frank, indicating the empty chair next to José.

"Gentlemen, thank you for coming out here. I hope I didn't inconvenience you." He looked at Frank, then José. It was José who first understood Rhinelander wanted an answer.

"No inconvenience," José said.

"I had some issues here that required tending to," Rhinelander responded. "You are familiar with congressional hearings procedures?

Frank and José shook their heads.

Rhinelander sat back in his chair and matched his fingertips together, hands forming a tent. "Hearings are a way that Congress gets testimony on a formal record. . . . *Sworn* testimony," he added with a prim, schoolmarmish severity. "And then Congress decides, based on that record, what laws must be passed, changed, or done away with."

"And we're going to have to testify?" José asked.

Rhinelander pursed his lips. "Not necessarily. I asked you here today to get some ideas as to what lines of questioning would be most beneficial."

"Who to?"

"Why, to the people of the District, of course," Rhinelander said loftily.

"Oh. Okay. How can we help?"

Rhinelander casually dropped his right hand beneath the desk, then brought it up.

Somewhere in the library, Frank imagined, discreetly placed microphones and videocameras had been alerted.

"Let's start with Kevin Gentry's killing. The papers are reporting a Colombian connection. What do you know about that?"

"That there isn't much there, Mr. Chairman," Frank said.

"What *is* there?"

"First, there's the business dealings."

"Which are?"

"Skeeter's and Pencil's dealings. You don't do big-time drugs in the District without connections. Either Jamaican or Colombian. Pencil's former girlfriend says he and Skeeter traveled repeatedly to South America. Then there was the weapon used to kill Skeeter and wound Pencil—"

"Yes, yes," Rhinelander said with a sour note. "The gun that also killed Kevin and"—Rhinelander pointed an accusing finger—"and reopened a case that your department had marked closed."

José ignored Rhinelander's charge. "So we have a connection between Skeeter, Pencil, and Kevin Gentry. Then you add the fact that Kevin Gentry had worked for CIA in Colombia and that somebody killed Pencil by cutting his throat and pulling his tongue out through the opening—what they call a Colombian necktie."

Rhinelander shuddered and ran his tongue across his lips. "Grotesque." Recovering, he turned his hands palms up. "But is that all we have?"

"So far."

"Brian Atkins might have something," Frank said. "Have you talked with him?"

The corners of Rhinelander's mouth curved up ever so slightly. He regarded Frank for a moment, then returned to José.

"Let me ask you this."

"Yes, sir?"

"Because you have no evidence doesn't mean there is no evidence. Might it be *possible* that there is more substantial evidence of a Colombian connection?

José nodded. "Yessir, it's possible."

"And *if* there is more substantial evidence," Rhinelander pressed on, "is your department best qualified to conduct the investigation?"

Frank watched his partner size up Rhinelander; he could feel José working out what he'd answer.

"A lot of ifs, Mr. Chairman." José began carefully, deliberately, a mason laying a foundation. "We're responsible for investigating homicides in the District of Columbia. If the perp . . . the perpetrator . . . is from another country and he's in the District, we'll apprehend him. If he's somewhere else, we'll get that jurisdiction to apprehend him. We may not be Interpol or the Bureau, but we know how to track down killers and take them off the street."

Rhinelander's tightened lips said he wasn't happy with José's answer. Rather than challenge José, however, he asked, "Do you have any suspects?"

"Not yet."

"No suspects." Rhinelander said it in a pious monotone, putting a mark against a mental checklist. "Any prospects?" he followed up.

"Sir, if we had 'prospects,' we'd have suspects," José said. "Way we work, we gather information. We put the pieces together. We're still gathering."

"Informants?"

Rhinelander's tone was maddeningly condescending, arrogantly dismissive.

Frank saw the muscle along José's jawline quiver. He stepped in. "People are talking to us."

Rhinelander toyed with a gold fountain pen, taking its cap off, making several exploratory dashes on a lined pad, putting the cap back on, settling the pen on the desktop. He looked at Frank, then at José.

"You realize, of course, that this is a high-visibility case?"

"We noticed," José said.

"And you realize," Rhinelander went on, "that my subcommittee funds the District government."

"Yes, we—"

"And you realize"—Rhinelander cut José off—"that along with funding we are responsible for oversight." He paused a beat. "Oversight," he continued in his prim, schoolmarmish voice, "means that we want to make certain those funds are properly spent." Another beat. "Do you appreciate that?"

José took a breath, then swallowed. "Yes, sir," he said, "we appreciate that. We really do."

Rhinelander weighed that for a moment before accepting it. Then he picked up the gold fountain pen and twirled it between his fingertips like a baton.

"Thank you for your time, gentlemen. It's helpful to have an appreciation of the state of play before we open the hearings. Cornell will show you out."

As though summoned telepathically, Cornell materialized in the doorway. Leaving the library, Frank looked back: Rhinelander was gone, and the bookcase door was just sliding shut.

José tossed the keys to Frank. Neither of them spoke until they were well down the parkway toward Washington.

"Feels like we been on a short trip to hell," José said dispiritedly.

"Some people are rich, Hoser, and other people just have money."

José smiled. "Not bad. Who said that?"

"Maggie Kearney's little boy Frank."

"That sounds like my daddy."

"Hoser, that sounds like a compliment."

THIRTY

Frank stood for an indecisive moment in the breakfast room, a CD of Handel's *Water Music* in one hand, *Johnny Cash, 1955–1983* in the other, and Monty wrapping around his left leg.

"Okay, what is it," he asked the cat, "Freddy or Johnny?"

Monty growled an answer, so Frank loaded up the Man in Black. Cash started out with "Hey Porter." Having made one decision, Frank wrestled with another. Freezer to microwave? Whip up an omelet? Call out for pizza?

The omelet won. From the refrigerator, Frank rescued four brown speckled eggs, two jalapeño peppers, several shallots, the butt of a Smithfield ham, and a wedge of extrasharp cheddar. He went back into the refrigerator for a half-bottle of a California Pinot Grigio.

Cash was driving his gravel-rich baritone hard with "Folsom Prison Blues," accompanied by waves of inmates' raucous cheering.

Frank notched up the volume. While the peppers and shallots sautéed, he grated some cheese, then cracked the eggs into a yellow-glazed mixing bowl. ". . . let that lonesome whistle," he sang with Cash in a monotone as he beat the eggs, "blow my blues away."

Monty eyed Frank as he slid the cooked omelet out of the pan onto a plate.

"Grandpa Tom didn't make this, you know," Frank warned the cat.

Monty's gaze stayed fixed on the plate. Frank shrugged, sliced out a portion, and minced it into Monty's bowl.

Ten minutes later, Frank had finished the omelet. Monty was sleeping by his bowl. Johnny Cash wasn't liking it, but was guessing things happened that way. A swallow of Pinot Grigio gave off a hint of pears and seductively called for a refill.

The phone rang as Frank drank the rest of the wine in his glass.

Caller ID said it was a District number, caller name unknown. Monty had rolled over onto his back, all fours up, mouth slightly open, making sleep attractive as only cats know how.

The phone rang again.

Bad Frank: *Ignore it, go for the second glass.*

Good Frank: *You're a cop, you're a cop, you're a . . .*

"Shit," he muttered, and picked up the phone.

"I'm calling for Detective Frank Kearney."

Bad Frank sneered as Frank cursed Good Frank.

"You got him."

"Can we meet?"

Confident . . . no kid. Bass baritone. Maybe black, maybe not, but American English.

"Sure. My office is at—"

"It's not good . . . coming to your office. Tonight somewhere? You call it."

"This's about?"

A heavy silence, then, "Kevin . . . about Kevin." Steely with a subtext of anger.

I want to tell you about the Kevin I know. I want to tell you because I want the ratbastard who killed him to roast forever in the hottest corner of hell.

"How do I recognize you?" Frank asked.

. . .

Nineteen imposing feet of solid Georgia marble, Abraham Lincoln watched over the republic he'd saved. Every time Frank stood in the Memorial it struck him that someday Lincoln was going to speak, and it would be a voice of sadness, pride, and hope.

The memorial was empty but for a Park Service guide in her Smokey Bear hat and two Oriental couples standing in front of the Gettysburg Address chiseled in the south wall, on Lincoln's right.

Frank checked his watch. He was several minutes early.

He walked over to the north wall. His eye traveled the familiar words of Lincoln's Second Inaugural Address. The first time he'd been here, it had been with his father. Tom Kearney had read the words to him. He had told him how thousands of people had stood in the mud beneath a gray and threatening sky in March 1865 to hear Lincoln. How it was that when Lincoln stood to speak, the sun broke through the leaden clouds to shine on the nation's savior. And how it was that Lincoln then stood in the shadow of death, at the hands of John Wilkes Booth little more than a month later.

" 'Let us strive on to finish the work we are in . . . to do all which may achieve and cherish a just and lasting peace.' "

The voice came from behind him and slightly to the right—the confident bass baritone.

Frank turned. The man stood like a pro running back, hands hanging loose but ready at his sides, body coiled slightly forward. Milk-chocolate skin, a thick black well-trimmed mustache. Scars above the eyes, and a larger, crescent-shaped ding on the point of his right cheekbone. The man held out a big square hand.

"I'm Bradford Sims."

"I'm—"

"Franklin Delano Kearney." Sims opened a credentials case. A holographic eagle seal floated across the photograph and a statement that Bradford Sims was an officer of the Central Intelligence Agency.

"Signed by Tenet himself," Frank said. "I didn't know you guys carried credentials."

"Most of the time we don't." Sims replaced the case inside his jacket.

"What do you do at the agency?"

"You know the D.O.?"

"Directorate of Operations," Frank translated. "The clandestine service."

"Unh-hunh."

"Nice night out." Frank motioned toward the Washington Monument and, farther, the Capitol's white dome.

Outside, the two men walked around to the back of the Memorial. Old-fashioned streetlamps along Memorial Bridge led across the Potomac to Arlington National Cemetery. There, just below the Custis-Lee Mansion, occasional glimpses of the flame at John Kennedy's grave site.

"You're running the investigation into Kevin Gentry's death."

"Yeah."

"We hear there're questions about Kevin and a Colombian connection."

"*We?*"

Sims gave Frank a level look.

"I came to tell you," Sims said, "the Agency's not involved."

Frank spotted a pair of runners coming across the bridge from Virginia. Two guys. Lean. Seven-minute pace. They'd probably angle off the bridge to his left, take the path down past the FDR Memorial. Then they'd have a choice: back into Virginia over the Fourteenth Street bridge or turn left by the Tidal Basin, pass the Jefferson Memorial. It would feel good, in the cool of the evening, hitting a stride where you felt you could run forever, your mind taken up with the running. He saw Sims watching the runners too, and he waited a moment.

Finally he asked, "Why do you think you have to tell me that? . . . That the Agency's not involved?"

"Talk's going that way," Sims replied, eyes still on the runners.

"All by itself?"

Sims gave him an appraising look. Frank wondered where Sims had gotten the scar on his cheek.

"All by itself?" Frank repeated.

"It's getting help."

"From who?"

"Our cousins on Pennsylvania Avenue."

"Why'd they do that?"

"Why does any bureaucracy do anything? Feather its own nest, get the fingers pointed somewhere else."

The runners had taken the path south. They were well out of sight now, probably passing the FDR Memorial.

"You knew Gentry well, didn't you?"

Sims's face lengthened. "I was his boss in Bogotá station."

"What'd he do?"

"My deputy. His real talent was as a case officer. One of the best I've seen."

"Case officers do . . . what?"

"Recruit agents . . . spies."

"Like recruiting informants?"

"Like . . . but not exactly like."

"What's the difference?"

"A case officer's got to be selective. His first question is, What do I need to know? Next question is, Who can get access to what I need to know? Third question's the toughest: How do I get this person to work with me?"

"Money helps," Frank said.

Sims didn't shake his head, but turned it slightly. "Sometimes. But not all the time." He directed an inquisitive glance toward Frank. "You've got informants," he said.

"Yes."

"You put them on the payroll?"

"No payroll. I can't afford it, and the city makes it hard to use their money."

"You'd rather have somebody motivated by something other than money?"

"Sure."

"Same with a good case officer. What's ideal is somebody with a dream or a beef, or maybe both. They work out better than a mercenary. They may not be as smart. They may not have as good an access. But you can rely on them."

"And Kevin Gentry could find those people?"

Sims smiled, and it seemed to Frank that the smile had behind it memories of other times and other places. "He was one of the best. Kevin had a nose for recruiting the true believers."

"Why'd he leave the Agency?"

"I didn't want him to. We talked . . . hell, we argued . . . about it for several weeks. He didn't feel that the Agency was doing enough in the drug war."

"Meaning?"

"Look," Sims said slowly, perhaps picking his way through a minefield of secrets, "the druggies were a new target for the Agency. If it had been up to us, we never would have gotten involved."

"Why?"

"The old-line Agency guys, the Ivy League Wasps, cut their teeth in the OSS in World War Two. They saw drugs as a law enforcement problem."

"Beneath their dignity."

Sims smiled ruefully. "That, and they were afraid of it, too."

"Why?"

"The money. Enough goddamn money to buy a country or two. The cartel bosses almost bought Colombia. You could lose your soul in the drug trade. You can't find out about the cartels by going to embassy receptions. Young Sammy Straightlace from Harvard or Yale would have to get chummy with the producers, the distributors, the street men. It was safer dealing with the commies and their nuclear weapons than it was dealing with the Colombians. The commies had rules. Tough rules, but they were rules. It was . . . *cleaner* . . . more fastidious."

"More honorable than law enforcement," Frank said with a touch of sarcasm.

Sims gave him a long, regarding look. "I didn't say that. My father was a cop here in the District. A good one."

"Retired?"

"Dead," Sims said, the hurt shadowing his voice. "Fought his way through Korea, then got killed here in the King riots . . . 'sixty-eight." He motioned toward Arlington National and the Kennedy flame. "Buried over there."

Letting out a deep breath that was almost a sigh, Sims picked up the Colombia thread again.

"When I first got to Bogotá, we were targeting the KGB in Latin America, the Cuban connections, the contras in Nicaragua. Then, when the Soviet Union crashed, the Ivy League mafia at headquarters sat back on their butts."

"Until the cartels caught somebody's eye."

Sims nodded. "The White House woke up one fine morning and found that the drug lords like Pablo Escobar had decided they wanted their own country and part of ours. Somebody had to do something to keep Colombia from becoming Cocaine Central. And so the president dragged the Agency into spying on the drug business." He laughed cynically. "There were heel marks all the way from Langley to Sixteen hundred Pennsylvania Avenue."

"And Kevin Gentry?"

"Like I said, he was one of the best. Same talents he used against the Soviets and Fidel he turned against Escobar and his pals. He built up a stable of solid-gold sources high inside the Medellín and Cali cartels."

"You guys finally got Escobar, didn't you?"

Sims didn't say anything, but a smile twitched at the corners of his mouth.

"So, after he left the Agency, you kept in touch with Gentry?"

"He was a friend."

"Officially?"

"The Agency can't do that kind of thing in the States."

"You're not supposed to," Frank said. "When'd you see him last?"

"Week before he was killed. We had dinner at a Tex-Mex place on the Hill."

"He doing anything that could get him killed?"

"Easy to do these days, give somebody a reason to kill you," Sims said. "Drive too slow, wear shoes somebody wants, be white, be black."

"That's not what I meant."

Sims looked at Frank as though trying to get behind his eyes.

"I know," Sims said wearily. "I know."

Silence stretched out until he took a deep breath. "Kevin had re-cruited somebody. A source."

"For?" Frank asked, feeling the adrenaline kick in and his pulse pound in his throat.

"He didn't say, exactly. I got the idea he was stoking up for some kind of investigation."

"Source have a name?"

"Sure. But Kevin didn't tell me, and I didn't ask." Sims paused. "Look, it was a couple of buddies eating tacos and drinking Coronas. Most of the conversation was guy stuff . . . football, women, jobs. The part about his source took up less than a minute. It wasn't anything you'd talk about in a bar."

"Male?" Frank persisted. "Female?"

Sims shook his head. "No idea . . . none."

"When do you think he recruited this source?"

Frank waited. Sims stared toward the river and the bridge with its lane of lights. Frank waited some more. Finally Sims looked at him.

"Summer 'ninety-eight." He nodded, as if confirming that some-thing inside had whispered the answer. "June, sometime."

Kevin Gentry was standing out in sharper relief now, but Frank still had the sense of being surrounded by something he could not see.

"Do you think," he began carefully, "there's any chance Gentry got involved in something he shouldn't?"

"Meaning?" Sims asked.

"Like you said, the money could buy a person's soul."

"No!" Sims cut off each word: "Absolutely . . . fucking . . . no!" Then, more softly, "There's only a few people I've trusted with my life. Kevin was one."

"I had to ask. Women friends?"

"Nobody serious. He was a refuge from a hatchet-fight divorce. Had a saying that second marriages—"

"Were a triumph of faith over experience," Frank finished.

Sims gave him a sidelong grin. "You've been there too."

"Anybody he was working with before he was killed?"

Sims thought, started to shake his head, then held it. "Woman, first name Elena. She ran one of those associations up on Dupont Circle." Sims worked on it more. "Institute for . . . ah, yes! Institute for a Free Drug America."

"You mean 'drug-free'?"

Sims grinned. "Nope. Free drugs. As I recall, they want to give the stuff away."

"Elena?"

"Yeah. Like I say, I don't think I ever had the last name."

Frank looked at his watch. "It's been a day."

The two men headed toward the front of the memorial. The floodlights had been turned off. The Park Service guide sat on one of the steps, filling in a report on a clipboard she held on her knees. Side by side, the two men went down the steps.

"By the way," Frank said, "he ever say anything about his boss?"

"Not really. I got the impression the boss was a guy who bought his way through life with other people's money. Kevin said once that Rhine . . . Rhine . . . ?"

"Rhinelander."

"Oh, yeah." Sims laughed. It was a good laugh, one that reminded you of Friday afternoons at a bar with a buddy, and a beer in front of you that was probably one too many but wouldn't matter until tomorrow morning.

"That Rhinelander's idea of heaven," Sims said, "was to be the best-dressed at a Hamptons wedding."

THIRTY-ONE

José pulled over to the curb in the 2200 block of P Street. He pointed to a dingy gray stone building across the street.

"Twenty-two-oh-oh."

A used-book shop took up the first two floors. Signs in the third- and fourth-floor windows advertised an orthodontist, a law office, and a holistic massage therapist. A sandwich sign on the sidewalk outside the bookshop promised Madame Jana's palm readings upstairs, no appointments needed.

"Nothing about free drugs," Frank said.

José switched off the engine and flicked open his seat belt. "Shit, Frank, they put up a sign for free drugs, we'd need an armored car and a Marine battalion to get us through the mob."

On a door at the rear of the third-floor hallway, a plastic frame held a yellowed three-by-five-inch card: "Institute for a Free Drug America—Please Knock."

Frank knocked. The paint-scrabbled door was surprisingly more substantial than he thought it would be. No sound from inside. Crystalline strains of a New Age score drifted from the direction of the

holistic massage therapist's suite. Idly, he let his eyes explore the
hallway. He almost missed the lens set into a shadowed recess in the
ornate crown molding behind him. He traced the molding. Several
feet away, another lens. This one he figured provided a long shot
down the hallway. He flipped open his credentials case, and held it
up and smiled for the hidden cameras.

A buzzing rattle shook the door. Frank turned the knob and
pushed.

In and to his right, a balding man with a frizzy fringe of iron-gray
hair sat at a desk. Frank guessed late sixties, early seventies. Olive
complexion, black eyes, sharp nose, the look of a fierce but weath-
ered hawk. He wore a black suit that might have arrived at Ellis Island a hundred years ago.

"Yass?"

"I'm Detective Frank Kearney." Frank offered his credentials and
motioned to José. "My partner, José Phelps."

The old man took in the credentials, then searched their faces. He
had the suspicious eyes of an émigré.

"And you want?"

"We would like to talk with Ms. Elena Navarro," Frank said.

The old man sat impassively for a moment, still measuring the two
in front of him. Then he pointed to two armless wooden chairs against
a wall.

"Sit," he ordered. Then, almost an afterthought, "Please."

The old man got up and opened a door behind him. Hand on the
knob, he angled his head around and gave Frank and José a severe
glance, as though to make certain they'd obeyed. He stepped through
and pulled the door shut with a solid click.

Earlier that morning, Eleanor had handed Frank and José a thin
folder.

"Elena Navarro," she'd said, "president of the Institute for a Free
Drug America. It's a 501(c)(4) outfit."

"A charity?" Frank asked.

"Charity's a 501(c)(3)," Eleanor corrected. "The IRS describes a (c)(4) organization as one that is operated to promote the common good and general welfare of the people of the community." Eleanor recited it as if reading straight from the tax code.

"Promote the common good by giving away heroin?" José had asked.

That had given Eleanor an opportunity to get in her second correction. "'Decriminalization' is the PC term," she'd said primly.

The door opened. The old man thrust his head in, looking even more hawklike.

"Come," he gestured with an impatient wave.

He led Frank and José down a passageway toward a closed door. On the right, a row of wire-meshed windows looked across an alley to a soot-crusted brick wall punctuated by a similar row of windows. On the left, a large bay of cubicles with what appeared to be a platoon of truant high school kids rapping on computer keyboards. A poster for Mel Gibson's *Braveheart* dominated a cubicle occupied by a white kid in dreadlocks. Someone had highlighted the banner—"Every man dies, not every man really lives." Next to Gibson, another poster, red background, with a bereted Che Guevara in black. Frank guessed that Che had been dead years before the kid at the computer was born.

"*'Hasta la victoria siempre,'*" Frank muttered, reciting the call to arms beneath Che's image.

"Ever onward to victory." The old man rasped out his dry translation without breaking stride. He knocked at the closed door, then opened it. He stood aside and with a curt gesture motioned Frank and José in.

Seated at her desk, Elena Navarro glanced up at Frank and José over a teetering parapet of books, newspapers, and magazines. To her right, one of those giraffelike engineer drawing lamps; to her left, a telephone with a massive speed-dial keyboard that looked capable of coordinating a small war or directing a shuttle launch.

She stood, and Frank saw that she was taller than he'd thought. She wore a white silk blouse and black slacks. Her black hair was pulled behind her neck, emphasizing her high cheekbones and delicate nose.

Same dark eyes and complexion as the old man, Frank thought. *Five-foot-eight, maybe five-nine . . . one-fifteen, at the most one-twenty . . . late thirties.*

Navarro smiled at the old man. *"Gracias, Bidari."* Her voice was a resonant contralto.

The old man stood in the doorway. He glared at Frank and José menacingly. When he pulled the door, his suit coat fell open. Frank thought he caught a glimpse of webbing at the left armpit.

Navarro smiled as the door finally shut. "Bidari was my father's best friend," she said, as if this explained something more. She pointed to a sofa, then sat down and crossed her legs.

"You are here about Kevin Gentry."

She spoke with such assurance and in such a precise classroom-honed English that Frank felt a rebellious impulse.

No, ma'am, we're here to sell you tickets to the policemen's ball.

Instead he asked, "How did you meet?"

"We met just after he became Congressman Rhinelander's staff director."

"That would have been . . . what? Early 'ninety-eight?"

"January. Just after the Christmas recess."

"And the purpose?"

"The Rhinelander subcommittee drafts and proposes narcotics legislation." Navarro laid it out slowly, patiently. She paused, then added, "Our institute is a proponent of changes in current narcotics legislation."

"Yeah," José said, in his let's-rumble voice, "you want to give the stuff away."

Navarro's eyes widened, and she cocked her head as if readjusting her initial measurement of the two men before her. She smiled, and Frank saw that she could be an attractive woman.

"No." The tone softened. "We are market-oriented. We advocate that narcotics be sold legally"—here the smile came on, slightly mocking—"much like alcohol, tobacco, and coffee."

"So I just drop into the Starbucks or 7-Eleven and pick up an ounce of blow?" José asked.

"Yes." Like the first, provocative flick of the matador's cape. Navarro sat back in her chair, relaxed, confident, knowing what would come next.

Frank waited for José to do what he knew José would do.

José thrust his head forward. "We got too many addicts now."

"Yes," she agreed, adroitly letting him slip by. "And if we legalize narcotics we shall probably have more."

Realizing Navarro was using his momentum against him, José pulled up short. "Right," he said, "so . . ."

Navarro made a small, polite "Wait" gesture with her right hand. "Please. Let me finish. We would see an increase in addiction. But we would destroy the narcotics business." A beat. "The *business*," she repeated. "Addiction is a *medical* disease. The illegal narcotics business is a *social* one. You cannot treat the two with the same medicine.

"Think about this." She leaned forward. "How much violence . . . how much killing . . . comes not from the drugs, but from the *business* . . . the illegal business of buying, distribution, selling?"

Navarro's cheeks had an excited flush, and her voice deepened.

"Narcotics do not corrupt. It's the criminal business that buys politicians and even . . . even police. We have our 'war on drugs.' And we have brave and principled people fighting it. Kevin Gentry was one. But it is a war we are losing. And when you are losing a war, you change your strategy."

"To preemptive surrender?" Frank asked.

"No. Merely rational recognition of human nature. Congress cannot outlaw sin. But it can keep evil people from making money from it." Navarro sat back and smiled ruefully. "But you did not come here to argue the merits of legalizing narcotics."

"You were close to Kevin Gentry," Frank said.

"Yes." No longer the missionary, Navarro brought her guard up.

"When he was killed, he was preparing for a subcommittee hearing."

Navarro answered cautiously. "Yes."

"The usual annual D.C. budget review."

Navarro's look said "Listen carefully." When she seemed certain she'd be understood, she spoke quietly. "Perhaps."

"Perhaps?"

"Kevin had it in mind to expose the drug business in the District."

"You knew this?"

"We helped him build a case."

"How?"

"I said we exist to put the illegal narcotics dealers out of business."

"Yes . . ."

"Those young people you see outside . . . they may seem like children. But they are very good researchers. We made this research available to Kevin."

"Research about the business? What in particular?"

"In particular the Juan Brooks empire and his successor, James Hodges. It was quite an enterprise, you know."

José looked doubtful. "Bunch of skinny kids on computers build a case on Skeeter?"

Navarro smiled. "Those skinny kids know the streets as well as computers. And we collect everything . . . things prohibited to you . . . rumors, hearsay. We even collect lies. Over time, patterns emerge, even in lies. And we are not bound to courtroom standards of evidence."

"Could we have a copy of what you furnished Mr. Gentry?" Frank asked. "Hard copy if we can, computer discs if we can't get that."

Navarro nodded and made a note. "That was two years ago. We will have to pull it together. Do you want an update?"

Frank shook his head. "Maybe later. Right now, we'd like to see what Mr. Gentry saw."

"The hearings Mr. Gentry was planning," José asked, "Skeeter Hodges and his crew going to be the feature attraction?"

"Yes. We did an extensive organizational and economic analysis."

"Economics?"

Navarro smiled cynically. "If the Hodges activities were legal, they'd be the third-largest moneymaker in the District behind the federal government and the Redskins."

THIRTY-TWO

Frank stirred two Equals into his coffee. "Who knows what evil lurks in the hearts of men?"

José shut his notebook and tucked his pen in an inside coat pocket. The only other customer in the Starbucks was a thin kid with a ponytail, sharing a table at the back with his parrot. The kid was busily writing in a journal, stopping to feed the parrot chunks of a sweet roll.

Frank sipped at the coffee. He'd read somewhere that during World War II, the Germans had had to make coffee from burnt acorns, and he often wondered if they'd sold the recipe to Starbucks. It was awful stuff, but at least Starbucks was consistently awful. You knew what you'd get wherever you went.

"The lady pulled your chain, didn't she?" he asked José.

José nodded. "Señorita's got *cojones*. A true believer." He stared out the window at the gray stone building across P Street. "Helluva thing," he said wistfully, "older I get, the more I wonder . . ."

"About?"

"Oh, things I used to know were so . . . rock-bottom certain."

"She got you thinking, didn't she?"

"Made me remember," José said, "something my daddy once told me about Jackson, Mississippi, back when he was a kid."

"Yeah?"

"Dry state then. No hard booze. Only three-two beer. You wanted hard stuff, you saw the local bootlegger. Night and day, trucks ran the stuff into Jackson from over in Louisiana, 'cross the river to Vicksburg. Folks finally got fed up and got wet/dry on the ballot. Preachers came out for dry. Raised hell on Sundays. Just before the elections, papers carried the story that the bootleggers were paying off the preachers."

"What happened?"

"Mississippi went wet. Bootleggers lost their asses."

Frank was about to say something, when José's cell went off.

José answered, listened, then flipped his cell shut. "R.C.," he said. "Has a show-and-tell down at impound."

We'd finished dusting for prints," Calkins said. He stood beside Skeeter's Taurus. Everything that would open was open: hood, trunk, all four doors, even the gas-filler hatch. The seats had been taken out. Halogen droplights illuminated every crevice.

"Nothing but Skeeter's and Pencil's. Then, when we were vacuuming for fibers . . ."

Calkins paused and stepped nearer to the car, picked up a yardstick, and pointed inside.

". . . we found this."

"This" was a heavy insulated cable running from the engine compartment, along the floor of the car, and disappearing into the trunk.

Calkins led Frank and José around to the trunk.

"Comes in here." He motioned with his chin.

Frank saw the cable snaking along the inner fender, then disappearing under the mat that covered the trunk floor. Calkins lifted the mat. The spare tire had been removed from the storage well. The cable ran into a curved section of the well. He reached down into the well, and with a metallic snap, the section popped loose to reveal a small compartment with a black box inside.

"Guts of a top-end Nakamichi cassette recorder." Calkins tapped the box with the yardstick. "Microphone pick-ups in the floor, head-liner, headrests."

José examined the box. "No buttons."

"Remoted to the car's regular sound system," Calkins explained. "Do some trickery like turning off the music, and you turn on the recorder."

"Skeeter and Pencil knew it was there?"

"Oh, yes," Calkins said. "Their prints all over it. I'd say they were the ones who installed it." He stepped to a workbench and picked up a brown paper bag, then held it open to reveal a cassette to Frank and José. "Skeeter's prints are on the cassette." He anticipated the next question: "But the tape itself is blank except for you, José."

"Me?"

Calkins smiled. "Has you asking, 'Who was the nine-one-one?' You must have keyed the recorder when you turned off the rap at the scene."

"Yeah," José said, "about a million years ago."

Calkins regarded the recorder in its hiding place with admiration. "They went to a lot of trouble."

"Car was his office," Frank said. "He had had more time, he'd probably have had a fax and a computer rig in there." He stared at the car, Skeeter's office, trying to work out the permutations, the pos-sibilities, trying to catalogue what was in front of him, integrate it into the jumble of fact, supposition, and downright hunches.

After this's over, we'll look back and wonder why it was we didn't see how everything fit and why we didn't understand it right away. And we'll tidy it up. We'll discard the implausible theories, get rid of the dead ends we screwed around with, forget about the rabbits we went chasing after. And maybe Hoser and I will lecture at the academy about how this led to that and that led to this and finally to how it all ended up with a closed case. And we'll screw up the rookies' minds, because they'll think that's the way things really happen.

THIRTY-THREE

Back in the office, Frank measured the Folger's into the coffeemaker. José had loaded the CD player, and Ella Fitzgerald launched into "Someone to Watch over Me." Leon Janowitz tilted back against the wall in the straight wooden chair, a bottle of Poland Spring in one hand, a dart in the other, surveying the Ipswich Fives board on the wall.

"Okay," Janowitz said, "Skeeter had a recording studio on wheels. Why?"

"You know, Leon." José eyed the dart in his hand warily, "some guy in Watergate once said this's a great town when you're the one askin' the questions."

"Better question, Leon," Frank said. "Let's go back to the Bayless Place shell casings. If Pencil killed Gentry, why'd he do it?"

Janowitz threw. Three pair of eyes watched the dart *thock!* into the board. A double eighteen. Janowitz grinned triumphantly.

"You're losing your touch, Leon," José said. "You missed the wall."

"This a test?" Janowitz asked. "Okay, try this. If Pencil killed

Gentry, it was because he and Skeeter found out that Gentry had gotten the goods on them."

"Or he was getting close," José added.

"Second question, Leon," Frank said. "How might Skeeter and Pencil have learned that?"

Janowitz picked up a second dart, studied the tip, lofted it experimentally, then looked at Frank. "Suppose they tumbled to Gentry's source?"

"And if they did," Frank came back, "what do you think they'd do about the source?"

Janowitz threw the dart, whipping it hard. A double twenty.

José got up from behind his desk and turned to the whiteboard behind him. From a beer mug he selected a red felt-tip marker. "A little profiling exercise," he announced.

He drew a round bullet on the board. "Okay," he asked Janowitz, "the ideal source . . . first attribute?"

Janowitz didn't hesitate. "Proximity. He's gotta be close to Skeeter and Pencil."

José jotted "Prox" by the first bullet. "Why 'he'?" he said.

"These guys don't buy PC. It's a boys-only club."

A second bullet, and "Male" next to that.

"Age?"

"Within several years of Skeeter and Pencil."

José entered "Mid-30s" against a third bullet.

"Fourth bullet's this," Janowitz said. "A longtime buddy. Somebody they'd trust. Been through the mill with them."

José capped the marker and ran his eyes down the board. Then he asked, "And how'd they tumble to the source?"

"Probably caught him in the act. Maybe meeting with Gentry, being in the wrong place at the wrong time."

"So they'd milk him for what he had." Frank picked up the lead. "Then what?"

"They'd pop him," Janowitz replied. "Look, guys," he said, "you tiptoed me through the tulips like a rookie. Where's this finger exercise heading?"

"Glad you asked, Leon," Frank said.

From a cabinet, José produced Eleanor's printout and handed the thick sheaf to Janowitz. "Given that profile, you might want to start here."

Janowitz got a put-upon expression as he took the printout. "So we find the needle in this haystack . . . then what? I mean, shit, we aren't going to be bringing Skeeter and Pencil into court."

"If we have to close the Gentry case administratively, we want it solid. Nobody's going to buy the fluff they did first time around."

"And then there's the matter of Skeeter, Pencil, and Pencil's woman," José said. "Somebody might just be around who did them."

"And maybe a Colombian connection?" Janowitz ventured. "Skeeter and Pencil made one bad deal too many? Or the cartels found a better outlet somewhere else?"

Frank gave Janowitz a sunny smile. "Like Hoser said, Leon, this is a great town for questions. Now we need to work out a few answers."

Janowitz hoisted the printout. "Take this back to my cubicle?"

"Yeah. By the way, how's your audit turning out?"

"Slow. Library of Congress archives just found the subcommittee's bank records and Gentry's personal files. I probably got a stack thicker than this"—he waggled the printout—"waiting for me. I'll run a quick scan tonight."

"Don't get wrapped up in too much night work," José said. "Department's cutting down overtime."

Janowitz grinned. "Mrs. Janowitz and I got some night work planned, and I won't put in for overtime."

Janowitz left.

José shook his head wonderingly at the closed door. "Kid sees the world through his dick," he said.

"Probably better than some other ways of looking at it," Frank said, beginning his end-of-the-day desk-clearing routine.

THIRTY-FOUR

Having woken early, Frank took a longer run: down Thirtieth to the river, then up the river path. Four miles past Fletcher's Boat House, he reversed course. Back home, Monty waited for breakfast. That taken care of, Frank showered, twisting and stretching under the needle spray, first hot, then cold, then hot again.

Finished shaving, he inspected his face. The eyes still clear, the gray still holding at the temples. The slightest ropiness along the jawline, the hint of puffiness beneath the eyes. Good for another day.

A stand-up breakfast at the kitchen counter: coffee made a bit stronger than usual, bran flakes with blueberries and skim milk. He opened the *Post.* The sad-sack Wizards had just hired Doug Collins, Michael Jordan's former coach with the Bulls. Collins and Jordan, reunited to re-create the old Chicago magic in Washington. Frank shook his head.

Second acts in American lives.

His eyes drifted to the masthead. Somewhat surprised, he found it was already Friday.

Two weeks since Bayless Place? Two . . . weeks?

Searching his closet, he found a favorite suit, a J. Press spring-weight navy wool that had the feel of cashmere. The phone interrupted him as he picked through his ties.

"Frank? This's Leon." Janowitz had an upbeat of excitement in his voice.

"You're up early."

"Yeah. I was driving in, thought you might still be home. Mind if I drop by?"

"Got some coffee left."

"I don't know if I can handle that. Be there in five."

Seated at the breakfast room table, Janowitz pulled out a folder, opened it, and handed Frank a booking mug shot.

"Who's this?"

"Likely prospect for Gentry's source."

A good-looking African-American kid stared back at Frank. Strong mouth and jaw, but a hint of fear in the dark almond eyes.

"Martin Moses Osmond." Frank read off the sign the kid was holding.

"Eleanor's pulling his file out of inactive storage," Janowitz said, "but here's what I could get from the abstracts: born 'sixty-eight. Conviction grand theft auto, 'eighty-six. Three other guys tried for the same offense." Janowitz paused for effect. "James 'Skeeter' Hodges—"

"Tobias 'Pencil' Crawfurd and Zelmer Austin," Frank finished.

Janowitz nodded. Rapping the printout for emphasis, he went on. "All four together at Lorton. That's where Skeeter made the connections that got him in tight with Juan Brooks. Skeeter, Pencil, Austin, and Osmond got out the same time, and got a franchise from Brooks. Osmond was picked up later, two charges possession intent to sell. Beat both. His P.O. noted that he warned Osmond about continued association with Skeeter and Pencil."

"The P.O.," Frank asked, "was . . . ?"

"Arch Sterling."

Frank knew Sterling. Too many parole officers got co-opted by what the PC establishment now called "clients." Sterling still thought of them as parolees.

"What else makes Osmond a likely?" he asked Janowitz.

"Had access, had a history with Skeeter and Pencil. Didn't quite fit one element of the profile, though."

"How do you mean?"

"He's dead, but it wasn't ruled homicide. His grandmother found him in his car. M.E. ruled it a heroin overdose. Interesting timing, though."

"Oh?"

"Died Monday night twenty-two February 'ninety-nine . . . about two hours after somebody popped Kevin Gentry." Janowitz sat quietly, watching Frank take that in.

Frank registered Janowitz's expectant look. "You've got more, don't you?"

Janowitz gave a low whistle. "I'm not going to play poker with you."

"You're an easy read. You wouldn't be here if the profile was all you had. And besides, you got your hand ready to pull another rabbit out of your L. L. Bean bag."

Grinning, Janowitz thrust his hand into the briefcase and came out with a yellow ledger sheet penciled with notations.

"I worked through the subcommittee's administrative expenditures—a real rat's nest. Anyway, starting in June 'ninety-eight, Rhinelander authorized Gentry to set up an account, something called 'Hearing Research and Analysis.' A lot of money went in, but no details of disbursements; no vouchers, no receipts. No documentation of any kind. Rhinelander closed out the account on twenty-four February 'ninety-nine—two days after Gentry bought the farm. No funds returned. Money disappeared."

"How much?"

"Best I could estimate, hundred twenty thousand. More than I make in a week."

"That'd be a nice payout for a source," Frank said.

Janowitz was peering into the depths of the bag. "Ah, yes," he muttered, pulling out a small manila envelope, which he handed to Frank.

Someone . . . Gentry? . . . had printed "Rch/Analysis" across the envelope flap. Frank shook out a key and a slip of paper.

"Receipt for a safe-deposit box at Riggs," Janowitz explained.

"Opened June 15, 1998," Frank said.

"Might be interesting to get a look. I checked the bank. We're gonna need a court order."

Frank returned the key and receipt to the envelope and slipped it into his shirt pocket.

Janowitz trailed a teaser, "Funny thing about Osmond," he said softly.

"Funny ha-ha?"

"He lived on Bayless Place with his grandmother," Janowitz said. "About half a block from where Skeeter bought the farm."

From the rising inflection and the look in his eyes, Frank could tell Janowitz was holding on to yet another card.

"A small world, Frank . . . Arch Sterling's background report on Martin Osmond? Martin and his grandmother were members of José's dad's congregation."

Minutes later, Janowitz stood on the sidewalk, holding his over-stuffed canvas briefcase, watching Frank lock up the house.

"Where'd you park?" Frank asked, when he had joined Janowitz.

Janowitz pointed down Olive, toward Twenty-ninth. "Just in front of you."

The two had gotten midway down the block when Frank's cell phone rang. He stopped to answer. It was Kate. He waved Janowitz on. Janowitz nodded and continued down the sidewalk.

"Catching the first shuttle out in the morning," Kate said. "Dinner still on?"

Charlie Whitmire and Murphy appeared down the street, return-ing from Murph's morning walk.

"I'll pick you up at National, and dinner's still on. You learn how Giuliani benched the squeegee men?"

"I learned that sometimes a mayor has to kick ass," Kate said. "Take care of yours."

Frank closed the phone and continued toward his car.

Up ahead, Janowitz had left the sidewalk and was in the street, stepping along the drivers' side of a line of parallel-parked cars. He was just passing Frank's.

On the sidewalk opposite, and farther down the block, Charlie Whitmire had stopped to let Murph sniff around the base of a maple.

Frank felt in his pocket for his keys, found them, pulled them out, and pressed the remote to unlock his car.

The world vanished in a blinding flash. A massive rippling sound, as if the earth had split under the impact of a cosmic jackhammer. A dirty cloud engulfed the street and shut out the sun.

For the thinnest slice of a second, Frank lost all orientation. Up, down, night, day, who he was, where he was, where he'd been going—all stripped away by the shock wave that threw him to the street.

Reflexively he struggled to his knees. A red blackness every-where. Security alarms from nearby houses and cars screeched and warbled. Panicked by his blindness, he felt a wetness on his face. He wiped his eyes with his hands and cleared away the blood. The street blurred into focus.

Litter and leaves stripped from the trees pinwheeled lazily down through the dusty haze. An odor of ash and scorched fabric. A green and white canvas awning hung from its frame, swinging back and forth in the secondaries from the shock wave. Frank's car leaned drunkenly nose first into the street, tires flattened, steel skin peeled back in all directions from the driver's seat.

A dark figure lay crumpled in the middle of the street. Frank got up. Pressing his palm against the gash over his eye, he staggered to-ward what had to be Janowitz.

From the opposite direction, Charlie Whitmire was running toward Janowitz, Murph barking in chase. In the distance, sirens. Up and down Olive, people began opening doors and venturing out onto front steps.

When Frank reached Janowitz, Charlie Whitmire was already there, kneeling in a pool of blood, tightening Murph's leash around what was left of Janowitz's right arm.

The ER doors crashed open as José pushed through.

"Frank! You okay?"

Frank sat with his legs dangling off a gurney, head tilted back. Sheresa Arrowsmith, examining flashlight in hand, peered into his eyes.

"Okay, Hoser," Frank whispered.

"He's had a concussion, multiple contusions of the chest, and enough stitches to make a quilt," Arrowsmith said, still checking out Frank's eyes.

"Leon?" José asked.

Charlie struggling with the blood-slicked leash. "He's bleeding," Charlie was saying. "He's bleeding," Charlie kept saying, over and over, and Frank knew what he was saying but he couldn't hear the words.

"Bad. Real bad."

Irritably, Arrowsmith lowered the flashlight and turned to José. "Mr. Janowitz is in surgery. I'm with a patient, and you're in the way," she said abruptly. "Go wait outside, José."

Behind her, Frank eased himself off the gurney, rocking slightly.

Arrowsmith whirled, and put a restraining hand on his shoulder. "We're admitting you, big boy."

Frank got his feet under him and gently pried her hand loose. "Not today, Sheresa. Just get me something for this goddamn headache."

Arrowsmith jammed the flashlight in her jacket pocket. "If there's anything worse than treating cops, it's treating men cops. You're too old to think you're bulletproof, Frank."

"I want to see Leon when he gets out of surgery."

Arrowsmith gave a surrendering shrug, and in a nearby cabinet found a small pill bottle and put it in Frank's hand. "They'll be bringing him into ICU." She waved the back of her hand at Frank and José as though shooing away two troublesome little boys. "Go on, get out of my ER."

Frank began feeling better in the corridor as they made their way toward the ICU.

"Who's handling the scene?"

"Hawkins has the place nailed down," José answered, and before Frank could ask, added, "and R.C.'s there, too."

"Leon's wife?"

"I called her."

"And . . . ?"

"She's on her way over. Didn't waste any words. Just 'Thank you' and hung up."

"Emerson?"

"Typical . . . First thing, he wanted a press release."

The ICU waiting room, small, windowless, and wall-scarred, had been a storeroom before the growing ICU business necessitated a place for relatives, friends, and police. Frank and José took two of the four hard plastic chairs, across from a battered rack filled with medical journals, pharmaceutical sales literature, and a handful of dog-eared travel magazines. To their right, the nurses' station was visible through a glass door.

José watched as Frank dropped deeper into a brooding silence. He let him go until it got too much for him. "You want some coffee? A Coke?" he asked.

It took Frank a second or two to register. "What?"

"Coffee? Coke?"

Frank shook his head.

"You need one of those pills Sheresa gave you?"

"Pill?"

"Headache?" José prompted.

"Oh," Frank said it slowly, as though he had to take inventory. "Yeah. I still have it."

José got up, stepped into the hall, and returned with a paper cup. Frank was back to wherever he'd been.

"Water," José said louder than he had to, and thrust the cup at Frank.

Frank took it and looked at José.

"I did it, you know."

José regarded him gravely. "You did . . . what?"

"I set it off. They must have had it rigged to the door lock. It was supposed to get me when I turned the key. I set it off when I did the remote."

José pulled his chair around to face Frank and sat so his knees almost touched Frank's.

"Yeah," he said carefully, "that's what they did. They must have wired it to the lock."

"And I pressed the remote when Leon was walking by, and I set it off."

José brought his face close to Frank's so their eyes were inches apart. He reached out and clamped one of Frank's knees in his hand.

"Frank," he said, leaning forward and biting off each word, "you listen to me. *They* put the bomb there. . . . *They* rigged it to the lock. . . . *They* did whatever happened."

"But Hoser, *I*—"

"Bullshit, Frank!" José rapped out. "No goddamn way you gonna put this on yourself! Pushin' a goddamn remote button on your car didn't do that to Leon. Bastards did who put the bomb there."

Frank looked into José's eyes for a long time, searching, then pulled back. As he reached into his pocket for the pills, his hand paused. Perplexed, he drew out a small manila envelope. It took him a second to remember Janowitz sitting at the breakfast room table, handing the envelope over.

Riggs Bank . . . court order.

He put the envelope away and fished out the container. He twisted the top off and shook out two white pills, then downed them with the cup of water. He crumpled the cup, sat back in his chair, and rested his head against the wall.

"Hoser, I feel like shit."

José squeezed his partner's shoulder. "You got a right, buddy."

"You oughta get over to the scene."

"Yeah." José hesitated, giving Frank a close once-over. "You sure you're okay?"

"I'll live."

After José left, Frank shut his eyes and waited for Arrowsmith's pills to kick in. He dozed off, his hand opened, and the crumpled paper cup fell to the floor. At the same time, machine-gun fire cut through his mental fog. He bolted upright in his chair, eyes open, and the machine-gun fire morphed into the insistent chirping of his cell phone.

He got the phone to his ear.

"Frank? What the hell?" Tom Kearney's concern came in at high volume.

"Dad . . ."

"Radio's talking about a bomb in Georgetown. Then Judith called me. Said your street was blocked off. Neighbors said you were hurt. . . ."

"I'm okay, Dad."

"Where the hell are you?"

"Hospital Center."

That reignited Tom Kearney's alarm. "I thought you weren't hurt!" he shouted.

"One of our guys is, Dad," Frank said patiently. "I'm waiting for him to come out of surgery."

"Any idea who did it?"

"Not yet, Dad. Not yet."

Frank was putting away his phone when Sheresa Arrowsmith entered, her arm around a woman. Petite, in her late twenties, early thirties, black hair cut short and shaped around her face. She wore jeans, a paint-daubed Ohio State sweatshirt, and Nike running shoes.

"Detective Kearney," Arrowsmith said softly to the woman. To Frank she said, "This's Esther Janowitz."

He's been in there nine hours," Esther Janowitz whispered to the clock on the ICU waiting room wall.

Frank watched the red second hand. All that could be said had been said. He and Esther Janowitz had been by turn withdrawn and almost maniacally chattering, only to drift off again into isolation. The clock notched another second, then another and another. And the near-silent ticking engulfed the tiny room.

He had told her all he remembered. How he and her husband had sat over coffee, how his remote had triggered the explosion. She had listened expressionlessly, and there was no way he could tell whether she blamed him for what had happened. If she was angry, the anger might come up later, but then it might never come up. She didn't impress him as a whiner or sniveler, and if she did bring it up, she'd come at him in-your-face hard. He didn't want it now, but he'd rather have it now than never.

He stepped outside to use his phone. He left a short message with Kate's answering service, then called José. Calkins was setting up for a twenty-four-hour operation. Robin Bouchard had offered the Bureau explosives team, and José had gone into Frank's to feed Monty.

Frank thought about calling Emerson, but gave it up when he realized he had nothing to say. He didn't want to get involved in a hand-holding exercise.

Back in the waiting room, Esther Janowitz put down the copy of

Condé Nast Traveller—"The Best Tapas Bars in Seville"—and gave Frank, a long, appraising look.

"Mind if I ask you something?"

"No. I don't," Frank said, wishing inside that she'd stayed with the magazine. *What* were *the best tapas bars in Seville?*

"Why did you choose Leon?"

It didn't come across as a baited question. Esther Janowitz seemed genuinely curious. All the same, Frank found himself vaguely troubled that she'd asked and that he'd have to answer.

"I don't know that I'm making the best of sense right now," he began slowly, talking to her and to himself as well. "Simple answer . . . I asked for Leon because José and I needed help. We'd worked with him on the Keegan case, and we thought he was a good cop."

He paused to gather his thoughts. "There's a not-so-simple answer too. I'm proud of being a cop. There've been lots of days I wish I wasn't, but on the whole, I like what I do, and I think it's important."

He searched for a word, a word that meant something. "It's a *worthy* job. A job worth doing. Something worth devoting a life to. And it's worth all the crap that goes along with it. And I guess when I see a young cop like Leon, it makes me feel good because I know when I hang up the badge, somebody is going to be out there wearing that badge who feels the same way I do about being a cop."

"A legacy?"

"Call it that. Why'd you want to know . . . why I chose him?"

A small, nostalgic smile played around Esther Janowitz's mouth. "I know why I chose him. And those reasons are good enough for me. I love him very much for those reasons. But it helps to know him better if I know how others see him."

"I didn't want him to leave the force."

"I know. He told me. He said it made him feel warm inside."

"Now I'm not so sure. Maybe New York . . ."

From the corner of his eye, he caught a flurry of motion in the narrow window set into the door to the ICU. A tall African-American man in green surgical scrubs came through a set of double doors, crossed the hallway, and entered the waiting room. He came over to Esther Janowitz.

"Mrs. Janowitz, I'm Dr. Michaels. They're bringing your husband out of surgery now. I expect a full recovery. We had some internal injuries to take care of. . . . There were facial lacerations, and . . ."

Michaels paused. Frank sensed a man about to step out on unknown ice. The doctor shot a glance at Frank. ". . . we . . . I . . . *I* had to amputate his arm."

Esther Janowitz gave no sign she'd heard. Her eyes widened as two orderlies brought a gurney through the double doors into the ICU. Without a word, Esther Janowitz brushed by Michaels and was at her husband's side.

That night, Frank couldn't sleep. Outside in the rain, R.C.'s techs were still scavenging the block for evidence, working below canopies flung up over high-intensity floodlights. In his bedroom, each time Frank closed his eyes he felt the presence of meaningless death, the slow, circling beat of dark wings. He lay staring at the ceiling, listening to the rain, measuring its rhythms on the roof.

He couldn't imagine ever having slept before or ever sleeping again. Soon he gave up. He got out of bed, slipped a pair of denim shorts on, and padded downstairs to the kitchen. Standing in the light of the open refrigerator, he drank deeply from a carton of milk. He wandered into the den, where he switched on a floor lamp and aimlessly began opening cabinets. One after another, he surveyed their contents, then closed them. Finally, in one, a thick album caught his attention.

He took it into the kitchen, retrieved the carton of milk, and sat at the table. He opened the album and it was Vietnam again.

A series of photographs: the building of the firebase near Ben Cat. GIs filling sandbags, digging bunkers, stringing razor-bladed coils of concertina wire.

In one photograph, he and Masek stood grinning into the camera, interrupted from their task of setting out Claymore mines. Masek held a curved book-size mine in his hand. They were both bare-chested and rail-thin, and their fatigue trousers were stained dark with sweat. A gold tooth glinted in Masek's mouth, and Frank wore a low-slung pistol belt. They looked rakish and impossibly young.

The pictures tugged at him—he was looking into a time when the firebase at Ben Cat still existed, before Masek became a name on the black marble wall, and when all that had happened to Frank had yet to happen to the Frank in the pictures. It was a time before the images became distorted by shattered truth and failed ambition.

Looking at himself, Frank wanted to whisper a warning to the young man he once was.

THIRTY-FIVE

The headache was a roaring, clawing dragon behind his eyes. Eyes shut, Frank crab-walked his hand across the nightstand until he found the plastic container. Cursing the nanny state, he managed to work open the childproof cap and roll out two capsules. He got them down dry, then lay back in half-sleep and listened to Monty snore on the other pillow. He heard the grandfather clock downstairs strike two. Only seconds later, he heard it strike seven.

The dragon had left, but the stitches over his right eye felt like dozens of needles thrust under his skin. When he sat up, a painful protest swept over him from the bruises covering his chest and arms.

Every joint creaking, he made it into the shower, then, after gingerly drying himself, in front of the mirror to shave. The stitches pulled his right eye open, while a world-class shiner surrounded his left eye and blood from a ruptured vein had turned the white of the eye a deep red.

"No Hollywood contract today," he muttered to himself.

Thirty minutes later, he hailed a cab at the corner of Thirtieth and M, and fifteen minutes after that, John Richardson, the department's dispatcher, was looking up at him.

"Jesus, Frank, you look worse than your car."

"Car didn't wake up with a head-popper this morning. You got something drivable?"

"You don't want to wait until we fix yours?"

"You and I aren't gonna live long enough, John."

Richardson checked his computer, running a finger down the screen. "We got a couple of confiscated vehicles. How about a Hummer? Leather, Bose sound, only eight thousand miles, no bullet holes?"

"Maybe when I move to Montana."

"You moving to Montana?"

"No. You got a spare Crown Vic?"

Richardson swiveled around, ran his fingers across a pegboard on the wall, plucked a set of keys, then turned back to Frank.

"Hummer matches your face," he said, holding on to the keys. "You look like the Terminator on one of his worst days."

Frank held out his hand. "I don't want to be in anything that looks like my face."

Richardson lofted the keys, and in an easy motion, Frank snagged them out of midair.

"Thanks, John." Frank put on his dark glasses, and smiled. "I'll be back."

Hummer might have been fun, Frank thought as he made his way across the Fourteenth Street bridge. He switched on the radio and there was Joe Madison. As he expected, Madison was waist deep in yesterday's bombing, grilling a hapless guest from Alcohol, Tobacco and Firearms.

Sorry, Joe.

The next preset put him in the middle of Mary Chapin Carpenter's "Can't Take Love for Granted." Carpenter's Marlboro-and-Jack-Daniel's throatiness came out warm and sexy, and he felt his tension ease as Kate's smile came to mind.

At Reagan National, Frank hurried past newsstands whose papers carried photos of his bomb-blasted car side by side with file shots of Leon Janowitz. He got to the US Airways gate just as the doors were opening.

Kate was among the first passengers off the shuttle. Catching sight of Frank, she stopped momentarily, obviously shaken, then rushed to him. She dropped her carry-on bag and hugged him, then, feeling him wince, stood back, eyes moist, and cupped his chin in her hand.

"You said a couple of scratches."

"Looks worse than it is. I was lucky. Leon wasn't."

She held him at arm's length, eyes going over his face.

"Frank," she whispered, "it was . . ." As though suddenly realizing how near to the brink they had stood, and how deep the abyss, she shuddered. A single tear ran down her cheek. ". . . it was so damn close."

She leaned forward and kissed him.

Five minutes later, they were driving north on the parkway.

"Favor?" Frank asked.

"Not here," Kate said.

He reached into his shirt pocket for what he'd started thinking of as Janowitz's envelope. He passed it to her.

She opened it. "Looks like a safe-deposit-box key."

"It is. From Kevin Gentry's office files. I want to see what's inside. We need a court order or something?"

"Unh-hunh. You'll want it yesterday?"

"That'd be nice."

"How about today? Even that'll be a push, getting a judge on a Saturday."

Frank swung off the parkway onto the ramp to the Fourteenth Street bridge and back into the District. He headed toward Kate's office.

"Have to do."

"What do I get in exchange?"

Frank glanced over and grinned, and for the first time that day he felt pretty damn good.

It was an improvised device employing a sodium perchlorate explosive." Renfro Calkins danced a laser pointer over the poster-size enlargement of what had been the front seat of Frank's car.

At the head of the conference table, Seth Tompkins raised a hand. "Improvised, Mr. Calkins . . . how?"

"Relatively simple, Your Honor," Calkins told the mayor. Around the table with him were Chief Noah Day, Randolph Emerson, Frank, and José.

"You can do it in a bathroom or kitchen. Take HTH, a common swimming pool chlorinating compound, boil it along with table salt. Run the mixture through a couple of filtering processes and you come up with sodium perchlorate crystals. Grind the crystals, then mix with petroleum jelly . . . Vaseline . . . and you've got a very dandy plastique explosive."

Calkins nodded toward Frank. "Your batch, Frank, was mixed with aluminum powder . . . obtainable at any paint store . . . that increased the explosive power, which also accounted for the bright flash you saw."

"How big was it?" Tompkins asked.

"Not more than a pound of explosive," Calkins answered, "perhaps even less."

Tompkins's eyes widened. "That small?"

"Enough if you know what you're doing. The explosive was formed into a shaped charge, much like a cone," Calkins explained. "The wide end was pointed toward the door and packed with lead pellets. Strictly an antipersonnel weapon. Officer Janowitz wasn't killed, because the driver's-side door shielded him from the pellets."

"So much for the device," Emerson said. "Any evidence of the origins?"

Calkins made eye contact with Frank, then with Emerson. "The design is one favored by bombmakers in the drug trade."

Frank knew what was coming.

"Colombian?" Emerson asked.

Persistent if nothing else, Randolph, Frank wanted to say. Instead, he asked, "Forensics, R.C.?"

"The bombmaker was a local."

"How'd you get that?" Emerson asked.

Calkins went to the easel, reached behind the photo enlargement of Frank's car, and brought out another enlargement, of an irregular-shaped orange and black object. He settled the photo on the easel and flashed the laser pointer over a series of numbers apparently impressed into the surface.

"The bomb's firing mechanism had its own power source," he said. "A nine-volt Duracell battery. We found this fragment. Note here"—the bright red laser dot danced across the figures—"these are the manufacturer's lot numbers. Duracell records the regional distributors to whom each lot is shipped."

Emerson frowned. "Yes?"

"We traced this lot to a distributor in Columbus, Ohio. The distributor's records show that it was broken into three separate shipments to retailers. One to a Home Depot in Montgomery, Alabama, and another to a Lowe's in Lexington, Kentucky, and a third . . . here in the District. The Home Depot over in Northeast."

The door to Tompkins's left opened, and an assistant slipped in and handed him a folded note.

Tompkins picked his reading glasses up off the conference table. He took his time when reading the note, then glanced around the table.

"A summons," he said, waving the paper. "The Honorable Frederick Rhinelander requests my presence in his office Monday morning."

Calkins, sensing his time onstage was over, folded his easel and began putting away his charts. Frank caught Emerson nudging Chief Day's elbow. Day sat without expression.

Emerson hesitated, then jumped in. "You know what he's going to want, Your Honor."

Tompkins raised an eyebrow. "Besides my head?" After enjoying Emerson's discomfort, he continued. "I suspect, Captain Emerson, he's going to put the squeeze on me to get this case solved."

Emerson nodded energetically. "I think you're right, Your Honor."

"Thank you, Captain," Tompkins said dryly. His sarcasm sailed over Emerson's head.

"Who do you want to go with you?" Emerson asked with the same suck-up enthusiasm.

"Who do you suggest, Captain?"

"Well," Emerson said, all businesslike, "myself . . . ah . . . Chief Day, of course. Perhaps Susan Liberman, our congressional relations specialist . . ."

"Quite an entourage, Captain," Tompkins said as he got up. "I don't think so." He got an amused look and pointed down the table to Frank and José. "I think these two gentlemen will be sufficient."

José looked down the block. Both sides of the street had been restricted to parking for official vehicles.

"We got wheels?"

"Yeah . . . blue Crown Vic over there." Frank pointed. "Richardson wanted to give us a confiscated Hummer."

"And you didn't take it? Shit, Frank, our chance to get a luxury assault vehicle and you turn it down?" José glanced around, checking for anyone within earshot. "Tompkins is gonna be hung out to dry. Steaks on it."

"Depends on how much Rhinelander squeezes him."

"Rhinelander's in the catbird seat. He gets prime time on the tube for beating up on the D.C. government. . . ."

"The D.C. punching bag . . ."

"And if we close the case, you can bet your ass he'll grab the credit for that, too."

"Helluva place, that Congress. You don't have to come up with solutions. . . . All you got to do is point fingers and piss and moan."

"And hire guys to raise flags on the roof."

How is he . . . ?" Frank asked. "Long-term prospects?"

Sheresa Arrowsmith stopped and leaned wearily against a column in the long corridor leading to the ICU. She pushed her glasses up to her forehead with one hand, and with the other scrubbed her eyes.

"That's two questions, Frank. How is he? He's still critical. Damage like that doesn't leave a clean wound. But Dr. Michaels saved the elbow and a little over three inches of the forearm."

"Meaning?" José asked.

"Meaning he's got a chance for a working prosthesis. One that can take advantage of the muscles remaining above the elbow. The second question, long-term prospects, that's harder. The best prosthesis can only do so much. Rest of it comes from the heart. Overall, for what he went through, he's lucky."

"Yeah," Frank said in soft irony, "lucky Leon."

In the ICU, a wave of smothering despair swept over Frank. Leon Janowitz lay almost lifeless, his face a waxy white. His right arm, encased in a pillowlike bandage, was elevated by an overhead traction device.

Esther Janowitz was curled up in a chair beside her husband's bed. Frank recognized the chair as one from the ICU waiting room.

Frank whispered her name.

Esther stirred, was still, then suddenly awake, eyes wide, taking in Frank, only slowly becoming aware of where she was.

"What . . . what time is it?" Then her eyes fastened on José. "You have to be José."

José smiled big. "Don't have to be, but I am. How's he doing?"

Esther stood and stretched, hand covering a yawn. "He came out of it for a minute or two this morning. Sometime around three." She smiled wryly. "He told me they were going to discharge him tomorrow. He's been drifting in and out since." She gave Frank a grave look. "Each time he asks about you."

"Me?"

"He thinks you didn't make it. I tell him you were okay. But I don't think it sinks in."

"Does he know what happened?" Frank asked.

"You mean about his arm?"

Frank nodded.

"No. Not yet." Forlorn, Esther shook her head. "I want to be the one to tell him, but I don't want to be the one to tell him."

Frank stared unhappily at his feet.

Her voice somewhat brighter, Esther said, "Let me see if I can wake him."

Before Frank could protest, she leaned over and put her palm on her husband's cheek and kissed him. "Leon," she whispered. Then louder, "Leon?"

Nothing.

Frank held up a belaying hand. Before he could say anything, Janowitz stirred, a slight flutter of the eyelids, then a weak cough to clear his throat. His eyes opened and made contact with Frank's. His lips moved.

Frank bent closer.

"Yes, Leon?"

"Frank," Janowitz whispered, "you look like shit."

"Thanks, Leon."

"You okay?"

"I'm good. How you feeling?"

"Spaced out . . . What happened?"

Frank exchanged glances with Esther, who nodded slightly.

"My car was rigged with a bomb," he said slowly. "It went off when I hit the remote to unlock it."

It registered gradually with Janowitz. Frank felt he could see the realization bulling its way into Janowitz's consciousness through layers of drug-suppressed pain.

"Bomb?"

Frank nodded.

Janowitz's eyes widened in alarm. His left hand scrabbled at the sheet.

"A bomb? I still got my . . ."

Esther leaned forward and took his left hand. "Everything's still there, sweetie."

Leon smiled.

José rolled his eyes toward the door. "We'll be back, Leon. Anything we can get for you?"

Janowitz was having trouble focusing, and his eyelids were fluttering rapidly. "Kill for some ice cream," he muttered, beginning to drift off. Then, making a visible effort to double-back into consciousness, "You guys check Martin Osmond yet?"

"Today or tomorrow, Leon," José said.

"Important," Janowitz mumbled.

"Today or tomorrow," José repeated.

Janowitz fought to keep his eyes on José and Frank. "You'll let me know?" he whispered.

"Sure," said José.

"No shit?" The words came faint, barely audible.

"No shit, partner," José said.

.   .   .

Frank turned onto Columbia Road, only partially paying attention to the early-afternoon traffic.

"I wonder how I'd take it . . . one minute walking down the street, the next thing waking up without an arm?"

José pushed his dark glasses higher on his nose with the tip of his finger. "You told him up front about the remote."

"I don't think it sank in."

"It sank in? *What* sank in?" José asked irritably. "That you blew his goddamn arm off? You wallowing in that self-blame guilt shit again?"

Janowitz's bloodless face came back to Frank. "Can't help it, Hoser, I couldn't keep my mind off what was underneath those bandages. Thinking about her having to tell him . . . about when he realizes . . ."

José shifted in his seat to get a better look at Frank. "You remember the first thing he asked?"

"No. What?"

"He asked about *you*. Even before he asked about his dick. And you remember the next thing?"

"Martin Osmond."

"Yeah. I'll ask Daddy to set it up for us to talk with his grandmother."

"Yeah. His file . . ."

"Eleanor ought to have it waiting when we get back."

By early evening, the headache had taken a recess. Two Tsingtaos, and the stitches didn't pull as much and the bruises didn't protest while Frank moved around the kitchen. As he opened a third beer, Monty sprang up to the counter and settled himself on the one space he'd claimed since he was a kitten. His eyes locked with Frank's.

"What's on your mind?" Frank asked.

You humans.

"What now?"

The way you live.

"And?"

The cause of most of your troubles.

"We walk on our hind legs?"

You make too many decisions.

"Decisions?"

You live in a way that requires too many decisions. You are so busy deciding, you don't have time to think.

"And the way you live?"

Monty got a bored look. *I have very few decisions to make. This lets me explore the universe. To travel in time. To watch the things in corners that you can't see. To talk with God.*

Frank took another sip of beer. "And what does God say to you?"

Monty drew his head back as if affronted. He leaped down and made for the front door. A second later the doorbell rang.

When Frank opened the door, a smiling Kate waved an envelope. "And what am I offered in return for this court order?"

"Spinach salad, cold poached salmon, snow peas amandine, and a wholesome selection of the best of Ben and Jerry's."

"Pretty good kitchen work for a banged-up detective."

"I did the salad. Dean and DeLuca did the rest."

Over dinner, Frank described Calkins's findings and the meeting with Emerson and Tompkins. When they were finished, Kate placed a "Stay put" hand on Frank's shoulder. She cleared the table, and then poured coffee.

"So this Osmond's the prime suspect for Gentry's source?"

"*If* Gentry had a source. So far, this case's a grab bag of suppositions and suspicions. According to Gentry's CIA pal, Gentry made
the recruitment in June 'ninety-eight."

"Any chance the Agency's dragging a red herring across the
path?"

Frank shrugged. "There's always a chance something's going on
under the blanket. The Navarro woman believes that investigating
Skeeter's operation was Rhinelander's idea."

"Your jackstraw game's getting more complicated."

Frank glanced toward the corner where Monty sat upright, a gray
sphinx, gravely staring back at him, as if to say, *See, human, you
make everything more complicated.*

"One thing about jackstraws," Frank said wistfully, "you jiggle
enough sticks and something happens. Problem is, sticks may not all
fall your way."

The image returned of the ICU and Leon Janowitz's waxen face
and bandaged arm.

"Leon?" Kate asked. "You can't keep beating yourself with that."

"Last night I sat here and went over the Vietnam album. First time
I've done that in years. I hated that goddamn war. But I loved the
guys around me. It was like we had a contract with each other . . . a
responsibility. To take care of each other. And when somebody got
wounded or bought the farm, each of us thought about it. Took everything apart . . . every move we'd made, every step we'd taken . . . trying to see where we might have screwed up."

"Shoulda, coulda, woulda can haunt you if you let it," Kate said.

Frank waved that off. "It was more than playing 'What if?' or
taking a self-inflicted guilt trip. More than a survivor syndrome. It
was self-preservation. You thought about those things so you might
keep them from happening again. Because you knew if you didn't
keep those things from happening, none of you would make it
through."

. . .

Angel of Death got that woman marked," Titus Phelps rumbled. "Husband got killed in that Korea War. Daughter smashed up on the Beltway. Grandson died in her front yard." He sat in the big arm-chair, head to one side as though listening to the echo of his own words. The echo faded and he slowly swung his head from side to side. "Angel of Death marked her," he repeated, with the weary air of a man who'd learned that truth had sharp edges.

"We want to see her tomorrow," José said. He sprawled on the sofa. Across the living room, Channel 4 was giving out the evening weather and traffic. Neither man was paying attention. From the kitchen came the sounds of cooking.

"What can she tell you?"

"I don't know. Won't until we talk to her. If she talks to us." He paused. "You mind calling her before we go over?"

"Mind? Yes, I mind."

"But you'll do it?"

"Yes," he said wearily, "I'll do it."

Weather and traffic went off. A clip of Timothy McVeigh, a cut of the Murrah Federal Building, its face obscenely stripped away, then again a clip of the unsmiling crew-cut McVeigh.

"Evil man," Titus Phelps murmured.

"You think he ought to die?" José asked.

"We all die."

"You know what I mean . . . the death penalty."

"For someone like him"—Titus Phelps's eyes remained on the TV screen—"for doing something like that . . . I do."

"But you been against capital punishment . . . always."

"All my life."

"But now . . ."

"I know . . . I know . . ." The man shifted in his chair to look at his son. "I used to think you get to some age, you get to some place where you've wrestled all your demons down . . . you're at the magic place where doubt goes away." He threw his hands up in a gesture of surrender. "I guess I'm still wrestlin'."

"You knew Martin Osmond."

Titus Phelps nodded. "Baptized him, buried him. In between, saw him in Sunday school, youth choir, league basketball." He ran his fingertips across his forehead. "Happens a lot. Everything seems to be workin'. Then . . . the street gets them."

"Street got Martin."

"His mother lived, he mighta been all right. But he tied in with that Hodges boy."

"His grandmother . . . ?"

"She did what she could," Titus said. "You get to a certain age, your chirrun get too fast for you to keep up."

José grinned. "I never got fast enough."

His father swatted a hand at him. "There were times. Times I had to run plenty hard."

"I know. I'm glad you did. You think Virginia Osmond finally gave up?"

Titus shook his head emphatically.

"Hunh! That woman doesn't know give up. She was on that boy to the last." He paused to think back. "There was a time . . . I thought maybe he'd get hisself straight, but . . . ." Titus's eyes strayed off into the distance, searching for a lost soul.

"She ever come to you about Martin?"

His father held up a hand. "That's something you ask her." As though he'd received a signal from the kitchen, he got up out of his chair. "Besides, supper's ready."

THIRTY-SIX

Your daddy called. Said you'd be over."

José nodded in a way that was almost a courtly bow. "Thank you for seeing us on a Sunday, Mrs. Osmond."

Erect, as if on parade, Virginia Osmond came up to just below José's shoulder. Her voice pulsed with a slight tremor, and her green eyes had a hollowed-out but luminous look.

"My partner, Mr. Kearney."

Osmond gave Frank a minimal smile and motioned the men inside. "I fixed coffee and biscuits," she said. "You don't mind? . . . Sitting in the kitchen?"

José nodded again. "Kitchen's the soul of the house."

Frank got an impression of scrubbed . . . clean . . . neat. Smells of furniture polish, floor wax, and years of baking. The living room: two armchairs, a breakfront bookcase, and a camel-backed sofa. On a small table between the armchairs, a lamp, reading glasses, and an open Bible. The lamp was on, and the reading glasses rested atop the Bible.

A floral hall runner led back to the kitchen.

It was a kitchen from the 1940s or 1950s: old-fashioned white enamel sink, refrigerator, and gas stove. A brightly colored oval rag rug covered much of the polished dark green linoleum. Four dowel-backed wood chairs waited around a sturdy harvest table. The only jarring note: ranks of prescription drug containers filling a stainless-steel surgical tray on the countertop.

Three places had been set at the table, two on one side, one on the other. Napkins, ceramic mugs, woven-rush placemats, cream, sugar, and a butter dish.

Osmond motioned to the two chairs. "Please."

Frank and José sat. Osmond brought a coffeepot from the stove and filled the three mugs. A second trip to the stove for a basket of freshly baked biscuits, wrapped in a napkin. She offered the basket to José.

He took it, unfolded the napkin, and offered the basket to Osmond. She mouthed a "Thank you" and picked out a biscuit. José took one and passed the basket to Frank.

José paid close attention to buttering his biscuit before he looked up and said, "Mrs. Osmond, we need to talk about Martin."

"Your father told me." Osmond sat quietly, her hands folded in her lap.

Frank started. "People say Skeeter Hodges was selling drugs. That he made a lot of money that way."

Osmond nodded warily. "Yes. People knew . . . they knew he was selling."

"And people say that Martin and Skeeter spent time together."

"Yes." The admission came out, dragged across years of pain.

Frank was about to ask Osmond if she knew of her grandson's dealing.

Of course she knows. What will it get you if she says yes? What will you do if she says no?

So instead he asked, "It bothered you, didn't it? . . . Martin spending time with Skeeter?"

Osmond gazed through him as though she hadn't heard. Then, almost inaudibly, "It bothered me a lot."

"Did Martin ever talk with you about Skeeter?"

She shook her head. "Only when I brought it up."

"And then?"

"And then he'd say they were just friends."

"Nothing about Skeeter selling drugs?"

Again Osmond shook her head.

"When was the last time Martin and Skeeter hung out together?"

"They were together the afternoon Martin died."

Frank asked, "So Martin and Skeeter Hodges were good friends?"

Osmond shook her head vigorously. "No. No they weren't. They weren't good friends."

"But they were seen a lot together. And Skeeter was there at the funeral."

"That didn't mean *good* friends. That Hodges boy was not good. Not good for Martin. Not good for anybody. He was a tempter. He beckoned to the bad that is in us all. He was a *bad* friend."

"And he beckoned to Martin?"

Anguish crossed Osmond's face.

"Yes. He beckoned. I tried to give Martin the strength to say no. I thought Martin had shed himself of Skeeter. But he went back. I failed him. I raised him from a baby. His mama died and I raised him and then I failed him."

"'Shed himself'?" José repeated. "When was that?"

"Almost a year," Osmond replied. "Almost a year to the day he got killed. He said he found Jesus." Her eyes went rheumy, and she sat so still she might have been stone.

"And he went back . . . when?"

"June that year," she managed in a pained whisper. "It was June."

José said gently: "You found him . . . that night he died."

"Yes."

"Tell us what you saw and heard."

Osmond closed her eyes. Her eyelids fluttered, then she opened her eyes. "It was late . . . late for me . . . almost eleven. I was reading." She gestured toward the living room, and Frank pictured the armchair and the lamp and the Bible.

"I hear Martin's car pull into the driveway. I don't hear him race the engine the way he usually does. I didn't think anything about it for a while. But I realize I heard the door slam twice. And I didn't hear him set his alarm . . . his horn always honked when he did that. So I went out, and he was in his car. He was lying down on the driver seat. He wasn't breathing. I ran into the house and called nine-one-one and then went back to the car. He still wasn't breathing."

Osmond fell silent. Just as José was about to prompt her, she resumed. "And then I knew . . . Martin was gone."

The old woman hugged herself, and rocked slowly back and forth, eyes distant, looking for something that she'd never see again.

"There was a sudden emptiness," she whispered. "It was like something took flight from inside me . . . and it flew right out of my life." Her eyes hardened. "They said Martin died of a drug overdose. They said heroin. But I knew Martin. I knew he would not do drugs." Osmond's hands began trembling.

José looked at Frank, who just looked back. There might be more. There probably was. But for now, it was time to go.

"Why now?" Osmond asked.

The question froze the two men as they pushed back from the table.

"Ma'am?" Frank was not certain he'd heard right, and if he had, what was Osmond driving at?

"Why now?" Osmond repeated. "My Martin's been dead two years. Nobody came to talk to me when it happened. Now you back about Martin. Is it really about Martin? Would you be here if it wasn't for that white man getting killed?"

The coldness penetrated the wall. It was something that writhed in Frank's guts, something he wanted to pass off to José. And because he wanted to, he didn't.

"No, ma'am, we wouldn't be here if it wasn't for that white man getting killed."

On Virginia Osmond's front porch, Frank pulled deep at the morning air. He felt José's hand gripping his shoulder.

"Jesus, Hoser." He had to work to get it out.

José's grip tightened. "I owe you one. You said the right thing."

"Telling her it makes a difference who gets killed?"

"Always has," José said, "always will."

Frank looked down the street, toward where Skeeter Hodges's Taurus had been parked.

"Truth always have to hurt?"

"No."

"Then somebody's gettin' our share of the good stuff to pass out."

"Think she's a forgiver?" José asked.

Years earlier, over beers at the Tune Inn, Frank and José had decided there were three kinds of homicide victim's relatives: forgetters, forgivers, and forevers. Forgetters put things behind them and moved on. Forgivers shed tears for the killer as well as for the deceased. Forevers never forgot and damn sure never forgave.

"I don't know," Frank said.

"Reads her Bible."

Frank remembered walking in . . . the Bible and the reading glasses. "I think an Old Testament woman." It was one of those things he'd say sometimes, not quite knowing how it came into his head or out of his mouth.

José nodded. "Daddy *teaches* the New Testament, but when he *preaches*, it's the Old every time."

Frank looked at the driveway where Martin Osmond had died. "She knows more than she's telling us."

"Everybody knows more," José said. "Everybody always knows more."

"Think she knew Martin was up to his ass in dealing?"

"Probably. Mothers know those things. They might not know everything there is, but mothers know enough."

"She was his grandmother."

"Mother, grandmother"—José shrugged—"same thing."

"Martin and Skeeter together the day Gentry was shot. Then Martin buys it later that same night."

José didn't seem to be paying much attention. He was looking up the street. "Spring gardenin' goin' on."

Two doors away, Edward Teasdale saw them coming and got up slowly from his knees. He stood waiting, a pair of gardening shears in one hand.

Ivy had grown through and over the chain-link fence surrounding Teasdale's front yard. The ivy was closely trimmed, so it made a low green wall around the azalea-filled yard.

Frank and José stopped on the sidewalk.

"Morning, Mr. Teasdale. I'm—"

"You're Kearney and you're Phelps," Teasdale said, pointing with the shears.

"You got a minute or two we can talk?" José asked.

"More about Skeeter?"

"Some him, some Martin Osmond."

"Martin?" Teasdale asked. "You talked to Missus Osmond?" he asked, making certain Frank and José had touched all the bases.

"Unh-hunh."

"Then what you need to talk with me for?"

"Martin lived here on the block," José said. "He died here. Maybe . . . just maybe . . . you can tell us something that can help us clear up some things."

Teasdale thought about that, then waved the shears at the front gate. "Come on in. Sit on the porch, you like. Or go inside."

"Porch's fine," José said.

The porch ran across the front of the small house. A low brick balustrade held flower boxes filled with geraniums. The four massive rush-bottomed wood rockers faced the street in a precise row.

Teasdale took an end chair and turned it to face the other three.

Frank eased himself into one of the chairs and pushed back slightly to test it. The big chair rocked smoothly. Just the right amount of motion with the least effort. He caught Teasdale appraising him.

"Rocks good," Frank said. "They cut the rocker rails wrong, chair won't rock right."

"Chairs over a hunnert years old. Wife brought those up from her daddy's farm down by Charlottesville," Teasdale said. "We'd sit out here summers. Friends come by . . ." Teasdale trailed off, thinking of a time he had had a wife and they could sit on their front porch and friends could walk down Bayless Place on a summer night.

Teasdale rocked a moment, then asked, "Why you asking about Martin? And why now? Two years later?"

José asked, "Anybody talk with you when Martin died?"

"No."

"You lived here, what . . . thirty-some years?"

"Six," Teasdale corrected, "thirty-six."

"And Martin . . . his grandmother took him in after his mother was killed?"

"Boy wasn't in school yet." Teasdale rocked back, eyes on the ceiling in recollection. "That'd be late sixties sometime."

"Different times then," José said.

"Last of the good times. Nobody knew what we'd see." Teasdale scanned Bayless Place, as if trying to recall it as it had been thirty years before.

"You saw him grow up."

Teasdale nodded. "He'd come up here. I'd give him a quarter to do chores. Weedin', cuttin' grass. Boy liked to work. He got older, taught him to take up for himself. Missus Osmond's a good lady, but there's things a boy got to learn from a man."

Sadness dragged at Teasdale's eyes.

"Bad," José said, "him dying that way."

"Bad, him gettin' messed up with people who do shootin' and drugs. Bible tells us about livin' by the sword."

"People say he and Skeeter were buddies," Frank said.

Teasdale gave Frank a skeptical look. "His grandmother say that?"

"No."

Teasdale studied Frank, then said, "Real battle was between Skeeter and Missus Osmond. Over Martin. She was always on that boy. I thought she'd won. Then . . ."

"Won? How'd she win?"

"She told me one day . . . a Monday . . . that Martin had found Jesus. Woman's face shined. Like she had a fire inside. Like a young girl almost, excited, giggly."

"Didn't last," José said.

"For a while . . . I thought maybe . . . Then Martin . . . he started hangin' out with Skeeter again."

"You remember when it was," José asked, "he found Jesus?"

"Year . . . about a year . . . before he died."

"He died February 1999," Frank said.

"That'd be about right. Sometime early 1998."

"You have any indication he was doing drugs himself?" José asked.

"No. You said you talked with Missus Osmond, she told you, didn't she . . . that Martin didn't mess with that shit?"

José nodded, like he'd heard Teasdale's question but wasn't answering.

Teasdale paused a beat. "I ask you something?"

"Sure."

"You after finding out about Martin? Or finding Skeeter's killer?"

"Both."

Teasdale cleared his throat and spit over the balustrade in the direction of the street. He stood and squeezed the gardening shears in the air as if to warm them up.

"Wouldn't waste my time on Skeeter. Justice done there. Sum'bitch got what he deserved. Got what he shoulda got long time ago."

Kevin Gentry recruited Martin Osmond," José said.

Frank nodded. The two sat for a time in the car on Bayless Place not talking, but putting Gentry and Osmond together.

"What happened was, Rhinelander and Gentry set out to bag Skeeter," José said. "With a little help from Señorita Free Drugs and maybe from his pals at the Agency, Gentry spots Martin Osmond as a potential source. Does his recruiting magic . . . persuades Osmond to go back into the business with Skeeter. Skeeter finds out . . . he and Pencil kill them both." José paused, then asked, "We got a time for tomorrow?"

"Tomorrow?"

"You, me, and the mayor . . . Rhinelander, remember?"

"Oh. Yeah. Tomorrow's Monday."

Oh Lord, give me a day when I don't have to dread the next day. A cottage on a Spanish hillside where you could sit under the olive trees and look across to Granada or up above at the impossibly blue Andalusian sky.

He realized José was staring in his side-view mirror.

"Angry man," José said, still watching as he fastened his seat belt. "Almost sounded like he lost a son."

Frank found Teasdale in the rearview mirror. The big man was savagely attacking the azaleas with the shears, cutting away the winter kill.

THIRTY-SEVEN

Monday morning, Frank and José stood under the Rayburn portico and watched Seth Tompkins blow into the horseshoe driveway in grand mayoral style: sleek black Lincoln with U.S. and D.C. fender flags snapping, two motorcycle escorts front, two rear, lights blazing.

"Looks like the Queen of Sheba coming aboard," José said.

The sight cheered Frank. It was like Ali making his way down the aisle to the ring. Coming on big, bold, and brassy, with absolutely no doubt about the outcome.

"Float like a butterfly," Frank whispered.

We ready, fellas?" Tompkins asked as Frank and José led him down the corridor to Rhinelander's offices.

"Politics your turf, Mayor," José said.

Tompkins grinned. "Turf? Jungle's more like it, José."

Marge, Rhinelander's gatekeeper, stood as Frank and José entered with the mayor. She opened a door into a short hallway.

"They're waiting inside, Your Honor."

"They?" Tompkins asked.

"The chairman and Director Atkins."

Rhinelander sat at his desk. He was swiveled around to face Atkins, who was in an easy chair to Rhinelander's left. Both men looked up as the door opened. Tension hung in the air as though a conversation had been cut off in mid-sentence. Frank guessed it had been Atkins who'd been talking—the FBI director seemed adrenaline-charged, while Rhinelander had a subdued, thoughtful air.

Rhinelander underwent a lightning transformation. A smile of appreciation flashed, a man awed by a particularly spectacular sunrise. "Mayor Tompkins! Thank you for coming!" he gushed.

He waggled an impatient hand at Marge. "Three more coffees," he told her.

He stepped out from behind his desk and shook hands with Tompkins, then Frank and José. "I see you've brought two of the department's finest, Mayor." He gestured toward a small conference table. "We'd be more comfortable here."

Taking his position at the head of the table, Rhinelander patted the place to his right. "Please, Mayor. Let me take this opportunity to tell you that you've brought a sense of dignity and honor back to your office."

"Thank you, Mr. Chairman."

Tompkins said it with a cool detachment, and Frank noticed that the mayor sat with his hands folded in his lap.

Concerned, Rhinelander turned to Frank. "And you, Lieutenant Kearney, you had a close call. I trust you're all right?"

"Yes, sir, I am. Thank you."

"And Leon?" Rhinelander asked. "How is he doing?"

"Still listed as critical."

Rhinelander shook his head in sympathy. "He worked well with my staff. A bright young man." He pointed to Frank. "You be sure to let me know—let me know *personally*—if there's anything we can do."

"I will, thank you." Frank felt a hot acid stabbing in his stomach. *Smarmy bastard.* Much more of this and he'd be reaching for the Maalox.

"In view of recent events," Rhinelander began, "I thought we might put our heads together and . . . ah . . . review the bidding."

"*Bidding,* Mr. Chairman?" Tompkins's inflection made 'bidding' sound frivolous.

If Rhinelander noticed, he gave no indication. "It would be most appropriate, I think, to reach a consensus on two issues. First"—he raised his index finger—"I believe we must define our problem. Second"—another finger—"we must agree on the assets we need to resolve the problem." He paused and looked expectantly at Tompkins.

"And the problem is?" Tompkins asked.

"Quite bluntly, Mayor, the problem is a widely held perception that we are getting nowhere in closing the Gentry–Hodges case."

Tompkins started to respond, but Rhinelander held up a hand.

"Please let me finish," he said almost petulantly.

He's cooked the meal, and by God, we're gonna eat it. Frank forced himself to take a deep breath and keep his hands away from Maalox.

"Let me lay out some fundamental elements," Rhinelander said, "and I think the task we face becomes clearer. The murder of this drug lord Hodges revealed that the District police department had not properly closed the investigation of the killing of my chief of staff, Kevin Gentry."

Rhinelander paused to look around the table. To his left, Atkins sat impassively, gazing off into space. Tompkins had an expression of studied neutrality. From the corner of his eye, Frank caught José's hands, busy rolling a ballpoint pen between his fingertips.

"We then discover that Kevin had been a CIA operative in Colombia. And there is the manner of Pencil Crawfurd's killing. These alone justified a hypothesis of a Colombian connection."

Rhinelander gestured toward Frank and José. "I appreciate, Lieutenants Kearney and Phelps, your department's reluctance to consider such a hypothesis. But now, we have a car bombing that nearly kills Sergeant Janowitz and you, Lieutenant Kearney. Add all this together and it would seem that we have the hallmarks of a Colombian operation."

Rhinelander turned to Tompkins. "Have I been inaccurate, Mayor?"

"No," Tompkins said glumly.

Rhinelander turned to Atkins. "Director Atkins?"

Clearly unhappy, Atkins nodded. "Unfortunately, I think you're right, Mr. Chairman."

"Now"—Rhinelander briskly slapped both hands palm down on the edge of the table, a man satisfied with the stage he'd set—"let me ask you this, Mayor . . . where are you now . . . this morning . . . in closing this case?"

Tompkins looked around to Frank and José. "Gentlemen?"

José and Frank exchanged glances, and José gave Frank a go-ahead nod.

Worse than a goddamn press conference. Frank took another deep breath while he hastily framed a basic vanilla response.

"We're developing a clearer picture of Kevin Gentry's activities and associations that may bear on his killing and his connection with Skeeter Hodges."

Rhinelander listened without expression, his eyes hooded behind the small round lenses of his glasses. "Is this . . . *picture* bringing you closer to closing the case?" He put a smirking accent on "picture."

"I believe so."

"You believe so," Rhinelander intoned solemnly. "When?"

Tompkins cut in. "Are you asking for a specific date, Mr. Chairman?"

Rhinelander smiled innocently at Tompkins. "Obviously, Mayor, we'd all like one. Just as obviously, though, I realize that's not doable." Turning his attention to Frank, he asked, "But can you tell me roughly? . . . A month? Two months? A year?"

Frank shook his head. "I can't tell you that either, Mr. Chairman. We could walk out of here this morning and run across something that'd wrap a ribbon around the case by dinnertime. But then again . . ."

"But then again," Rhinelander picked up, "it could join the other cold cases in your extensive files." Without waiting for an answer, the congressman continued. "So it's a matter of running down things? Exploring possibilities?"

"Yes, sir."

"A lot of dead ends too, I imagine?" Rhinelander was obviously building a case but trying, unsuccessfully, to camouflage it under a tone of empathy.

"Dead ends too, sir," Frank acknowledged.

"I understand," Rhinelander said, "that when the department was forced to reopen the Gentry case, you and Lieutenant Phelps pooh-poohed your superior's recommendation to create a task force."

José leaned forward, looking down the table at Rhinelander. "Frank and I have been on the force a total of fifty years, Mr. Chairman. We've never seen a task force do much more than get in its own way."

"So it was a judgment call that restricted the investigation to you and Lieutenant Kearney?"

"And Detective Janowitz."

"Oh, yes . . . the young man who is recovering from losing his arm." Rhinelander made it an accusation. He turned to Tompkins.

"Your Honor, let me tell you what my thinking is."

"Please do, sir," Tompkins said, a chill in his voice.

"I think we have a case that has escalated in complexity. From the unremarkable shooting of a drug dealer on the street we have moved to attempts by an international criminal cartel to assassinate American law enforcement officers on the streets of our nation's capital."

Rhinelander angled his head toward Tompkins. "Are you with me so far, Mayor?"

"I'm with you." Tompkins's tone dropped several more degrees.

Rhinelander nodded in satisfaction. "And solving such a case depends, as Lieutenant Kearney observed, on tracking down possibilities and checking out dead ends . . . yes?"

Tompkins nodded.

Sitting back in his chair, Rhinelander touched his fingertips together just below his lips, looking very judgelike.

"My thinking is that when a case grows so large in scope, so complex in detail, we must devote more assets to solving it." Rhinelander paused, then launched further into the assault. "It appears, Mayor Tompkins, that your police department, having initially assigned too few assets, is now behind the curve. There is an irredeemable loss of credibility because of the handling thus far. Meanwhile, the case has expanded far beyond your ability to deal with it."

Tompkins answered with a flinty silence.

"Let me explain the position I'm in, Mayor Tompkins," Rhinelander said. "I'm responsible for appropriations for the District of Columbia."

"I'm well aware of that, sir."

"And I'm certain, you're aware, then, that the curse of government is that there is never enough money to do everything for everyone."

Tompkins nodded curtly.

"And so, my subcommittee must make decisions. Set priorities on who gets what," Rhinelander said with a sigh of regret. "And I do not believe it is good government to reward incompetency."

"There *is* a point, Mr. Chairman?" Tompkins said.

"Come now, Your Honor." Rhinelander spoke with a let's-do-business edge. "The District has great needs. Schools . . . medical care . . . Head Start . . . shelters for the homeless . . ." He threw his hands up. "The list is endless."

Lacing his fingers together at his chest, Rhinelander set aside the stick and offered the carrot.

"I am willing to work with you on these problems, Mayor Tomp-kins," he said in a conciliatory tone. "But it will be very difficult for me to convince my colleagues to fund these needs when the District government's credibility is threatened by blatant examples of the in-efficiency of its police department."

Tompkins was silent for a small eternity. A vein pulsed at his tem-ple, and it wouldn't have surprised Frank if the Mayor had walked. Then Tompkins blinked rapidly several times and the vein stopped pulsing.

"What do you want, Mr. Chairman?" Tompkins asked, his voice leaden.

"For the District's good, Mayor, we need to get this case behind us. We need more assets, and as well, we need new thinking . . . new eyes. And that's why I've invited Deputy Director Atkins here." Rhinelander paused. "I believe the best course is to have the Bureau take over the Gentry and Hodges cases."

Atkins had the uncomfortable look of a man who wished he wasn't there. He quickly added, "With, of course, local assistance from your department, Mayor Tompkins."

Rhinelander got a beatific smile. "Of course, Mayor, of course."

In a wordless procession through the Rayburn corridors, Frank and José accompanied Tompkins to the horseshoe driveway where the Lincoln and the motorcycle escort waited.

An aide opened the rear door for the Mayor. A visibly disheart-ened Tompkins turned to Frank and José.

"Gentlemen, I'm sorry. That crap Rhinelander handed out was undeserved."

Frank wanted to reach out and squeeze the man's shoulder, but he didn't. He said, "I guess politics is being satisfied with half a loaf, Your Honor."

Tompkins ducked into the backseat. He smiled cynically out at

Frank and José. "Half a loaf? Sometimes, fellas, politics is being sat-isfied with one goddamn slice."

Frank and José watched as the mayor's convoy made its way down the drive, turned right, and disappeared down South Capitol Street.

"No question how Rhinelander knew about that task-force shit," José said.

Frank nodded. "Nobody ever accused Randolph Emerson of not knowing which side his toast was buttered on."

José's cell phone chimed. He answered, then, covering the mike pickup, whispered, "R.C."

"You're where?" José asked into the phone.

A pause.

"We'll be right there," he told Calkins. He folded the phone and turned to Frank. "We both gettin' absentminded."

It came to Frank: The court order in his jacket pocket . . . Renfro Calkins waiting for José and him at the Riggs Bank. "After that crap in there"—he jerked a thumb back over his shoulder—"last thing I feel like doing is pushing a car that's run out of gas."

"Aw, come on," José urged, "our chance to give the Bureau a little local assistance."

ç

Across Pennsylvania Avenue, half a block east of the White House and opposite the U.S. Treasury, Riggs Bank is Washington's oldest private financial institution. Riggs financed Samuel Morse's inven-tion of the telegraph. Abraham Lincoln opened his Riggs account weeks after Jefferson Davis closed his. And court order or not, Riggs took care that its safe-deposit boxes remained as secure as its bil-lions in assets. It was early afternoon before a vice-president ushered Frank, José, and Calkins into a small vaulted room.

The Riggs vice-president watched with rapt attention as Calkins opened his print kit, dusted the exterior of the steel safe-deposit box, and lifted the prints. When he had finished, Frank and José placed the box contents in a heavy cardboard carton and signed the releases that returned the box to the bank.

Six hours and four carafes of coffee later, Frank tossed his pencil down, cupped his chin in his palm and surveyed his desk, cluttered with notes, crumpled papers, and a take-out container that earlier had held a prosciutto and Taleggio cheese sandwich. Three hours before, R.C. had called in with a preliminary: unsurprisingly, he'd found several sets of Gentry's prints on the exterior of the safe-deposit box. Martin Osmond's had appeared as well, on the packet of receipts and, of course, on the will and the cassettes.

Frank glanced at the whiteboard, covered with a hash of dates, times, names. He felt a sudden weariness welling up, a soul-deep exhaustion that had nothing to do with the hour or the stress of the day. He imagined he saw it too in José's eyes.

"Why'd it happen, Hoser?"

"I think that's pretty clear," José said in a flat, leaden tone.

"No," Frank disagreed. "*What* happened's clear. Why . . . ?" He asked.

José got up and stretched. "The U.S. attorney's satisfied with what happened. We called Atkins. Question is, we gonna let Emerson know?"

Their eyes met.

"Well," José said with a conspiratorial smile, "I *had* to ask." He paused, then asked, "How about Tompkins?"

Frank decided that José was working way ahead of him.

"Think so, Hoser," he said. Then, assurance building, "Definitely."

THIRTY-EIGHT

Just after nine, Frank found a parking place on Virginia Avenue opposite the Watergate complex. José got out and stood on the sidewalk, looking up at the tall yellow stucco building that was now a George Washington University dormitory.

"Lost a real piece of American history there," he said.

Frank followed José's gaze. The dorm once was a Howard Johnson's. And not just any HoJo. This was the Howard Johnson's where Nixon's dirty-tricks team planned their break-in of the Democratic Party's campaign headquarters in 1972.

"I always wondered about those guys," Frank said as he opened the car trunk. "I mean, two of those guys . . . E. Howard Hunt, G. Gordon Liddy." He lifted out the small tape deck. "I don't think we would have made the cut: J. Adams Phelps and F. Delano Kearney don't have quite the same ring."

Brian Atkins opened the door. He wore faded khakis, a chambray work shirt, and Top-Siders. Over his shoulder, Frank took in a large, softly lit living room. Two dove-gray sofas faced each other, framing a powerfully colored red and blue Persian carpet and a low, intricately carved Chinese bamboo-and-elm table. Against a wall, a very good seascape oil hung over a black lacquer sideboard.

"Gentlemen, come in." Atkins smiled. He momentarily eyed the tape deck Frank had slung over his shoulder, then turned to lead them to an enclosed balcony. Four teak chairs looked out on the Potomac, black and glistening in the night, and in the distance, headlights raced across Key Bridge between Rosslyn and Georgetown. In the background, jazz played on an unseen sound system.

Frank noticed a highball glass on the coffee table between the chairs.

"I'm having a little medicinal scotch," Atkins said. "You guys?"

"Beer?" José semi-asked.

"Pilsner Urquell? Tecate?" Atkins offered. "I've somehow accumulated a regular United Nations in the fridge."

"Anything cold," José said.

Frank nodded. "Same here."

Atkins disappeared, and Frank stepped closer to the glass wall of the balcony. Five stories directly below, Rock Creek Parkway. To his right and at a greater distance, Georgetown Foundry and the waterfront, and, somewhere in the darkness, the bench where he wished he and Kate were sitting now.

"Music too loud?"

Frank turned. Atkins was setting two Tecates and frosted mugs on the coffee table.

"Monk's never too loud," José said.

"This's early Thelonious," Atkins said as the three settled into their chairs.

"Riverside label," José furnished. "With Gerry Mulligan?"

Atkins silently saluted José with his scotch. He watched as the two men filled their mugs. Then he was all business. "You guys didn't come here for beer and jazz."

Frank sipped his beer. It had a bitter metallic taste. "No, we didn't." "You said there's something new."

"Some background first?" Frank asked. Getting a nod from Atkins, he put the beer down on the coffee table. "In the files we're going to be turning over to the Bureau, there're interviews in which two people told us that shortly before his death, Kevin Gentry was investigating Skeeter Hodges's operation."

Atkins's eyebrows lifted slightly. "Investigating?"

"In preparation for congressional hearings," José said.

"That's . . . interesting."

"You didn't know?" Frank asked. "Neither Gentry nor Rhinelander said anything to you?"

Atkins smiled. "Hell, they may have and I just forgot or didn't pay attention at the time. Some committee on the Hill is always talking about investigating something or somebody."

"And then we go back to the weapon that killed Skeeter," José picked up. "Two years before the shooting on Bayless Place, the same weapon was used to kill Gentry . . ."

"And the shell casings that you found on Bayless had Pencil's fingerprints," Atkins finished. Then, as if making a mental note to himself, "That pistol . . . if we only knew where it went . . . where it is now."

"We may never know," Frank said. "But there are some things we do know."

"Oh?"

"We know that Gentry recruited somebody inside Skeeter's organization."

"And how do you know that?"

"Gentry told two people, who then told us . . . a guy he'd worked with at the Agency and the director of a think tank."

"The insider has a name?"

"Martin Osmond," Frank said

Atkins got a reflective look. "The name's familiar . . ."

"He's dead," José said. "Died of a heroin overdose the same night Gentry was shot."

"So, two men, both dead for over two years." Atkins sipped at his scotch, then shook his head. "We're seeing a replay of the old adage that dead men tell no tales."

"But they leave things behind." Frank pulled the safe-deposit key from his pocket and laid it beside his beer on the coffee table. "This is to a safe deposit box Kevin Gentry maintained at Riggs Bank," he explained. "Leon Janowitz found it in Gentry's files in the Library of Congress archives."

Atkins leaned forward, picked up the key, examined it, then put it back on the table. "And in the box?" he asked.

"A number of things," Frank said. "A hundred and twenty thousand in cash. And Martin Osmond's will."

"A . . . will?"

"Osmond knew the game he was playing," José said. "He left the money to his grandmother."

"And in a box controlled by Gentry," Atkins said.

"Gentry kept receipts," José said. "Payouts began in June 'ninety-eight. They came out of a subcommittee account."

Atkins held up a hand. "Let me guess . . . The payments totaled a hundred twenty K. So it's obvious . . . Gentry slipped up somehow. Or maybe Osmond. Anyway, Skeeter and Pencil decide to take them out."

Frank nodded. "That's part of it. Some loose ends . . . like who killed Skeeter and, later, Pencil and his lady friend?"

"And who nearly killed you and Leon Janowitz?" Atkins added. "We'll be nailing all that down."

"Maybe we can help you," José said.

Atkins pointed to the key. "That certainly did."

"That box was full of surprises."

Something in Frank's voice brought Atkins's eyes up. "Oh?"

Frank pulled an audiocassette from an inner coat pocket. "This isn't the original," he explained. "It's a copy of one Osmond made from the original . . . a cassette that Skeeter and Pencil recorded." He put the cassette on the coffee table, next to the safe-deposit key. Then he reached down and brought up the portable tape deck, flicked it on, and inserted the cassette.

"This'll be interesting," he said, as he pressed the Play button.

A hammering rap blasted from the small tape player.

Atkins winced.

Frank turned the volume down. "A recorder in Skeeter's car was picking this up. This was in June 'ninety-two."

"I still don't . . ." Atkins said, frowning.

The tape went silent. Then a burst of static. The sound of a car door opening. Frank pressed the Pause button.

"The first voice is Skeeter Hodges."

"How you doin'?"

It was a cruel, sly voice of arrogance and condescension.

Frank pressed the Pause button again.

Atkins stared at the tape deck, seemingly hypnotized.

Frank reached for the Play button, waited, and looked into Atkins's eyes. "And the next voice is yours."

"You called about a deal."
"Yeah. You want Juan Brooks?"
"Yes."
"You know who I am?"
"You're James Hodges. You give me Brooks . . . what do you want?"
"I walk. Me, my friends Martin Osmond, Pencil Crawfurd."

Frank punched the Stop button. Atkins had a thousand-yard stare—a man who'd seen a wished-away hell suddenly reappear, yawning open at his feet.

"You and Skeeter cut the deal," Frank said, dispassionately, even sadly. "He'd turn in Juan Brooks. You'd get the publicity. And he'd inherit Brooks's outfit."

"And then Skeeter kept helping you." José's tone was less sympathetic, a tone borrowed from his father's pulpit. "Skeeter would finger his competition. You'd shut them down. You'd put another notch in your badge, Skeeter'd add another piece of turf."

Atkins sat emotionless, rocking ever so slightly in cadence, matching what he was hearing against some internal master record.

"You kept the heat off Skeeter," Frank said in a hoarse whisper. "Warned him whenever the posse was saddling up."

"Skeeter didn't do the glitz that Juan Brooks did," José said. "Even so, as he got bigger, it got harder for you to keep the heat off him."

Frank leaned forward sympathetically. "Two years ago, Gentry and Osmond almost broke it open."

Atkins nodded, a stricken, haunted look on his face.

"But you and Skeeter managed a last-minute save," Frank continued almost soothingly.

José jumped in. "What happened then, Brian? Skeeter and Pencil get too ambitious? Too grabby?"

"You decide to take them out?" Frank followed closely.

"You screw up and don't get Pencil," José tacked on.

After the staccato buffeting, Frank and José sat silently for a second or two. Atkins brought his hand up and rubbed his eyes.

José picked up. "Pencil's alive. You know you have to get him, and you know you have to get control of the case."

"So the Colombian connection," Frank continued. "Part was already there . . . Gentry's time in Bogotá, his Agency connection. You added the necktie and bomb touches."

"And you killed Pencil's woman when she came in on you tossing the house," José said.

"Looking for this." Frank touched the Eject button and held up the cassette.

Atkins stared at it, then into Frank's eyes.

A chance to top off a career as more than a mid-level agent. Years of watching others catch the brass ring. And then the chance to take out Juan Brooks. To get your portrait in the director's corridor. What would have happened, Brian Atkins, if you hadn't taken the deal?

Atkins finally spoke. "We've been in this business a long time, the three of us," he said, talking like he'd just joined two friends at a bar.

"Yes," Frank said, "yes, we have."

"They want us to clean the sewers for them." Atkins spoke with a mix of sadness and resentment. "And we do. We go about it the best way we know how. We make a profession of it . . . cleaning the sewers. And sometimes . . . sometimes in the sewers one finds a diamond in the shit."

Slowly Atkins got to his feet. Silently, he held his hands out. Frank locked on the cuffs.

"You're going to have to make a helluva case," Atkins said in an almost jovial, professional manner.

"I think we have enough, don't you?" Frank was working to be equally professional about it.

"You got most of it down," Atkins admitted.

"Most?"

Atkins grinned as if enjoying a private joke. He shook his head. "Most," he repeated, adding, "except . . . I didn't shoot Skeeter."

EPILOGUE

With difficulty, Frederick Rhinelander managed a welcoming smile. "Mayor Tompkins!"

Tompkins nodded curtly and, without invitation, took his seat in one of the chairs facing Rhinelander's desk. Tompkins held a leather portfolio in his lap.

Rhinelander looked past the mayor to Marge, who was leaving. Rhinelander wanted her to turn so he could send the private eye-signal to extract him after a minute or two. But she closed the door behind herself without a backward glance.

The unhappy congressman turned his attention to Tompkins. He cleared his throat. "The trial . . . a shock . . . Brian Atkins." Rhinelander shook his head and got a profoundly perplexed look. "Who would have thought?"

Tompkins didn't answer right away, and his silence and stony gaze intensified Rhinelander's sense of dread.

"Who would have thought?" Rhinelander repeated.

"You should have thought, Mr. Chairman." Tompkins's tone was that of a priest administering last rites.

Rhinelander's mouth worked silently through several cycles. "Should have thought *what?*" he finally managed.

"Oh," Tompkins said, "you should have come out with the truth."

Rhinelander stared speechlessly.

"You see," Tompkins continued, "Kevin Gentry was working for you when he began investigating Skeeter Hodges's operation."

"But," Rhinelander protested, "I didn't know everything Gentry was doing."

"You knew he had recruited an informant inside Skeeter's organization, and you knew he was paying that informant."

"No!" Rhinelander's voice rose.

"Yes." Tompkins said quietly. He reached inside his portfolio for a sheaf of papers, which he tossed onto Rhinelander's desk. "Photocopies of payment authorizations. A hundred and twenty thousand dollars in subcommittee payments to Martin Osmond."

Rhinelander made no move toward the papers, yet eyed them as if a snake had suddenly materialized on his desk.

"You'll find your signature on each payment authorization."

Rhinelander started to say something, but Tompkins held up a restraining hand. "The original authorizations have fingerprints on them . . . yours."

Struggling for composure, Rhinelander went on the offensive. "So I signed them. So Gentry was conducting an investigation. So what?"

"So, I suspect that if an energetic investigator followed the trail far enough, he would find that you told Brian Atkins about Gentry's recruitment. And from there Atkins told Skeeter Hodges, and that in turn led to the murders of Gentry and Osmond."

"No one is going to investigate a congressional committee," Rhinelander said weakly.

"And the sun won't rise tomorrow." Tompkins laughed derisively. "Wake up, Mr. Chairman. Never underestimate the lure of a Pulitzer

Prize. The newspapers in this town have brought down bigger men than you."

Rhinelander was breathing deeply, and his face had taken on a sallow bluish tint.

"And don't think other congressional committees wouldn't hesitate to get some prime TV time," Tompkins continued. "Such as the Senate Select Committee on Intelligence, chaired by Senator Daniel Dugan Patterson. Coincidentally, I had breakfast with him this morning. He asked me to remind you of his deepest regard for Kevin Gentry."

Rhinelander sat motionless, drained of resistance. "What do you want, Tompkins?"

"I want your resignation from Congress."

Incredulity, then fear flashed across Rhinelander's face.

"A deal!" he said, with a burst of desperation-fueled energy. Words came in a tumbling frenzy as he upended the pork barrel. "You want the education plus-up? The new sewage plant? Bond guarantees for building those clinics? Shelters for . . ."

Tompkins stood and looked down on Rhinelander with contempt.

"No deal, Rhinelander. I want you out of my town."

José pushed open the door to the office, Frank close behind.

Feet on Frank's desk, Leon Janowitz sat cocked back in Frank's chair. With an easy motion, he threw. The third dart marked a solid single eighteen.

Janowitz turned and grinned. He held up his prosthetic throwing hand and wriggled the lifelike fingers.

"The Bionic Darter."

He tilted forward and stood up. "Welcome back. I hear you two got Atkins a permanent room in the gray-bar hotel."

José shut the door. "You're supposed to be on convalescent leave."

"That was a helluva trial. I had to come in and welcome the conquering heroes."

Frank hung up his jacket and loosened his tie. "We'd still be working it if it weren't for you."

Janowitz smiled modestly. "Luck."

"Plans?"

"The mayor offered to put in a word or two up in New York. One of the investment firms that handles the District pension plan."

"That's good of him."

"The least he could do," Janowitz bantered. "After he shot my chance to go to work for Frederick Rhinelander."

"So it's the Big Apple," José said.

"No. I turned him down."

"Oh?" Frank asked.

"Turned him down on the New York thing," Janowitz amended. "Asked him if he could use a one-armed detective."

"What'd he say?" José asked.

"Said I'd have to talk with you guys . . . said that you'll be doing the hiring."

The phone rang before either José or Frank could follow up.

Janowitz answered, listened, eyeing José, then Frank. He stood straighter. "They're both here, sir. . . . Who? . . . Where? . . . Yes, sir, I'll tell them."

Janowitz hung up. "Your dad," he said to José. "Said he's at Virginia Osmond's. Says you and Frank get over."

A somber Titus Phelps answered the door.

"Back here." And he led Frank and José to Virginia Osmond's bedroom.

A fleshy, medicinal odor filled the small room. Eyes closed, Virginia Osmond lay under a patterned quilt. The months had ravaged her: her hands had wasted away to bony claws, and a green undertone dimmed her rich brown skin. A middle-aged nurse who'd been sitting bedside got up when the three men entered, and left after patting Osmond's cheek.

Photographs in silver and gold frames stood on a night table. A high school graduation picture of Martin Osmond in cap and gown. A fading studio portrait of a handsome man in uniform, who Frank assumed had been Virginia Osmond's husband. A picture of a younger Osmond with a still-younger woman standing on the steps of the Bayless Place house. The younger woman held a baby.

Her daughter and Martin.

"Virginia," Titus Phelps said, "they're here."

Osmond opened her eyes.

"I can see that, Titus," she said in a thin, papery voice. She smiled at José. "You have a handsome, handsome son."

She raised her hand a fraction off the quilt.

"Come closer," she whispered to José and Frank.

The two men stepped to the side of her bed. José put his hand over hers.

Virginia Osmond smiled. "I want to give the two of you an old woman's blessing. . . . My Martin didn't die a bad man."

José bent close to her. "No, ma'am," he said, "he died a hero."

"I knew," Osmond said. "I *knew.*" Her eyes searched José's. "I waited to see . . . I knew . . ."

"Yes ma'am."

She slipped her hand from under José's and gestured to the night table. "In the drawer."

José hesitated, then opened the drawer. Over his partner's shoulder, Frank saw the pistol.

Glock 17.

José and Frank exchanged glances, then turned to Virginia Osmond.

"Night they killed Martin . . . after I called the ambulance . . . I went back to him," Osmond said. "I saw the gun on the seat beside him."

Her voice strengthened, tapping some last reservoir of energy.

"Heard the sirens . . . don't know what went through my head . . . I knew the gun was bad. Took it. Hid it in the little shed I have for my garden things."

Osmond was quiet for a moment. "They said Martin died of drugs. They said heroin." She shook her head.

"But I knew Martin. I knew he had nothing to do with drugs. Later . . . I went through his things. I found an envelope with my name on it and a note inside."

Osmond's eyes drifted away as though she were trying to see the note again.

"All it said was, 'Anything happens to me, go see Mr. Kevin Gentry. Don't tell police.'" She shut her eyes, then opened them. "I read the papers and saw on the television. . . . Mr. Kevin Gentry was killed the same night as my Martin."

Osmond looked at José as if seeking confirmation.

"Yes, ma'am, this was so."

Seemingly relieved, Osmond nodded.

"I knew . . . all that time . . . that Hodges boy had something to do with Martin's death. And that white man's too. But I didn't trust anyone. Not you police. I guess I'd a done nothing except pray for Martin, hadn't been for that Hodges boy coming over here to Bayless Place, sitting in that car with that loud music. Him and his friend, that Crawfurd boy, looking us over."

"Yes, ma'am," José breathed, knowing what was coming next.

"Then I got the cancer. Like it was a signal from the Lord. I had to right things before I joined Martin."

"Yes, ma'am."

"And so I did."

The last of her vitality draining away, Virginia Osmond gestured feebly toward the night table.

"Martin . . ."

José picked up Martin Osmond's graduation photograph and placed it in Virginia Osmond's hand. She clasped the frame to her breast, then looked up at José and Frank.

"Thank you," she whispered.

And so she died.

http://dc.gov/index.asp

News for Immediate Release

Government of the District of Columbia	John A. Wilson Building
Citywide Call Center: (202) 727-1000	1350 Pennsylvania Avenue, NW
TTY/TDD Directory	Washington, DC 20004

August 29, 2001

Mayor Announces Police Department Retirements

(Washington, D.C.) Mayor Seth Tompkins announced today the retirements of Police Chief Noah Day and Police Captain Randolph Emerson.

"Retirements of such men," the Mayor said, "are always occasions of mixed emotions. Such men will be missed. They have long been law enforcement institutions. I wish them happiness and godspeed in their well-deserved retirements."

....

* This document is presented in Portable Document Format (PDF). A PDF reader is required for viewing. Download a PDF Reader or Learn More About PDFs

THE WASHINGTON POST
Thursday, August 30, 2001

METRO
In Brief

THE DISTRICT

DCMPD Under New Management?

Mayor Seth Tompkins, having announced the surprise retirements of Police Chief Noah Day and Homicide Captain Randolph Emerson, is about to pull another rabbit (or two) out of his hat.

Insiders say that Tompkins is preparing to nominate Detective Josephus Adams Phelps as Chief of Police and Franklin Delano Kearney as Chief of Homicide.

Phelps and Kearney, longtime partners in . . .